D0021356

THE N.O.A.H. FILES

I AM THE WALRUS

THE N.O.A.H. FILES
I AM THE WALRUS

NEAL SHUSTERMAN
&
ERIC ELFMAN

LITTLE, BROWN AND COMPANY
New York Boston

Copyright © 2023 by Neal Shusterman and Eric Elfman

Cover art © 2023 by Jim Madsen. Series lettering by Sammy Yuen. Cover design by Karina Granda. Cover copyright © 2023 by Hachette Book Group, Inc. Interior design by Carla Weise.

Little, Brown and Company
Hachette Book Group
1290 Avenue of the Americas, New York, NY 10104
Visit us at LBYR.com

First Edition: April 2023

Little, Brown and Company is a division of Hachette Book Group, Inc.
The Little, Brown name and logo are trademarks of Hachette Book Group, Inc.

The publisher is not responsible for websites (or their content)
that are not owned by the publisher.

Little, Brown and Company books may be purchased in bulk for business, educational, or promotional use. For information, please contact your local bookseller or the Hachette Book Group Special Markets Department at special.markets@hbgusa.com.

Library of Congress Cataloging-in-Publication Data
Names: Shusterman, Neal, author. | Elfman, Eric, author.
Title: I am the walrus / Neal Shusterman & Eric Elfman.
Description: First edition. | New York : Little, Brown and Company, 2023. | Series: The N.O.A.H. Files ; 1 | Audience: Ages 8–12. | Summary: "Noah Prime discovers he can exhibit the traits and access the abilities of animals and must use them to fight back against those who are hunting him." —Provided by publisher.
Identifiers: LCCN 2022019865 | ISBN 9780759555242 (hardcover) |
ISBN 9780759555259 (ebook)
Subjects: CYAC: Genetic engineering—Fiction. |
Animal defenses—Fiction. | Survival—Fiction.
Classification: LCC PZ7.S55987 Iam 2023 | DDC [Fic]—dc23
LC record available at https://lccn.loc.gov/2022019865

ISBNs: 978-0-7595-5524-2 (hardcover), 978-0-7595-5525-9 (ebook)

Printed in the United States of America

LSC-C

Printing 1, 2023

FOR ERIN, JOELLE, JARROD, AND BRENDAN
—NS

FOR ROBBY
—EE

<FOBE Interrogation>
<Noah Prime>
<Security Code Sapphire>
<Part 1 of 3>

"WELL, AT LEAST NOBODY DIED," NOAH PRIME SAID.

He offered up a half-hearted grin and tried to shrug, but the various cuffs and chains that held him firmly to the chair made shrugging difficult.

"Believe me, Mr. Prime," said his interrogator, "in this world, there are worse things than death."

All he knew about the woman questioning him was her name: Agent Rigby. Noah had never heard of the secret government agency she was with, nor did he know who or how many were watching them through the huge one-way mirror that nearly overwhelmed the small room.

"I suppose you want to know about the volcano," he said. "And the monsters that crawled out of the duck pond."

From the look on her face, it was clear she didn't even know about the monsters yet. Darn.

Even so, she played it cool. "You could also tell me how

that Cadillac ended up stuck in a water tower a hundred feet from the ground," she said. "But let's start with why you're dressed as a caveman."

"Uh . . . it's the newest look," he said. "You should give it a try."

He heard a muffled guffaw from beyond the mirror—because clearly the idea of Agent Rigby's intimidating dark suit replaced by prehistoric furs was just too absurd for her colleagues—but she was not amused in the slightest. She sat on the edge of the table, her hard demeanor softening—or at least pretending to soften. "Noah," she said, "I know this can't be easy for you. But trust me when I tell you that cooperating with us will be the best thing for you, considering your current circumstances."

"Aren't I supposed to have a lawyer?" he asked.

"This isn't that kind of interrogation," Agent Rigby said with a little grin.

"So, what kind of interrogation is it?"

"The kind where the uncooperative don't fare very well."

Noah took a deep breath, which was also difficult against all his restraints.

"Could you at least tell me where we are?" he asked.

"The Bella Vista Correctional Medical Facility. But where you are is much less important than why you are. Or, for that matter, what you are," she said. "What are you, Mr. Prime?"

"That's not an easy answer," Noah told her. "But whatever you think I am, you're wrong. Dead wrong."

1

Sitting on a Froot Loop

BEFORE THE VOLCANO, AND THE MONSTERS, AND THAT MISERABLE business with Stonehenge, Noah Prime sat at the breakfast table, scowling into his Froot Loops.

"So you'll learn to adapt," said his mother.

"I don't want to adapt," said Noah.

His younger sister, Andi, looked up from her corn-flakes and shook her head. "Don't be such a baby," she said. "Motocross is a waste of time."

Noah's instinct was to strike back, but he wouldn't give his sister the benefit of knowing she'd pushed his biggest button.

Living in Arbuckle, Oregon, home of nothing in partic-ular, with a population of six thousand extremely pointless people, had only one bright spot as far as Noah was con-cerned: a fantastic motocross course.

Noah had been riding since he was eleven. He loved the

noise, and the smell, and the mud. But mostly he loved the total freedom he had on the track, and he delighted in mastering the control he needed to keep from overdosing on all that freedom and wiping out.

Then, a month ago, it was announced that the course was going to be bulldozed to erect condominiums. And if that wasn't bad enough, someone broke into their garage and stole Noah's motocross bike.

"Maybe this is all a sign," his mother had said.

A sign of what? Noah had wondered. *That the universe doesn't like me?* But he already knew that. It seemed as if everything had been stacked against him for as long as he could remember. Like when he was younger and they tore out the town's only ice rink just as he was starting to get really good at hockey. Every time he started to stand out at something, it was taken away before he could truly shine.

"Lemonade, Noah. Lemonade," said his mother. She often talked like that, using shorthand for longer expressions. She added some extra milk to his bowl, which she always claimed had too much cereal and not enough milk for his growing bones.

"Mom," he said, "when life gives you this many lemons, there's only so much lemonade you can make, okay?"

"You're such a drama queen," his sister said to him.

"Will you stop it, Andi—this is none of your business."

Andi turned to their mother and whined, "Mom, Noah's being disparaging."

In response, their mother poured a few more cornflakes into Andi's bowl, which was mostly milk.

"He's upset, honey," their mother said. "We'll cut him one piece of slack."

Noah gritted his teeth. "Slack doesn't come in pieces." He slammed down his spoon, having absolutely no appetite for breakfast, and knowing that his mother would complain that he wasted so much cereal.

"You know," she said, "there are lots of other things you could do with your time."

"Like what?" he said, then turned to Andi. "Study, like her?"

"It wouldn't hurt you to bring your grades up," his mother said.

"Dad says my grades are adequate."

"In case you didn't know," explained Andi, "that's not a compliment."

"But you know what, whenever I do something better than adequate, it gets taken away from me. I bet if I started getting perfect grades, the school would burn down."

"Don't be silly," their mother said with a grin. "It would just be condemned."

"Ha-ha." Then he grabbed his backpack and stood up.

"Leaving already?" his mom said. "Isn't today a late-start day?"

He could have made a disgruntled comment about not wanting to be at the table with his "perfect" sister, but he didn't even have the motivation for snark. "I'm going out to Dad's workshop—I promised I'd help him this morning."

• ● •

"Comfy?" Noah's dad asked.

"Why does it matter?" Noah responded, lying down.

"A thing still matters, even if it technically doesn't matter."

"That makes no sense," Noah said.

"Just tell me if it's comfortable."

Noah rolled his shoulders, then moved his legs, feeling how his body swished against the blue silk padding. "Yes," he told his father definitively. "If I was a dead guy about my size and weight, I'd be very comfortable spending eternity here."

"Excellent," his father said, grabbing a tape measure from his workbench. "Now, don't move; let me take a few more measurements."

That was okay with Noah. Not that he particularly enjoyed being in one of his dad's designer coffins, but he wasn't lying. It *was* comfortable. Far more comfortable than its future occupant would ever need.

Noah's father hadn't set out to be a coffin maker. He was a cabinetmaker of the old Craftsman style, creating museum-quality furniture. Then some terminal rich dude asked him to make a coffin. It was all the talk at the funeral. "My, what a lovely casket," all the rich and famous had said. "Wherever did you find it?" The widow dropped his father's name, and within days, orders started rolling in. Suddenly, purchasing your final resting place years in advance became a trendy thing among the movers and shakers. And so ToDieFor Woodworks was born. Today's model was made of rare knotty alderwood, trimmed in mahogany and gold leaf, for a real estate tycoon who was roughly Noah's dimensions: a little short, but with broad, muscular shoulders. The guy might not actually cash in his chips for years, but at least now he'd have the peace of mind of knowing he had a comfortable box of fun waiting for him.

"What if the guy gets fat or something before he croaks?" Noah asked. "I mean, this thing is tailored like a suit for him, right?"

His dad winked. "He can always order a new one."

Noah smiled. For a man who had such a morbid sort of business, his dad was the least morbid person Noah knew. He was the kind of guy who happily hummed classic rock tunes while he carved his wood. Although Noah did once catch him humming "Another One Bites the Dust."

As his father checked around him, measuring the spaces where the padding left little gaps, Noah changed the subject.

"By the way," Noah said, as if it was something that just casually came to mind, "I checked, and there's a moto-cross club in Portland."

His dad sighed. "Noah, we already discussed this. Portland is more than an hour away."

"We can always move."

"You'd really want me to uproot the whole family for this?"

"You can make these things anywhere—I mean, you ship them all over the world anyway, right?"

"Mom would have to start a whole new floral business from scratch. Besides, it would traumatize your sister."

That made Noah laugh. "Andi wouldn't be traumatized by nuclear war."

His father retracted his tape measure and put it on his workbench. "I'm sorry, Noah, I really am. But for the time being, you're going to have to find a new—"

"If you say 'hobby,' I'm going to scream."

"I was going to say 'passion.' I know you think you'll never love anything as much as motocross, but that's what you thought about hockey. You're the most resilient kid I know."

He looked at Noah, no longer for measurement, but to take in the whole of his son. "I promise that you'll find something new to throw your heart into—and it will expand you as a human being in ways you can't even imagine."

"Blah blah blah."

His dad sat down next to him, and Noah sat up. "Do you think this is what I expected to be doing?" his father

8

asked. "Creating works of art that will only be used once, and will never be seen again?"

"You always say you love what you do," Noah reminded him.

"I do," his dad said. "But it took me a while to get there. I had to accept that this world is an impermanent place. Nothing lasts forever, and nothing should. Things change. That's not always a bad thing."

"This time it is," Noah insisted.

"Maybe you're right," his father admitted. "But ask the question again a year from now. Your perspective might change."

"Maybe," Noah had to concede, "but a year is a long time to wait."

His father smiled. "Not in the grand scheme of things." He stood up and knocked on the casket. It resounded tuneful and true, like the body of a guitar. "I have to head into town for some supplies—do you want me to give you a ride to school?"

"Nah, I'll walk," Noah told him. Then he lay back down to experience the zen of his father's craft.

• ● •

Noah found himself in a recurring dream. It always seemed to come back when he was stressed by the world. He was in a raging river. Ice-cold water churning, churning. He couldn't breathe, yet he *could* breathe. He couldn't swim, yet he *could* swim. He kept leaping, then getting smacked back down by the current, until finally he made his way to the surface, but it wasn't exactly the surface—because water was still pouring onto his face. He leaped again and again, until he realized he was fighting the current of a waterfall. He couldn't fight the force of a waterfall, yet he could. He was. But it was exhausting, and it felt like it would never end.

"Dreams are random neurons firing in your brain," his friend Ogden had said. "But those neurons are connected to the ones you've been using while you're awake...so a dream is only one step removed from reality."

He had told Ogden that, in fact, Ogden was one step removed from reality, and that he had to stop speaking geek, and speak English.

"What I mean," Ogden had said slowly, as if to an idiot, "is that what you dream is a metaphor for what's going on in your life. Fighting a current means that you feel like life is pushing you backward and drowning you."

Noah had to admit that Ogden was right—which he was half of the time. The other half, he was spectacularly wrong. Like the time Ogden convinced himself the beehive on a tree behind Noah's house was swarming with something other than bees.

"They're fuzzy like bees, but they have a slender thorax like wasps," Ogden had said, proclaiming them a new species of murder hornets—which the Primes had taken exception to, since they hadn't tried to murder anyone yet. In the end, Ogden agreed to charge them with a lesser crime, calling them manslaughter hornets—and he kept throwing rocks at the hive every time he came over, to provoke them and prove his hypothesis.

As it would turn out, that tendency for Ogden to be either ingeniously right or spectacularly wrong was a coin toss that Noah's life would soon depend on.

• ● •

Noah awoke from the latest version of his waterfall dream. It took a couple of moments for him to realize he wasn't in his bed. Where was he? Oh no!

He sat up, then pulled himself out of his father's latest artwork.

"No! No! No!" It was only the fourth week of school, and Noah already had three unexcused tardies. He pulled out his phone and checked the time. Nine minutes until the bell rang. And his first period was a science quiz he could not miss!

He grabbed his backpack, racing out the workshop door. His mom had already left with Andi, probably thinking that either Noah had walked or his dad had taken him. No one was home to see his morning fail.

Their home had once been a farmhouse surrounded by a few acres of land, but those fields had long since gone to seed. The only plants that grew with intention were the

11

ones in his mother's greenhouse, where she cultivated rare and exotic orchids and the like.

Noah hurried out of the barn where his father had his workshop and raced down the dirt path out of the woods to the main road. There was no sidewalk, which made running all the way to school a hazard, what with morning drivers speeding around curves to get wherever they were going. Cities didn't have a monopoly on stressful motorists. Luckily, it was less than a mile. If he pushed himself, he wouldn't be too late, but he'd definitely break a sweat that would probably overwhelm his deodorant. At moments like this, he regretted his decision not to have a regular bike, because for a motocross rider, any other bike was an embarrassment.

His science quiz was about the brain, and as he raced to school, he tried to review the facts in his own brain.

Thalamus, hypothalamus, medulla, cerebellum.

The evergreens before him began to get thick. Since when were there so many trees in his way between home and school?

Lobes of the cortex: frontal, parietal, temporal, occipital.

Yes, but which was which? He was sure that his science teacher, Mr. Kratz, would make them fill out a diagram. He grabbed a branch, pushing off of it. A minivan sped by. Someone had spray-painted "Loser" on the roof. He wondered if the family even knew.

Right hemisphere, left hemisphere, joined by the corpus callosum.

He came up on the school much more quickly than he expected. Occupying his mind must have made the trip seem faster. If he was lucky, he might be able to make it through the door before the late bell!

But he wasn't lucky. Instead, his morning fail became a full-fledged crash and burn.

"CAN I HAVE A BATHROOM BREAK, AGENT RIGBY?" ASKED NOAH.
"Seriously, after all this interrogation, I really need one."

He shifted in his chair. His chains rattled. Agent Rigby sat down at the table across from him, ignoring his request.

"When you were six years old, you drowned."

"Almost drowned," corrected Noah.

"Should have drowned," said Agent Rigby. She looked at the report as if she hadn't already looked at it a dozen times. "It says here you fell into a raging river and were swept away."

"I really don't remember that," Noah told her. "I was very young."

"They expected to find your body downstream. Instead, they found you two-miles upstream, sitting next to the belt of a salmon conveyor, crying your eyes out."

"Wouldn't you?" Noah asked.

She spared him a single glance, then violently flipped a page.

"When you were ten, you fell off a cliff. You do remember that, don't you?"

"It wasn't a cliff," Noah told her. "It was a bluff."

"Your friends thought you were dead. Until you showed up at home as if nothing had happened."

Noah once more tried to shrug against his bonds. "It wasn't as steep as it looked," he said.

"Perhaps not," conceded Agent Rigby. "But that doesn't explain the dent in the roof of a car below." She slammed down a picture of a Hyundai that looked as if it had been struck by a boulder just about the size of a human being rolled into a ball.

He had not known about this part. He remembered that something had broken his fall. It felt kind of like a mattress. And he remembered wandering off a little bit dazed and walking all the way home because he thought his friends had left him. And, as Agent Rigby said, when he got home, he acted as if nothing had happened, because in his mind nothing had.

"Care to explain?" Agent Rigby asked, pointing at the picture of the dented car.

Noah shifted in his bonds. His arms were aching, his neck hurt, and he had a terrible itch on his nose. "You know," he said, "you might want to loosen these cuffs and stuff, because if it starts to hurt too much, it's not going to be pretty."

Agent Rigby glared at him and stood up. "Are you threatening me, Mr. Prime?"

"No," he said honestly. "I'm just saying stuff happens, you know?"

"Like the 'stuff' that happened to your town?"

"Hey, not all of that was my fault," he said. But even that was telling her too much. "Now can I go to the bathroom?"

2

La Dropp

UNLIKE NOAH, SAHARA SOLIS WAS NEVER LATE TO SCHOOL. Her life ran on a tight schedule, like a train. But, like a train, when you're late for one station, you're late for all of them. Such was her morning.

She had done the inexcusable thing of setting her alarm for PM instead of AM. And when she did wake up, she was already twenty minutes behind schedule. Try as she might, she was unable to make up that lost time.

Also unlike Noah, she did have a bicycle. But since she always pedaled to school at full speed, she wasn't going to make up any time by pedaling faster.

Knowing she had less than a minute before the late bell rang, she locked up her bike and ran toward the main entrance—

Where she encountered Noah, who brought her down with the force of an asteroid killing off the dinosaurs.

Her shoulder seemed to burst in pain, and her knee was scraped and bleeding. When she looked at her attacker on the ground next to her, he appeared about as oblivious to his effect as the aforementioned asteroid.

"Whoa," he said, looking at her. "Are you okay?"

"What's wrong with you?" she shouted. "And where did you come from anyway?"

"I—I was running to the door. I must not have seen you."

"No! *I* was running for the door." She pointed at the trees. "*You* jumped on me from up there!"

He helped her up. And although she didn't want to accept his assistance, she did out of reflex, before she could stop herself.

She rolled her shoulder. The sharp pain was starting to fade, but not entirely. This was not what she needed. If she lost the slightest range of motion because of this, she'd be ruined for this weekend's gymnastics competition. She could not allow her body to be compromised by some kid who thought he was Tarzan.

"I'm sorry," he said, but "sorry" just wasn't cutting it this morning.

And to add insult to injury, the late bell rang.

"Great," she said. But the word seemed to come out in a kind of harmony, since he said it, too, at the exact same moment.

"Jinx!" he said with a grin.

But that wasn't cutting it, either.

"What are you, five years old?"

"Hey," he offered, opening the door. "We'll go to the office together, and I'll vouch for you. I'll say it was all my fault."

"It *was* all your fault."

"Right, so maybe I'll get an unexcused tardy and you'll get off."

She walked a little faster than he did into the office, trying to keep him out of her peripheral vision. She had neither the time nor the patience.

"It's Savannah, right?" the boy asked.

Now there was salt, added to insult, added to injury.

"*Sahara*," she corrected. "Like the desert."

His mistake struck her a little more deeply than she wanted it to. This was, after all, a small town. Wasn't everyone supposed to know everybody?

"Sorry," he said again. "I guess we move in different circles."

"I don't move in circles," she told him. "I move in a straight line." Which, she realized, may explain why a lot of the other kids didn't really know her.

• ● •

Noah tried to play over in his mind the moment of their collision. How could he not have seen her? He didn't remember running up the front steps. All he remembered was crashing into her and then being on the ground.

It wasn't exactly a memory lapse; it was more like a gap in space-time. As if he had teleported to the front of the school, and into her path, because what else could explain how quickly he had gotten there?

In the end, they were each given an unexcused tardy, and Sahara went off to get a Band-Aid from the nurse for her knee.

Noah wondered why he hadn't really noticed her before. Maybe it had to do with that straight line Sahara was talking about, he speculated. When you're more interested in the destination than the view, not only do you miss a lot, but a lot misses you.

When he finally arrived in science class for the quiz, the period was nearly over.

"You're late," sang out Mr. Kratz.

"Sorry," Noah said for like the tenth time today. "Crazy morning. I fell asleep in one of my dad's coffins." Which brought some snickers from the kids around the room who knew what Mr. Prime did.

"Wonderful," said Mr. Kratz, with a sarcastic glare. "A family of vampires."

"What? No! Never mind." It wasn't the time or place for an explanation.

Mr. Kratz handed him the quiz and looked at the clock. "You have four minutes left."

"Yeah, yeah."

Noah sat down, looked at the page, and took a long,

slow sigh. The quiz was about the spinal cord, not the brain. He wondered if his life could possibly get worse.

It could.

• ● •

The only bit of luck Noah had that day was that Coach Bostic, head of the phys ed department, had been Noah's hockey coach all those years ago. He knew about the killing of motocross in Arbuckle. And although the school didn't like to let kids enter a sport a month into the school year, Coach Bostic was willing to make an exception.

"What sport are you thinking about?" the coach had asked him.

Noah didn't have an answer for that. It had never crossed his mind that he would ever have to choose another sport to be in.

"I don't know. What sport might need me?"

Coach Bostic gave him a slightly disgusted look. "All of them," he said.

And so, over the next three days, Noah spent afternoons on the basketball court, the soccer field, and the wrestling mat in the gym.

The results surprised even Noah. In basketball, he had the agility to move himself around much taller kids and sank more baskets than anyone expected him to—including himself.

In soccer, the coach, a bit irritated at being ordered to give Noah a try, stuck him in the goal, hoping he would be humiliated enough as goalkeeper to leave with his head hung low. Instead, he stopped every ball that came at him in the scrimmage, denying even their best players a goal.

And in wrestling, although he knew nothing about strategy or actual moves, he was remarkably skilled at not getting pinned.

All three coaches wanted him, but he found he had no interest in their sports.

"I hate you," his friend Ogden said when Noah told him he wasn't going to join any of those teams. "The rest of us would kill to have game like you. And you just want to throw it away."

It wasn't that Noah wanted to throw it away. And it wasn't news to him that he was naturally good at sports. He'd always known he could sink a basket or catch any size ball heading in his direction.

The thing was, people enjoy sports because of the challenge of it. But for him, it held no more challenge than tying his own shoelaces. Once he knew he could do it, it was nothing special.

He supposed he enjoyed hockey when he was younger because of the added complexity of being on skates and the speed of it. When he rode motocross, he never felt as if he was competing against the others; it was more about challenging himself. And he couldn't deny that the unpredictability and danger inherent in motocross gave him a rush that other sports didn't.

22

Ogden was not an athlete. He was not a popular kid, and he alternately envied and despised those who were. Ogden's interests were in more esoteric things, like designing his own board games, and collecting vintage PEZ dispensers, and memorizing facts about bizarre animals, such as the northern leopard frog, which uses its eyes to swallow its prey. And, of course, anything to do with dinosaurs—which arguably made him the town's biggest fan of FossilFest—a celebration unique to Arbuckle and its amazing fossil history.

Ogden's parents often said he was "on the spectrum," which meant he was a bit autistic. This never bothered Ogden. Everybody's on one spectrum or another, he figured, which Noah supposed was true.

"My parents exist on a love-hate spectrum," he once told Noah. "Although right now, it's closer to the 'hate' end." They were both math professors at Arbuckle College, but they had perpetual trouble balancing their own equation. They had been married, then divorced, then married again, then divorced again. Now they lived in identical tract homes across the street from each other, and they shared custody of Ogden on a schedule that had something to do with prime and non-prime numbers.

Noah and Ogden had been friends for as long as Noah could remember, and he discovered that their friendship had the added benefit of keeping away kids who ranked high on the shallowness spectrum.

Ogden volunteered at the local animal shelter. After his wrestling tryout, Noah joined him, helping to wash some of the animals. As it turned out, wrestling humans was much easier than wrestling wet dogs.

"If you're good at every sport you try," Ogden said, "you should pick something that's not common. You're more likely to get a college scholarship for an unusual sport. It's never too early to start thinking ahead."

"There *are* no unusual sports in Arbuckle," Noah pointed out.

The husky-Labrador mix they were bathing performed a skillful shake that left them both drenched in suds.

"Maybe I'll create my own sport," Noah added, "like you create games."

"Great," Ogden said, who didn't get that Noah was joking. He pointed to the dog. "Maybe you can create a hybrid, like Mimi here. I've often wondered what skydiving combined with lacrosse would look like."

"Great," said Noah, laughing. "We could call it La Dropp."

Although they both agreed it was impractical, Ogden said he would draw up a cost analysis that night.

• ● •

The next morning at school, Noah encountered an unexpected glitch in his sports tryouts. It was during that weird midmorning no-man's-land that some schools call "snack" or "recess" or, more pretentiously, "nutrition," when students have twenty minutes instead of five to get to their next class. But since it was not enough time to do anything of value, most kids just hung around in the hallways.

Noah made the mistake of walking into an empty stairwell alone. But he wasn't alone for long.

"Hey, Prime!"

He turned around to see a kid come into the stairwell behind him. Noah recognized him as one of the basketball players. He was tall, blond, and ugly in a rare kind of way, with harsh features that were getting harsher as he matured.

"That was some amazing ball you played the other day," the kid said. Noah now remembered that his name was Roger.

"Thanks, Roger."

He seemed pleased that Noah remembered his name. "The coach asked me to talk to you. To let you know that the team would love to have you."

Noah was a little bit wary. He sensed that the coach hadn't asked Roger at all—but Roger was taking it on himself to do this, because then he could claim he was the one who got Noah to join.

Then another voice entered the conversation.

"Nice try—but it's not happening. The soccer team has dibs." It was one of the soccer players. One of the school's cool kids, who was a known fashion time traveler. That is, he dressed in clothes about ten years out-of-date, although they were actually next year's styles, so he was always simultaneously behind and ahead of the times.

"Whadaya mean, dibs?" said Roger. "He tried out for basketball first!"

"*You* just had him do drills!" said the soccer dude. "But *we* put him in an actual scrimmage!"

Roger turned to Noah and glared at him. "You are *not* joining the soccer team!"

"No, he's not," said yet another voice. "He's joining the wrestling team."

It was, of course, a kid from wrestling. He had spiky hair and thick, padded shoes that were much too big for his feet, making him look a little like Sonic the Hedgehog.

"Our coach already has you on the roster," said the wrestler.

"You can't do that!" growled Roger.

"Too late," said the wrestler. "It's a done deal."

Through all of this, Noah couldn't get a word in edgewise.

Roger, with growing rage, turned to Noah, scowling, and poked him in the chest. "You're not wrestling! You hear me, Prime?"

Noah knocked his poking finger away with a kind of wax-off karate slap. That didn't go over too well.

These three, Noah realized, were not the captains of their teams. These were the kids who acted as if they were

26

in charge but had wisely been passed over for leadership positions. And it just made them angry.

"Are you seriously telling me that you're turning down a golden invitation to the basketball team—the most successful team this school has?"

"Successful?" said the soccer dude, laughing. "Your record last year was three and nine."

"Which," pointed out Roger, "is better than the soccer team."

"And explains why you're choosing wrestling," said Sonic. "It's both an individual and a team sport. We might not win many meets, but you'll definitely shine in your own matches—and no one can take away those wins."

Now it was the soccer dude's turn to get in Noah's face. "Is there something wrong with you? It's . . . UN-AMERICAN to not want to play a ball sport!"

Noah saw where this was going long before they did. Used to be, in an old-school world, bullies would corner you in stairwells and strong-arm you into giving them your lunch money. Nowadays they cornered you in stairwells, offered to buy you lunch, and when you didn't eat it, they rammed it down your throat.

"For your information," Noah finally said, "I'm not gonna do any of your sports."

"What? You're going for another sport?" asked Roger. "What is it, swimming? Track?"

"Skydiving lacrosse," said Noah. "Now get out of my face."

But they didn't get out of his face. They only pressed tighter, cornering him. Roger turned toward the other two.

"Can you believe this guy? The disrespect? The attitude?"

"He thinks he's better than us."

"Yeah."

"He comes waltzing into our sports, humiliates us, and walks away."

"He has no right to do that!"

"Yeah."

Roger turned back to Noah, jamming him in the chest with his finger, much harder this time. "Relationships are built on respect, and I don't see any from you!"

Noah pushed him away, hard. Roger bumped into the soccer dude, who bumped into the wrestler, who yelped because his huge shoe got stepped on.

Roger looked at Noah, incredulous. "Did you just hit me?" he said. "Did *you* just *hit* me? Excuse me, but that's bullying, and we have a ZERO tolerance policy at this school for bullying, whether it's physical or psychological— and right now, you're guilty of both!"

"We oughta teach him a lesson," said the soccer dude.

"Yeah," said the wrestler.

Roger grabbed Noah by the shirt and pushed him hard against the wall. "We're gonna show you what we do to bullies."

When Noah was younger, and bigger kids pressed their advantage as bigger kids often did, Noah would launch countermeasures that let everyone know he was not to be messed with. Ogden called it "going Wolverine." It would usually earn Noah detention and a good talking to by the vice-principal, but it had always been worth it. Kids who knew him knew he couldn't be pushed around.

It had been years since he needed to go Wolverine on anybody, but he was more than ready to do it with these clowns. He felt the adrenaline coming on, the tingling in his ears, the heating of his cheeks—but before he could throw that first punch, something else happened. Something he was not expecting.

Suddenly, both his arms pulled up like a T. rex's, the fingers on both his hands curled, and he fell. He didn't just fall, he keeled over—like a bike with a broken kickstand.

He was now on the ground, on his side. Every single muscle of his body was locked—he couldn't speak; he couldn't move. His eyes remained open, but he couldn't even blink.

"Jeez, whad'ja do to him, Roger?" asked the soccer kid.

"Nothing. I didn't do anything."

"He's right," said the wrestler. "Dude just dropped on purpose."

"Get up!" demanded Roger. "You can't do that! Get up!"

But Noah didn't move. He *couldn't* move. It was horrible.

"Man, you're freaking me out!"

"Roger, what if there's something wrong with him?

29

What if he had a stress heart attack like our math teacher last year?"

The wrestler backed away, already wrestling his way out of the situation.

"There's nothing wrong with him," insisted Roger, but he didn't seem so sure. He nudged Noah with his foot. "You think you're funny? You're not funny."

Noah did not think any of this was funny. But even if he did, he wouldn't have been able to laugh.

"C'mon, man," the soccer kid said to Roger. "He's not worth it."

Roger clearly was itching for a fight, but he couldn't fight a kid lying on the ground. So he gave up. "You're right," he said. "Let's not waste our time."

And just to make sure he had the last word in a conversation in which Noah had barely uttered a word at all, Roger said, "You need help." Then he added, "My mother's a therapist. I'll get you her card."

Once they were gone, the bell rang and kids flooded the stairwell. No one stumbled over Noah; they just avoided him, as if he was part of the scenery.

"What's up with him?" kids asked one another.

"Probably a dare," someone suggested.

"I hear the drama class is doing this weird performance art thing."

"Didn't someone vomit right there yesterday?"

"Last week, they were singing *Hamilton* in the trees."

"No, seriously, right where his cheek is."

And the last person to pass him in the stairwell was none other than Sahara.

"What are you doing?" Sahara asked.

Finally, Noah got enough control to be able to speak, if not move.

"I don't...know," Noah responded.

In a moment, he was able to flip a wrist, then shake an arm, and the momentum of that was enough for him to sit up and look at Sahara.

"That's not normal, right?" he said, getting to his feet.

"I get the feeling that you and normal don't live in the same area code."

Which made him laugh. Not because he found it funny, but because of the absurdity of it. He always saw himself as pretty "normal" in the broadest interpretation of the word. But to Sahara, he was fringe material. And not even clean fringe, but the dirty kind that drags in the mud when you walk.

She strode away in her straight line.

"You should go wash your face," she called back to him without turning. "A kid vomited there yesterday."

3

Monkey Brains and an Alligator's Belly

"It's called 'conversion disorder,'" Ogden said, as they did research in the computer lab during lunch. "It used to be called 'hysterical paralysis.' But since the word 'hysterical' derives from the Latin *hystericus*, which has to do with a woman's uterus, it was considered sexist to call it that. You'd be amazed how many words—"

"Ogden, wrangle."

It was their agreed-on code word for when Ogden got off topic.

"Right," Ogden said. "No matter what you call it, it's psychological. Unless, of course, it's not. Then it would be a brain tumor."

"You're not helping," Noah snapped at him.

"You asked me a question, I gave you an answer. Don't blame me, blame Google." Ogden put up his hands in a "who knows" gesture. "Maybe when you found yourself cornered, your monkey brain kicked in and decided the best course of action was to play possum."

Noah knew about the monkey brain. It's the part of you that is best known for saying, *It seemed like a good idea at the time.*

"Yeah, but monkeys are monkeys, not opossums," Noah pointed out.

Ogden considered that. "True," he said. "But don't forget, all mammals share ninety-two percent of their DNA."

• ● •

After school that day, Noah went down to the motocross track, which sadly wasn't a track anymore. Bulldozers had leveled the many hills and dips of the course. Concrete slabs and cinderblock walls were already being erected.

It was hard for him to reconcile the fact that something that had already left the world still existed so clearly in his mind.

The construction crew was already gone for the day by the time Noah arrived at the fenced-off parcel of land. Noah never saw himself as the destructive type—but just outside the fence, there was a pile of rocks that had been excavated. And all that yellow heavy machinery seemed to mock him like an attack force of miserable mechanical enemies. After he threw the first stone, it became easier to throw more, like skimming stones in a lake. The equipment was virtually indestructible, but it sure felt good to hear the hefty clang when a rock connected with its target.

So focused was he on his angry endeavor that he didn't even notice the car pull up behind him.

"Vandalism may feel good in the moment," a voice said, "but is ultimately very unsatisfying."

Noah turned to see a man about his size standing next to the open rear door of a big chauffeured Cadillac. Not quite a limo, but close. The man looked Asian, with a dark complexion that suggested the southern part of the continent. He wore an expensive-looking suit and a bright, busy tie that seemed much less reserved than the rest of him. "This happens to be my property, and you happen to be trespassing."

"I'm outside the fence, so technically I'm not trespassing," Noah pointed out. "And besides, I didn't break anything."

The man strode closer. "Intent to do harm is, in fact, enough to press charges."

Noah shrugged. "So, what are you gonna do now? Have me arrested for not breaking your bulldozers?"

The man grinned. "You're cheeky," he said. "And you also look familiar. Where do I know you from?"

"I don't know—do you keep a file on all the people whose lives you ruin? Maybe you know me from there."

Then the man gasped, as if reaching some grand realization. "Ah yes," he said. "Now I know. Now I know, indeed." But he didn't explain himself.

"Well, are you going to tell me?" Noah asked.

"You're much younger, wearing a Pokémon T-shirt, next to your sister, who refused to smile!"

Noah had a vague memory of that shirt—and a whole lot of memories of his sister not smiling.

"It's a picture framed in your father's showroom," the man said. "I recently commissioned a casket from him."

Noah finally put two and two together: This man he stood eye to eye with. A build not all that different from his own.

"Right," Noah said. "Yeah, I tested it out. It's comfortable."

"Good to know," he said. Then he looked at the work machines. "So, what do you have against me and my construction site?"

"I ride motocross," Noah informed him. "Or at least I used to."

Now the man got it. "And I have ruined your beloved pastime."

"You could have built your condos somewhere else."

Then the man picked up a rock and hurled it over the fence. It hit the bucket of a backhoe with a solid clang. "The land was for sale at a reasonable price." Then he turned around and headed back to his car. "If you want to blame someone, don't blame me," he called back. "Blame your father."

35

"My father? What are you talking about?"

And the man said, "He's the one who convinced me to buy it."

• ● •

Sahara's shoulder was still a little sore from her collision with that Noah kid earlier in the week. She iced it and heated it and iced it again, with the single-minded determination that she would not allow something so ridiculous as a boy falling on her from the trees to interfere with this weekend's gymnastics competition. And in spite of what he said, he *had* fallen on her from above—there was no question in her mind. The only question was, What was he doing up there?

And after today's display in the stairwell, it was clear the kid had issues. She wanted absolutely nothing to do with him. Except for the fact that she couldn't stop thinking about him. Which was ridiculously annoying, like when you have a song you don't even like stuck in your head, torturing you from within.

What was this kid's deal? After finishing her homework that afternoon, and before her evening gymnastics practice, Sahara spent a few minutes doing some online reconnaissance. He had told her his name was Noah, and when they had gotten their tardy slips, she had noticed his last name was Prime. She did a search for his name on multiple social media platforms. You could learn a lot about a person from their digital footprint.

She found profiles for seven Noah Prims, and four Noah Preems, but not a single Noah Prime. So she tried using just his first name and adding their town as a search parameter. Still, he didn't turn up.

Curiouser and curiouser, as her mother would say when she encountered something strange. Not everyone liked social media, but whether they liked it or not, everyone she knew had a profile. Everyone but this kid.

She resolved to put Noah Prime and his infuriating behavior out of her mind. And she would. Just as soon as she looked him up in her elementary school yearbook.

• ● •

It was raining by the time Noah got home.

His mom had made a pot roast for dinner, but she cooked the vegetables separately because Andi wouldn't eat foods that touched each other.

Noah had no appetite.

His father came in from his workshop smelling of wood instead of varnish, which meant he had started on a new project. Noah always associated that woody smell with his father. He even knew the smells of different woods his father worked with. Today it was cherrywood.

Noah had a good poker face. He could hide his emotions

37

well when he wanted to. As dinner began, no one suspected how truly furious he was, how betrayed he felt. He waited until his parents asked him about his day, which they always did.

"Something really interesting happened today," he said. They waited, but he took his time, chewing a piece of meat and swallowing it first. "I ran into the guy who bought the motocross course."

"Mr. Ksh? What do you mean you ran into him?" his father asked, looking a little suspicious.

Noah didn't answer the question. He'd let his dad figure it out.

"He told me something interesting," Noah said, cutting another piece of meat and chewing it slowly. He watched his father, then finally said what was on his mind. "He told me it was your idea for him to buy the course and get rid of the track. He told me you were the one who told him to do it." Then he caught his mom looking over at his dad, and he realized the truth.

"You knew, too? You both knew?" Noah stood up. "Why? Why would you do that? Motocross is the one thing I truly love, and you took it away from me." His eyes filled with tears, and this time he couldn't push them away and hide his emotions. "I hate you!" he told them. Then he stormed out.

"Noah, wait," his father called after him, but he wasn't about to listen to anything his father said.

He went to his father's workshop. Several projects were

38

in various stages of completion. Mr. Ksh's was done and pushed to a corner, soon to be delivered. An artsy conversation piece until the day he'd get shoved inside it.

Noah grabbed a heavy steel gouge from his father's workbench and walked over to the casket. Noah hefted the tool and prepared to dig a deep gouge into the wood, so deep his dad couldn't repair it, so deep that he'd have to do the whole thing over.

But Noah couldn't do it. It wasn't as if his body froze the way it had in the stairwell that morning. It was his mind that froze. No matter how angry he was, he couldn't bring himself to vandalize his father's work.

He dropped the gouge on the floor, cursed into the wood-scented air, and kicked up sawdust.

"Noah . . ."

He turned to see his father standing there. He had no idea if his father had seen what he had almost done.

"Leave me alone," Noah said. "You have no right to talk to me after what you did."

"I can understand how you'd be upset," his father said, picking up the gouge from the floor and returning it to the workbench. "But you don't know the whole story."

"I know enough," Noah said.

"Do you?" his father asked, turning back to face him. "So, did Mr. Ksh tell you the entire conversation I had with him?"

"He told me enough. That it was your idea for him to get rid of the course."

"No," said his father. "It was my idea that he buy the course. It was up for sale, and no one knew what was going to happen to it. So I suggested he buy it and build it out into a full-fledged motocross stadium."

This was not what Noah was expecting to hear.

"Turns out he only took half of my advice," his father continued. "I guess condos are more profitable than motocross."

"Is that the truth?" Noah asked, still not entirely ready to believe it.

"What do you think?" responded his father.

Suddenly, Noah didn't know how to feel. His anger still felt like a fever. And even though he now knew what had really happened, the feeling didn't go away. Instead, it turned inward, and now he was furious at himself for misjudging his father.

"Come back to dinner," his father said.

Noah shook his head. "I'm not hungry."

"Noah, in this world, things aren't always what they seem. You need to remember that."

Then he left Noah alone to grapple with it.

• ● •

That night, Noah tossed and turned, unable to sleep. He had humiliated himself twice today. Not only in front of his whole family at dinner, but also in the stairwell in front of Sahara.

And he still had no explanation for the way he had seized up in front of those three jerks.

Well, it was all in his head, one way or another. Although he didn't particularly like the idea of having to get checked for a brain tumor, or even telling his parents about it.

"See if it happens again," Ogden had suggested at school. "And if it does, you have to tell someone. Because if you don't, I will."

There was a gentle knock on his door, and then his mother opened it and peered in. Sometimes he would pretend to be asleep when she did that, but not tonight.

"Hey," he said.

"Trouble sleeping?" she asked.

He nodded. "Rough day."

She pulled up a chair and sat beside him.

"I don't want to talk anymore," he told her. "I'm sorry I said I hated you."

"Already forgotten," she told him. "And I'm sure it won't be the last time anyway."

She sat there with him for a few moments, then said, "Remember when you were little and couldn't sleep? How I would rub your tummy and it would always put you out?"

When he was little, it had been their bedtime ritual and private joke: He was a baby alligator, and she would rub his tummy and put him to sleep—because alligators had that sleep reflex.

"Mom, I'm fourteen. I'm too old for that."

"I know," she said. "I was just trying to help."

41

He thought about it for a moment more, then rolled over onto his back. He was in that place where he was beyond tired. That place where your mind is too stressed and your body is just too tired to fall asleep. "Maybe just this once," he told her.

She gently began to rub his belly, as she had done all those years ago, and like an alligator, he was asleep in ten seconds flat.

• ● •

Meanwhile, nearly seven thousand miles away, another boy who, not coincidentally, was also named Noah, lay on a gurney in a hospital in Buenos Aires, Argentina.

"*Estuviste en un accidente de auto,*" he had been told. "You've been in a car accident."

He had no memory of it. The last thing he remembered was being in his room at home. And suddenly he was here.

"But how did it happen?" he asked the nurse, a woman with a kindly smile, although there was something very strange about her eyes. Over the past few months, odd things had been happening to him. Things that he not only couldn't explain but was afraid to talk about.

Like the time he found himself squealing for no reason and was somehow able to "see" through walls. Or the time he pounced on his sister's guinea pig and ate the poor beloved *cavia*, fur and all.

Car accident? he thought. He didn't even know who had been driving the car.

"My family?" he asked the nurse. "Are they all right?"

She fiddled with a string of pearls around her neck, which seemed strange for a nurse on duty to be wearing. "Don't you worry about that right now," she answered.

Which was not the thing he wanted to hear.

He was rolled down an empty hallway and into a room with a large humming device that he recognized as an MRI machine. There was something strange about it. But, like the nurse's eyes, he couldn't quite place what it was.

"We'll need to make some scans," the nurse told him, "to make sure you're all right."

"Will it hurt?" he asked.

The nurse took his hand. "Not at all," she assured him. "Although it may be a bit loud. Just try to relax, and stay absolutely still," she said. "It will be over sooner than you know it."

The orderly shifted him from the gurney to the MRI platform. There was a faint mechanical vibration, and the platform began to slowly slide into the doughnut-shaped machine until his entire body was inside. And then the nurse closed the lid, sealing him in.

He didn't know that MRI machines even had lids.

He was in complete darkness now, and at that moment it occurred to him how strange this all was. He hadn't seen anyone besides the nurse and the orderly who had wheeled him down the hall into the MRI room. Shouldn't a hospital be bustling with people?

Well, maybe it was the middle of the night. He had no idea how long he'd been unconscious.

Then he realized what was strange about the nurse's eyes: While the MRI machine had a lid that shouldn't have been there, her eyes should have had lids . . . but didn't.

Not knowing what to do with this odd bit of information, he put it in the back of his mind and got back to the business at hand. He tried to remain absolutely still as he had been told.

The nurse was right. It was completely painless.

• ● •

The nurse let the machine run for ten seconds. Much longer than was necessary, but she wanted to be absolutely sure. Then she had the orderly open the lid.

Inside, on the narrow bed of the machine cleverly disguised as an MRI scanner, were approximately two pounds of white ash spread out across the surface.

The "nurse" sighed. "You'd think we'd be able to come up with a vaporizer that actually vaporized, instead of leaving behind such a mess. Clean it up," she told her associate.

Then she went off to a prepare a report that would let the home office know that N.O.A.H. Tercero had been neutralized.

<FOBE Interrogation>
<Noah Prime>
<Security Code Sapphire>
<Part 3 of 3>

THE INTERROGATION ROOM WAS GETTING UNCOMFORTABLY *warm, and Agent Rigby was not letting up. Noah was sweating in spite of all his attempts to remain cool. Ogden would call it "secreting." If so, Noah had no clue what he was secreting. He recalled that poison dart frogs secreted a deadly nerve toxin when under duress. Cane toads secreted hallucinogenic slime that people would lick to get high. None of those things would be of use to him now.*

Agent Rigby did not break the slightest sweat in spite of the heat. Perhaps she had had her sweat glands removed. Or perhaps she was a robot, like a certain other person he knew. Probably not. That robot had seemed much more human than Agent Rigby.

Now Agent Rigby just sat there pretending to be patient, when clearly she wasn't; she was waiting for Noah to slip and give her even more information.

"Where are Ogden and Sahara?" Noah finally asked.

"Your friends are being dealt with accordingly," Agent Rigby said. That did not sound good. He wondered what sort of tortures a deep-shadowed organization such as this would employ.

"If you cooperate," Agent Rigby said, "I promise you that your friends won't be harmed."

Even if Noah believed her, he still knew he couldn't give them what they wanted, because (a) they wouldn't believe him anyway, and (b) if they did, he'd spend the rest of his life being poked and prodded and vivisected piece by piece, organ by organ, in the name of science.

No, as long as he remained an unknown quantity—as long as they didn't know what they were dealing with—he and his friends were safe. All the more reason to stall and buy time by teasing her with information that wasn't at all useful.

"It's hot in here," Noah said.

"Really?" said Agent Rigby, "I haven't noticed."

"You should make it cooler, or I'll start losing all my body hair."

She perked up at that. "So, then, have you been exposed to radiation? Is that what you're telling me?"

"No. But if it gets too hot, I'll probably blow my coat."

"Excuse me?"

Noah sighed. "Haven't you ever had a dog?"

"I'm more of a cat person."

"Yes, I sense that about you. Although I'd think you were more the type to drown kittens rather than keep them."

There was another guffaw from behind the one-way mirror. Agent Rigby shifted her shoulders and pursed her lips, bristling like a disgruntled cat.

"Anyway," said Noah, "in hot weather, huskies and other cold-weather dogs blow their coats. They shed like crazy."

"You're not a dog," observed the woman.

"No, I'm not. But stress can make a person lose their hair."

"Maybe I should turn up the heat and see what else happens."

Noah shook his head. "Whatever happens, I can promise you it will not be good for you."

"I think I can handle myself."

"How can you, when you're secretly terrified of what I might do?" Because as unreadable as this woman was, Noah could sense the fear she was trying to hide. Not just a fear of him, but of the larger unknown that he might represent.

Agent Rigby laughed at last. "Noah, nothing about you terrifies me."

"Then why am I chained to the table with like fifty pounds of titanium? Why is the entrance to this building a vault door that's a foot thick? Why did you show up with a SWAT team to bring me in? Or is that your organization's standard procedure for dealing with fourteen-year-olds?"

Agent Rigby took a long look at him before she spoke again. "These precautions are for your own protection."

Now it was Noah's turn to laugh. "In case you haven't

47

figured it out, I don't need protection. In fact, protecting myself is kind of my specialty."

"Really? So why don't you tell me about it?"

But Noah would not be baited into revealing anything he didn't want to.

"Has my blood work come back?" he asked, changing the subject. Agent Rigby gave him an almost imperceptible nod, or maybe it was an involuntary flinch. "What did it tell you?"

Agent Rigby pursed her lips again. "It was ... inconclusive."

Noah grinned. "Blood tests are pretty straightforward. What couldn't it conclude?"

She leaned back in her seat, crossing her arms. "It just so happens that our gene sequencer is down at the moment."

"I broke it, you mean."

She scoffed at that. "Noah, you're really having delusions of grandeur if you think a single drop of your blood could break such a highly sophisticated machine."

But he saw right through her, and she knew it. So she dropped all pretenses and leaned closer. Not close enough for him to reach her, but close enough to make it clear this was her endgame.

"Noah, whoever interrogates you next won't be nearly as pleasant as I am," she said. "For all of our sakes, please tell me what you know."

Noah forced his shoulders to relax, then looked her in the eye, trying to make sure she understood that he was telling her the truth. "What I know," he said, "is a drop in the bucket compared to what I don't know ..."

4

The Champagne
Brunch Club

THE INCIDENT WITH SAHARA HAD LEFT NOAH WITH HIS FOURTH
unexcused tardy, landing him in mandatory Saturday
school.

Mr. Kratz, his science teacher, was perpetually on Saturday school duty. He did this not because he cared, but
because Kratz was determined to curry enough favor with
the school board to have something named after him.

"Well, if it isn't our resident vampire," Mr. Kratz said,
turning a page of his book. "Have a seat, and no talking for
the rest of recorded time."

Noah took a seat in the back of the room, in front of
an ocean mural featuring a pod of dolphins. It was a mural
that proved, beyond a shadow of a doubt, just how terribly
untalented were the youth of Arbuckle.

The room was sparsely populated with the usual sus-
pects. Slackers and wisecrackers and kids who looked like

they would rather be sold for their organs than be in Saturday school.

To his right was Bryant Goldman, who, at last week's football game, thought it would be a good idea to milk the school mascot. Unfortunately, the guy in the cow suit was not at all happy about the experience.

In front of him was Magda Greaver, who took it upon herself to steal all the dead things in the biology lab's specimen jars and give them a burial in the middle of the baseball field. Then, just in case no one had noticed, she sat herself in the middle of the little graveyard with her cello, playing Mozart's Requiem. It got her a full article in the local paper, which is exactly what she wanted. It also got her a quartet of Saturday schools.

And to Noah's left was Kaleb Carpenter, who, due to some sort of issue with spatial perception, had a Mohawk that was about one inch off-center. His geometry and spatial awareness problem also left him accidentally bumping into kids in hallways on a regular basis, then getting into fights about it, landing him in Saturday school—although Noah suspected the hallway bumps weren't always accidental. Kaleb seemed to like fights—even when he lost them, which was more often than not. And unlike everyone else there, he seemed to enjoy Saturday school, which suggested that he was a true glutton for punishment.

Kaleb turned to look at him. "So, what you in for?" he asked.

"Tardies."

"Boring," said Kaleb. "Hardly even worth it. Well, welcome to the Champagne Brunch Club." Then he high-fived Noah but missed.

Noah quickly deduced that Saturday school was called the Champagne Brunch Club because Mr. Kratz spent most of the day drinking something bubbly from a Perrier bottle that was clearly more relaxing than sparkling water.

Around the time the second hour bled into the third, Mr. Kratz stood up suddenly and stalked toward the kids. "Goldman!" he said sternly, holding out his hand. "Hand over your phone."

Bryant Goldman, who had been staring at the cell phone he was holding under the desk, looked up, surprised.

"Hand over your cell phone," Mr. Kratz repeated. "Now."

Noah watched the scene playing out with increasing anxiety. What if Mr. Kratz decided to confiscate everyone's cell phone? That's how these things usually go, right? Especially if Bryant ticked him off. Although Noah wasn't using his phone, the edge of it was sticking out of a very shallow pocket in his jeans. He just hoped Mr. Kratz didn't notice it. Or him. Noah slouched a little in his chair, wishing he could disappear. Not entirely, but just enough to be passed over by Kratz's all-seeing eyes. And the moment he thought that, he felt his skin start to tingle the tiniest bit.

Bryant handed the phone over reluctantly. "But I was using it for research, for a report."

Mr. Kratz glanced at the screen. "Really? Cat videos?"

"My report is on unusual feline behavior."

That's when Kaleb leaned over and said to Noah, "Dude, you okay? You're looking kinda sick."

"Yeah," said Magda, turning to Noah for a better look. "You look nearly as gray as that dolphin behind you."

"Huh?" Noah said, then turned around to see the oddly smiling dolphins in the mural behind him. When he held up his hand in front of one of them, his skin tone wasn't all that different, kind of bluish gray. It must have been a weird trick of the fluorescent lights, which at times could make people appear almost any unhealthy shade.

"Dude, if you're about to pass out, put your head down on the desk first, unless you want a nasty bruise on your forehead," Kaleb said with an unsettling grin. "I know this from experience."

"No talking, Carpenter," said Mr. Kratz. Then he looked directly at Noah. "Prime, you're looking a little unearthly," he said. "I was only joking about the vampire thing—but now I'm not so sure."

"I'm fine," said Noah, more irritated than anything. He put his hand down on his desk, and he noticed that it had changed to a different shade. More like the color of the desk.

Mr. Kratz kept a slight distance, as if worried Noah might projectile-vomit in his general direction. "If you're sick, you should go home. You can make up Saturday school next week."

52

"I said I'm fine," Noah told him.

In his frustration, he felt heat come to his ears, and normal color must have returned to his face, because Mr. Kratz said, "You were holding your breath to feign being ill, weren't you?"

"What?" Noah had never even considered the concept.

"Nah," Kaleb said, "you turn purple if you do that, not gray. I know this from experience."

Mr. Kratz threw Noah a half-hearted glare, gave him the universal "I've got my eyes on you" gesture, then returned to his place at the front of the room.

As soon as he was enthralled once more with his book, Noah turned around and put his hand on one of the dolphins on the wall, trying to will his hand to turn the same bluish gray again, but it stubbornly remained his regular skin tone. Maybe it was just the light after all—although the more he thought about it, the less he believed it. But if it wasn't that, then what else could it have been?

Then he glanced toward the front of the room, and he saw Mr. Kratz watching him with interest. And although the teacher didn't talk about it for the rest of Saturday school, he was true to his word—or at least his gesture—and kept his eyes on Noah more than anyone else in the room.

5

Just Another Oxymoron

As Noah walked out of the Saturday school classroom that afternoon, he shook his head to recover from the flatness of the day's monotony, as well as the weirdness of his unexplained chameleon-like behavior. What was that all about? Did he even want to know? When he heard applause coming from the gym, he wandered over to the entrance to take a look, partly out of curiosity and partly to get some momentary relief from his own thoughts.

There was a gymnastics meet going on inside, with engaged spectators in the stands, most of them, no doubt, the parents of the participants. There was an array of gymnastics equipment spread about on the floor, with multiple events going on at the same time.

And then he saw Sahara. She was warming up in front of a piece of equipment. He didn't even know the name of it until a voice came over the PA and announced it at the start of her event. The uneven parallel bars. Right. He remembered watching the Olympics with Ogden once, and Ogden was obsessing over them. "How can something be uneven and parallel at the same time?" he had said. "It's an oxymoron. Like jumbo shrimp or military intelligence."

Sahara's turn came, and she jumped up, grabbed the higher bar, and swung her legs wide, turning half a revolution on the bar, then extended her body straight up and froze there for a moment. She swung back down, changing her grip—a quick hand over hand—then swung up and over the pole one more time before deftly slipping to the lower bar, her body sliding gracefully through the air like a diver defying gravity. There was a fluidity to her movements that was simply beyond words. For a final flourish, she swung up and over, then released her grip, twisting her body around as she flipped her feet over her head one last time before she hit the mat, sticking a perfect landing. Instantly, all the spectators—including Noah—burst into applause.

After leaving Saturday school, he had wanted to be as far from Arbuckle Middle School as possible. Well, not anymore.

This was a joint meet, so there were men's events, too. They had a different kind of grace than the women's gymnastics events. More about strength and precision than artistry. These were arguably the most muscular boys in school—even more so than the football players, who were more about building bulk—but with the gymnasts, who were more or less Noah's size, it was all core and upper-body strength.

There were those who clearly struggled at their events, but there were some gymnasts who, like Sahara, made it look easy. That was the trick, wasn't it? Making it look like you could do it in your sleep. Noah wondered how hard it actually was. The closest he'd come to actual gymnastics equipment was a trampoline gym years ago, where kids bounced out their birthday cake sugar until someone inevitably got hurt, and the parents decided it was time to go home. He had enjoyed it and was pretty good at it. "You're a natural," the people who ran the place had said. But his mom told him they were just trying to sell them trampoline classes.

When the meet was over, before they began to put the equipment away, Noah made his way out onto the gym floor and looked up at a pair of rings hanging on cables. The rings competition was the most demanding of the men's events. They were about seven feet off the ground, and all the gymnasts had needed a boost to get up there. Noah couldn't see why—he jumped up and grabbed them on his first attempt...

But as he tried to pull himself up, he realized how difficult it was. The strain on his arms and shoulders was sharp and instantaneous, and it was quickly evolving into pain. This wasn't just hard, it was downright impossible! Clearly,

56

he had pulled himself up the wrong way, and now his shoulders felt as if they were tearing out of his sockets—but if he let go now, he'd be completely off-balance, and he'd hit the mat hard enough to break something. He had to position himself better just to let go. When he glanced up, he could see people in the stands. They were pointing at him. They were laughing—but worst of all, he saw Sahara watching, too. He had made a fool of himself in front of her twice already, and this would be a third time. He felt his face going red from both the strain on his arms and the embarrassment. This was a bad idea in a long string of bad ideas he'd had lately—and with the pain and embarrassment, a tingling came over him. He knew that feeling. He always felt it when he was about to begin a motocross race. It was a surge of adrenaline. He could feel his fight-or-flight response engage. He could drop to the ground, enduring whatever physical damage and humiliation that would bring . . . or he could fight to salvage the moment and actually try to hold himself upright on the rings.

He decided to throw caution to the wind and go with it—and the instant he made his decision, he felt the pain in his shoulders subside. He hoisted himself up higher between the rings, then tried to imitate some of the moves he had seen the male gymnasts attempt. He didn't know the names of the moves, just what they looked like. There was one he called "the Superman"—in which you held your body completely horizontal, using only the strength of your arms and core to do so. He managed it. And to his surprise, it wasn't all that hard.

Next, he held his arms out straight to the side but kept his body completely vertical. He called this the "Flying Jesus," because it kinda looked like being crucified without a cross. It didn't feel that hard, though—it felt kind of... natural. He swung into a handstand, then let the momentum of his body take him into a series of revolutions—like a swing flying over the bar. He revolved over and over until he felt dizzy and decided it was time to get off this ride. He couldn't be sure which way was down anymore, and when he let go of the rings, for one horrible moment, he thought he'd built up so much momentum that he'd go shooting up through the corrugated steel roof of the gym. He twisted, trying to find the ground, his body torqued around like a spring, and when he finally got his bearings, both of his feet hit the mat at the exact same moment. He found himself standing upright, perfectly balanced, and facing an audience that had begun cheering. He looked behind him, wondering what had happened to cause their reaction, except there was nothing behind him but a few stunned students staring at him, slack-jawed. The applause was for him! Whatever he had done, they liked it. He had faked his way through it well enough for people to think he actually knew what he was doing!

Mr. Snyder, the men's gymnastics coach, came running

up to him, his eyes sparkling like a fanboy's. "Kid, I'm speechless! Where on earth have you been hiding?"

"So, that was good?" Noah asked.

"Good? I think that was the best rings display I've ever seen!"

"Oh. Okay."

"Are you with a private club? Who's been coaching you?" Then he became suspicious. "Did Stretch Meyer from Portland GymWorx send you? Is this some sort of joke?"

"No, Coach," said one of the gymnasts, "I know him—he's in my English class."

That's when Sahara stormed up to him. If she was impressed, it was hidden behind an iron wall of anger.

"How did you learn to do that?" she demanded.

Noah shrugged as if it was nothing, because it kind of was. "I didn't. I just copied what the other guys did."

"*Copied?*" she wailed. "You just performed an Azarian Roll into an iron cross! Then a tucked double felge into a triple back twisting dismount!"

Noah shrugged again. "Yeah, so?"

Suddenly, she grabbed his arm, and squeezed his left shoulder. "Where are the muscles?" she demanded. "Where's the hair?"

"What?"

She pointed an accusing finger at him. "When you were up on those rings, your deltoids and biceps were *huge*.

They were bulging out of your shirt! And your arms were *hairy*! Like a *high schooler*!" Then she reached a conclusion and turned to the coach. "It wasn't him up there! It was some sort of trick! It *couldn't* have been him!" But everyone had seen it. Maybe Sahara refused to believe her own eyes, but no one else did.

Noah decided that this was an odd way to be the center of attention, and it had the exact opposite effect on Sahara than he had hoped it would. Then, as if the moment wasn't awkward enough, Coach Snyder went down on one knee like a groom about to propose. He looked at Noah with wide-eyed sincerity and said, "Son, do you want to be on the gymnastics team?"

What else could Noah say but "I do"?

• ● •

That night, the Prime family celebrated Andi's birthday—an event that Noah always forgot until it was thrust upon him, and he had to scramble for a present that didn't seem as if he was scrambling for a present. This year, he got her a game download, so he didn't have to go out to buy it, or wait for it to arrive in the mail late.

As always, Andi requested they have dinner at Rick E. Ricotta's—which had the worst pizza in the long, sad history of animatronic-character-themed pizza establishments. The only good thing was they allowed you to have different toppings on every single slice of your pizza. Unfortunately, the toppings always spilled over onto the other pieces, creating misery and strife for all involved. They also offered a selection of truly surreal toppings, like tomato-flavored gummy bears and Parmesan Alpha-Bits.

"You're ten years old—that's too old for Rick E. Ricotta's," Noah had told Andi before they left for dinner.

"Shut up!" Andi had snapped back. "It's nostalgia."

"You're ten years old—that's too young to be nostalgic."

Nevertheless, a birthday was a birthday, and so Rick E. Ricotta's it was.

"Think of it this way," his father said as they waited for their pizza. "Better here than in Saturday school, right?"

"Not really," Noah said.

And as if to prove his point, the robotic band of Rick E. Ricotta's poorly conceived cartoon characters (Gorgonzola Gorilla, Mozzarella McMonkey, Havarti Hippo, and Rhino LeRoquefort) launched into a spirited but slightly off-key rendition of "Food, Glorious Food."

After far too long a wait, a dude in a Gorgonzola Gorilla costume delivered their underwhelming pizza.

"So," Noah said as everyone dug in, "I think I found my new sport." He paused for dramatic effect. "Gymnastics."

This would have been followed by crickets, had they not been drowned out by the animatronic band.

"Are you sure you want to rush right into something?" his mom asked.

"Your mother's right," said his dad. "Your grades have

61

to come first. Have you thought about taking a year off from sports?"

Noah just gaped at them. "I thought you'd be happy for me, that I'm finally moving beyond motocross."

"We are, honey," said his mother. "We just want to make sure you're not rushing your decision."

Then Andi took a bite of her artichoke-and-Fritos pizza and said, "Didn't some kid get decapitated last year in, like, Kentucky or something during a gymnastics competition?"

Noah glared at her and said, "(A) that's extremely rare, and (B) we're nowhere near Kentucky." Then he turned to his parents. "I want to do this," he insisted. "I mean, I'm good at it."

"I'm sure you're good at anything you put your mind to, Noah," his father said. He shared a look with his mother, then said, "And if gymnastics is it, then we'll support it."

"But don't expect any sympathy from me when your head flies off," said Andi.

The fact that his parents weren't enthusiastic about it bothered Noah. But not quite enough for him to wonder why they'd be that way.

• ● •

Ogden was sitting on their doorstep when they got home, bouncing his knees impatiently.

"Of all days, you had to pick today to go to Rick E. Ricotta's?"

"It's my sister's birthday. I had no choice."

"There's something I need to show you."

While Noah's mother and sister went off to nurse acute indigestion, and his father retired to his workshop, Noah and Ogden went to Noah's room and sat in front of his computer. Ogden tapped a few keys and brought up a YouTube video with the caption "Get a load of this guy."

It was a clip of Noah's impromptu performance on the rings at the gymnastics competition—someone in the stands had caught it on their phone and posted it. As they watched, Noah heard for the first time how the audience's initial stunned reaction turned into an enthusiastic roar. He saw for himself how the muscles of his arms and upper body bulked up as he went through some impressive moves. And yes, as Sahara had accused, his arms were hairy.

"Ogden, what the hell is going on?"

"I'm not sure," Ogden said. "Further research is necessary."

That didn't bode well, because when Ogden did research, pain was usually involved, only some of it accidental.

"What was going through your mind during your little Olympic performance?" Ogden asked.

Noah shrugged. "Nothing. I was trying to imitate stuff I'd seen, and my body just knew what to do."

"Were you feeling confident? In control?"

Noah shook his head. "Stressed out. Like I was in over my head and was about to make a fool out of myself—but then I didn't."

"Interesting . . ."

"Interesting?" mocked Noah. "That's all you got?"

"For now. Let me know the next time something weird happens."

But as it turned out, Ogden would be there to see it. And so would about two hundred others.

6

Like the Plague

SCHOOL DANCES WERE ONLY SLIGHTLY HIGHER ON NOAH'S LIST of undesirable activities than dinner at Rick E. Ricotta's. Nonetheless, he had promised Ogden he'd go with him to the next one, which happened to be the following night. Sunday was the only night of the week that the gym wasn't occupied with other activities—thus, the school had no one but itself to blame for sleep-deprived kids come Monday morning.

"I'm sick of standing in the corner alone," Ogden had told him. "This way, we can stand in the corner alone together." Which was another oxymoron.

Ogden claimed he was building up momentum until he reached the glorious moment when he would actually ask a girl to dance. There was no telling how close that moment was, but Ogden was determined to get there.

As there were seven dances scheduled for the school

year, someone had the bright idea to have each one celebrate a different continent. The theme of this particular
continental cotillion was Antarctic Adventure. The deco-
rations featured hundreds of sparkling white snowflakes,
and as the gym was perpetually cold, it just added to the
illusion—as did all the blue lips, since too much food color-
ing had been added to the glacier punch.

Noah and Ogden weren't exactly in the corner, but they
were on the sidelines with a gaggle of other kids. The dance
floor was filled with what Ogden called "the early adapt-
ers." In other words, kids who quickly warmed to awkward and unnatural social situations. They either danced
with partners or gyrated alone as detached ions in the test
tube of human experience.

Noah was not one to dance alone, and although he
didn't really have a problem asking girls to dance, he didn't
want to abandon Ogden on the sidelines.

"I may achieve critical mass tonight," Ogden informed
Noah. This was Ogden-speak for "I might ask a girl to
dance." Turns out he didn't have to, because a girl whose
intensely blue lips telegraphed an overdose of sugar
approached the line of wistful wallflowers like an Antarctic blizzard, and she grabbed the first available hand.

"Dance," she said.

The hand was Ogden's, and he was helplessly swept out
onto the dance floor, plunging into the tumultuous sea like
a calving glacier.

Noah would have been content to watch the spectacle of Ogden attempting to dance—but then he spotted Sahara across the gym. Her dress was green, which clashed with the theme of the dance—and now that he had seen her, he could not unsee her. No matter where he looked, her green figure punctuated his periphery. She was, perhaps, the only girl there who he felt nervous asking to dance. That annoyed him, so he decided he wouldn't be like Ogden, waiting until he mined enough nerve from the depths of his soul. He would cross the gym and ask her now. When she invariably said no, he would at least know that he had tried.

She eyed him warily as he approached.

"Hey," he said.

"What? I can't hear you!"

"HEY!" he shouted.

"OH, IT'S YOU!"

Noah couldn't help but notice that she looked at his arms, as if checking for hairiness that was not there.

"NICE DRESS!" he said.

"WHAT?"

"YOUR DRESS! DEFINITELY NOT ANTARCTIC! YOU'RE MAKING A STATEMENT!"

"FYI, IT'S NOT ON PURPOSE. IT'S THE ONLY DRESS I HAVE THAT DOESN'T MAKE ME LOOK HORRIBLE."

"I DON'T THINK ANYTHING COULD MAKE YOU LOOK HORRIBLE."

"WHAT?"

"I SAID—"

"NEVER MIND," she screamed. "LISTEN, IF YOU'RE GOING TO ASK ME TO DANCE, JUST GET IT OVER WITH BEFORE WE BOTH LOSE OUR VOICES."

"SO, DO YOU WANT TO DANCE?"

"NO."

"NO? THEN WHY DID YOU MAKE ME ASK?"

"SO YOU COULD GET IT OUT OF YOUR SYSTEM."

Which, as Noah had already noted to himself, was exactly the reason why he had come over here. That meant that Sahara really understood him. And it made him want to dance with her all the more.

Sahara apparently got that, too, because she said, "YOU ASKED THE WRONG QUESTION. DO I *WANT* TO DANCE? NO: THERE'S WAY TOO MUCH PERFUME AND BAD COLOGNE ON THE DANCE FLOOR. BUT *WILL* I DANCE? SURE." And she stepped out onto the dance floor with Noah.

The DJ was in the middle of a set of '80s songs. He was attempting a mash-up of "Freeze-Frame" and "Cold as Ice." They were two songs that didn't mash up so much as they beat one another with chairs like professional wrestlers.

Noah gamely started to dance, but due to the mixed-up mash-up, he couldn't find the beat and ended up ineffectually shuffling back and forth—which is what most of the other guys were doing, but he usually had better rhythm.

He saw that Sahara was faring much better, defying the mismatched beat.

The mash-up came to a merciful end, but it segued into a slow song, and Noah knew he had to make the decision: Back self-consciously off the dance floor or sweep Sahara into his arms.

"So," said Sahara.

"So," said Noah. He was never one to back away from a challenge, so he put his arms around her waist, she draped hers over his shoulders, and they joined the few, the nervous, the slow dancers.

"You're not terrible at this," Sahara told him.

"Thanks."

But as not-terrible as he was, there were some moments that could not be avoided. About two minutes into the dance, he achieved the most feared literal misstep of a school dance. His left foot came down on Sahara's toes.

"Ouch!"

"Oops! Sorry."

He could feel his ears and cheeks going red from embarrassment—but the feeling didn't stop there. And Noah knew that something odd was about to happen that he had no power to stop—like the moment you know, without question, that you're going to hurl.

Noah let Sahara go, and he backed up. Then he ducked his chin down so hard the back of his neck hurt.

"What are you doing?" she asked.

"I don't know."

Then he lifted his chin so high his Adam's apple hurt, and he began slapping his hands to his sides over and over.

"Are you choking?"

"No."

"Is this a new dance I should know?"

"I don't think so."

Then suddenly his words left him, and out of his mouth came a bizarre rhythmic shrieking that made everyone else on the dance floor turn in their direction.

Now he found himself swinging his head side to side, then dipping it, raising it, and letting loose with the same shriek again. The moment was beyond horrific. It was worse than any anxiety dream he had ever experienced. Yet as strange as all this was, there was a wordless part of him that was telling him this was a perfectly natural, normal thing to do under the circumstances. It was a part of him that refused to pay any attention to the rest of his brain—or to the strange looks he was getting from Sahara and everyone else around them.

"Dude, what's your deal?" someone said.

His answer was another shrill squawk.

"Noah," said Sahara. "Stop it, you're really freaking me out!"

As he looked at her, he had an overwhelming urge to

jam his nose into the soft white feathers on her neck—which was strange, because Sahara had no such feathers—and so, rather than give in to the urge, Noah decided it was time to call it a night.

"Gotta go," he squeaked, then raced out a side door and didn't stop running until he got home.

• ● •

Middle school science teacher Q. Theodore Kratz was not a "Mister." He was a "Doctor." He had a PhD in experimental biology, but did anyone care? Not in the slightest. No matter how many times he had corrected people, no one called him Dr. Kratz, and he finally gave up expecting them to. He considered it part of his punishment. His penance for his greatest failure.

Just one mistake! One mistake had cost him his career in cutting-edge biotechnology, casting him out of the highest levels of the scientific world in shame. And now he was a science teacher at a middle school in the middle of nowhere.

Well, that was going to change.

Noah Prime was going to be his ticket back to his high-paying, high-power, high-tech job with the Federal Office of Biological Experimentation (FOBE). Imagine! A human chameleon that could change color at will! The military applications alone would get Kratz on the cover of half a dozen top secret magazines that no one had enough security clearance to read. *Those* were the magazines worth being on!

That would surely overcome his one mistake. And it wasn't even a big mistake. Just a few measly strands of a mutated virus got released. And just because that particular virus tended to cause extra limbs to grow on frogs, it didn't necessarily mean it would do the same thing to humans. And even when it did, was that such a bad thing? They really didn't have to torch the entire building because of it—that was clearly an overreaction.

But that was then, this was now. New opportunities for redemption lay before him, thanks to Noah Prime.

Kratz had seen Noah enter the dance and kept a close eye on him. He didn't even have to do it secretly, because as a party chaperone, it was his job to watch the students closely and cast warning glares at anyone who seemed to be having a suspicious amount of fun.

For about twenty minutes, he observed Prime on the sidelines with that irksome boy Odin, or Oren, or whatever his name was. While that boy seemed about as nervous as someone about to leap off a cliff into shallow water, Noah Prime did not seem nervous at all. Nor did he change color to match the room.

Kratz, momentarily distracted by the disco ball, which had begun to spin, took a moment to look up at the spotlights and strobes haphazardly installed above for the dance. The reluctant science teacher in him studied the temporary wiring and scoffed. Amateurs! If the entire student body were electrocuted because of slipshod wiring, he could storm into the principal's office tomorrow and proclaim a hearty "told ya so." They should have let him handle the engineering aspects of this event. But even here, he was unappreciated.

It was while he was riding this particular train of self-pity that his attention was called back to the dance floor by a series of piercing shrieks.

Was someone being electrocuted? Is that what was happening?

Sadly, no—it was just Prime, who had slipped onto the dance floor while Kratz wasn't looking.

Cursing himself for his wandering attention, Kratz pushed past a few other teachers and several students to get closer. He didn't want to miss anything. The signs of . . . *chameleon-itis*, as he had begun to think of the boy's condition, could be subtle, he knew.

The boy was performing some kind of strange new dance, or teen ritual, perhaps. He was slapping his sides while putting his head through strange gyrations and emitting a piercing shriek at his dance partner. *Kids today*, Kratz thought, shaking his head.

He continued watching for signs of chameleon-itis. If only the boy would stop moving in such a rapid, unpleasant way, Kratz might have a better chance of spotting something unusual about him.

But no. The boy suddenly left the dance floor and ran out a door. Not once did he appear to change color in any way.

"Mr. Kratz," said one of the other teachers, "could you please go over and taste the punch—we suspect that one of the students may have poured in something... problematic."

Kratz sighed. One little mistake, and here he was policing a spiked punch bowl. All right, yes, it's true that after his little mistake, one of his lab assistants did grow an extra hand out of the side of her neck. But it was a small hand. No bigger than a baby's hand, really. Did he deserve to be fired for *that*?

Kratz resolved that he would watch Noah Prime tomorrow and the next day and the next until he knew enough about the boy's chameleon-itis to win back the favor of people in high places. In the meantime, he went over to the punch and tasted it. He tasted it a lot.

· ● ·

Sahara couldn't fall asleep that night. She was, to say the least, disturbed by Noah Prime's strange display on the dance floor. And yet there was something about it that left her dazzled in a not entirely bad way.

She wanted to talk with someone about it—but this was not something she could discuss with her friends. She did not have the kind of friends you could share personal things with unless you wanted those personal things broadcast to the entire school.

She couldn't talk to her parents, because she did not have the kind of parents who were good with this sort of thing. They were all about avoidance. They avoided uncomfortable situations, avoided uncomfortable people, and steered clear of all kinds of uncomfortable conversations. If asked for advice, it would always be the same: Whatever the problem was, she should avoid it.

"Why trouble yourself with an odd boy?" they would say. "Just stay away from him."

It irked her—perhaps more than Noah Prime irked her. Because, truth be told, Sahara tended to gravitate toward odd boys. She didn't want to, but she couldn't change her interests in that regard. Maybe it was because her life was so organized and regimented, all the corners of her life neatly tucked in every hour of every day. She feared that this gravitation toward the quirky was not an adaptive trait, and she suspected it might bring her much trouble later in life.

In sixth grade, there was a boy whose face was ever-so-slightly asymmetrical. One eye a tiny bit higher than the other. A nose that was almost imperceptibly off-center. She found herself occasionally wondering what a mildly crooked kiss from him might feel like.

In seventh grade, there was a boy who had an unusual obsession with llamas. Llama sweaters, a llama backpack, a little silver llama on a chain around his neck. She was interested in him right up until the day she found out that his name was Hector Lamas. Turns out he was much more intriguing before there was an ordinary explanation for his odd obsession.

And now there was Noah Prime, a boy who dropped down on her from trees, froze in stairwells, and had bizarre but strangely enticing convulsions on the dance floor.

Avoid him! her inner voice told her. *Avoid him like the plague!*

But she already knew she wouldn't listen. And it irked her.

7

Market Research

"You're home from the dance early," Noah's mother said as he walked in.

"Oh . . . uh . . . the dance was for the birds," he replied, heading toward his room quickly so he wouldn't have to face any more questions. Clearly, something was terribly wrong with him, and he knew he'd have to tell his parents about the various weird . . . behaviors . . . that had come over him lately—but he didn't want to freak them out as much as he was freaked out. He wanted to get more information first.

He shut the door to his room, opened his laptop, and found a health website. Then he typed in his latest weird behavior.

"Involuntary screeching, uncontrollable arm and head movements."

The website returned an alert reading:

Brain tumor suspected. Get help immediately!

Just like Ogden said—but everyone knows that it was always a good idea to get a second opinion. So he went to a different health website and typed his symptoms in again, wording them a little bit differently. It returned this message:

Stroke suspected. Get help immediately!

But what if it was all in his head? That is to say, not a tumor or stroke, but more of a mental disorder. So he clicked to a psychological self-assessment website, entered his symptoms, and got back this message:

**Subscribe to our newsletter
if you wish to proceed!**

As Noah had no intention of subscribing to anyone's newsletter, he went off looking for other sites, but every place he went offered him gloom and doom and forced subscriptions. He gave up on the web, resigned to the concept of having to actually tell his parents about all this. Noah took a deep breath, opened his door, and went back to the living room.

"Mom . . . ," he began.

And at that moment, the doorbell rang.

"Can you get that, honey?" asked his mom.

Noah, relieved by the delay of the inevitable, went to open the door. It was Ogden.

"I've figured it out!" he said.

Noah was not surprised. Ogden figured out things on a regular basis. He figured out that gravity is an illusion, and it works only because everyone believes in it. He figured out that a majority of rock stars are holograms and don't actually exist. He figured out that evolved dinosaurs were planting random fossils in places like Arbuckle, just to mess with us. With all that in mind, Noah was doubtful, but it was always worth it to hear Ogden out, because his theories were so detailed you could almost believe them.

"I'm all ears," Noah said.

"Actually, you might be," Ogden responded, "in the right situation." Then, with profound seriousness, he went with Noah into his room and closed the door to make sure no one else could hear what he had to say.

"Okay," Noah said, "spill it."

"What you did at the dance was classic behavior," Ogden told him.

Noah shook his head. "Only if by that you mean classically humiliating."

"You didn't let me finish," Ogden said. "What you did at the dance was classic behavior...for an emperor penguin seeking a mate."

"Excuse me?"

"Observe!" Then Ogden turned to Noah's computer and pulled up a video.

On the screen, a pair of penguins faced each other on a field of ice. One penguin (presumably the male) lowered his head to his chest, then raised his face to the sky as he began slapping his flippers against his side. When the penguin began emitting a piercing mating call, Noah hit pause on the video. He had seen enough.

There was no question that the male penguin was doing *exactly* what he had done at the dance—and although Noah knew he shouldn't let it bother him, he did notice that the female penguin seemed much more receptive to the male's attention than Sahara had been.

Ogden leaned away from the computer screen, a triumphant look on his face, and said, "When under emotional or physical stress, you take on the traits of different animals! Defense mechanisms, instinctual responses"—he raised his eyebrows—"mating rituals."

"That's ridiculous!"

"Many ridiculous things are true," Ogden pointed out. "Humans share fifty percent of their genes with bananas! It rains diamonds on Saturn! Froot Loops are all the same flavor!"

"Are not!"

"Are, too—look it up!"

There was no arguing with Ogden sometimes, but this

theory...it was...it was...Actually, it would explain a lot, wouldn't it?

"When you froze in the stairway, you were being pushed around by three other kids, right? You reacted by playing dead. You weren't just playing possum—you were *being* one!"

Noah started running some of the other "events" through this new lens. "And what happened to me on the gymnastics rings! How I was suddenly so good at it—and how my arms got hairy...."

"Like an ape, or monkey."

"You mean I'm turning into different animals?"

"No," Ogden said, "not turning into them. But you *are* taking on some of their most important traits."

Noah shook his head. "No. As usual, you're adding two plus two and coming up with twenty-two."

"Then I'll prove it!" Ogden said. "But we have to put you in a stressful situation first."

"I'm not already in a stressful situation?"

"Apparently not stressful enough." Ogden smiled, then hauled back his hand and slapped Noah across the face, full force.

"Hey!" Noah said. "That hurt!"

"Not enough," said Ogden. "We have to find a way to release the animal!" He looked around the room, grabbed a baseball bat, and held it over his shoulder.

"Ogden! Hold up!" Noah said, taking a step back.

"Right," Ogden said, putting down the bat. "That might have other unintended results." He took a moment to consider, then said, "I have a better idea. There's something we'll need at the supermarket."

"What?" Noah asked.

"You'll see."

"The supermarket closes at ten, and it's already nine thirty."

"Perfect!" said Ogden. "It's mostly downhill—you can ride on my handlebars."

• ● •

When Fresh and Tasty Supermarkets merged with the Funky Donkey chain, it took on an ill-advised new name. Now Arbuckle, Oregon, was served by Fresh and Funky. Although there were indeed times that things were more funky than fresh.

It was a nearly ten when Noah and Ogden entered the market. To their right was the "unappetizing department," as Noah's mom called it, filled with questionable deli meats and trays of bleu cheese that hadn't actually started off bleu.

And on their left, the produce section tried hard, but it couldn't produce anything more than a hearty "meh."

"We're closing in five minutes," said the lone checker, without even looking up from her phone to see them. She was clearly annoyed that she'd have to remain for the duration. "Make it quick."

"We intend to," said Ogden, and he led Noah back to the meat department.

Meat was Fresh and Funky's one crowning glory. In fact, Arbuckle made great strides to distance itself from the vegan ways of Portland by being Oregon's meat mecca, featuring everything from venison to ostrich to aardvark—although no one ever actually purchased it...but they *could*, and that's what mattered.

Just beside the meat case was a door that led to the mysterious back of the store, where only employees were allowed. It featured a large sign reading UNAUTHORIZED ACCESS PROHIBITED.

When Noah was little, he used to believe that they kept the animals back there and butchered them with chainsaws purchased at the hardware store next door. It was the subject of many a childhood nightmare.

"Come on," said Ogden, heading for the door.

Perhaps it was a flashback to one of his butchering nightmares, or maybe just a twinge of intuition, but Noah hesitated.

So Ogden got behind him and gently pushed, but that made Noah all the more resistant.

"C'mon—what are you waiting for?"

"You still haven't told me why we're here."

"It's a show-don't-tell kind of thing," Ogden said,

which served to make Noah curious enough to cross into the dreaded back room. Still, he couldn't help but hold his breath as he stepped through the door, even though his first glimpse of the secret chamber was utterly disappointing: stacks of cardboard boxes of fruit, an assortment of brooms, and a few handcarts. But then he saw where Ogden was heading.

The freezer.

Ogden pulled the silver handle of the walk-in freezer and swung open the door. Frost poured out like a Halloween fog machine, revealing entire sides of beef hanging on hooks that looked as if they were ripped right out of Noah's worst butcher nightmare.

"Ogden, there's a reason why this place is prohibited and unauthorized. I mean, like, what if the Night Butcher catches us or something?"

"Work with me, Noah," Ogden said. "And there's no such thing as the Night Butcher," he added. "At least, I don't think there is. Come on, help me."

Ogden moved through the icy fog and into the freezer, but Noah stayed at the threshold, feeling gooseflesh already rising from the cold in spite of his hoodie.

"I'm not going in there until I know what you—"

And then came a thud. Actually, more like a *whomp!* And the sides of beef began swinging and bumping into one another as if they had come to life.

"Help!" he heard Ogden call. "One of them fell on me! Noah! Help!"

Noah sighed, and it came out as a blast of steam in the cold air. If someone had told Noah that he'd be rescuing Ogden from a frozen meat attack, he would not have . . . No, actually, when it came to Ogden, he *would* have believed it. This was exactly the kind of thing Ogden was famous for.

"Ogden embroils people in absurdity," Andi once said, during one of her "I-read-the-dictionary-for-fun" days.

The side of beef was so huge, Ogden was completely hidden beneath it.

"Only you, Ogden," said Noah, "could be decked by half a dead cow."

It was even heavier than it looked. Noah had to use all of his strength to get enough leverage to flip it, and once he did—Ogden wasn't there.

And then, behind him, he heard a voice.

"What are you doing here?"

But it wasn't the voice of the Night Butcher. Noah turned to see the last person he expected to run into that night. It was none other than Sahara. Of all the industrial freezers in all the world, why did she have to walk into his?

• ● •

Sahara Solis suffered from what she called "I.I.I.," or Ignoramus-Induced Insomnia, which was always brought on by somebody doing something brainless, which then flapped around her mind like a bird that flew in through a window, couldn't get out, and was now knocking every stinking knickknack off the shelf, leaving a mess that no one but her would have to clean up. Stupid bird.

The ignoramus of the evening was Noah Prime. Why did she have to dance with him? Why did he have to act so weird on the dance floor? And why could she not stop herself from thinking about him?

There was only one way to let the bird out of the house, she knew. She would have to confront him. Not tomorrow, or the next day, but right now. Bottom line: She knew she would not get any sleep that night until she either slapped him or kissed him. She wouldn't know which of the two urges would prevail until she was in the moment. All she could hope was that whichever it was, it would be satisfying enough to allow her to go home and sleep. So she quietly slipped out of her house and pedaled all the way to the farmless farm where Noah lived.

She heard voices coming from a window, and when she moved closer, she recognized Noah's voice and the voice of that kid he hung out with. She couldn't hear a lot, but she was able to deduce that they were having a heated conversation about the zoo.

"We have to find a way to release the animals!" it sounded like Noah's friend said. And then they left, not even seeing her there.

Sahara was beyond curious now. What were they up to? The nearest zoo was hundreds of miles away. Wait—didn't Noah's friend work at the local animal shelter? Were they going to set all those poor strays free? That was actually admirable. She could get behind that—maybe even help them. But as it turned out, they weren't going to the shelter. For some reason, they rode right into the parking lot of Fresh and Funky. She let them go in the store first, then followed about a minute behind them.

"We close in four minutes," said the uninterested checker.

"Did you see two boys come in here?" Sahara asked.

The checker shrugged, tapping away at some phone game that made her appear intently focused and yet entirely uninterested at the same time. "Someone came in. I think they left already."

But Sahara knew they had not left.

Then she heard what could only be described as a *whomp!* from the back of the store, and she knew exactly where to find them.

"What are you doing here?" she demanded when she cornered Noah in the freezer, wrestling a side of beef—which took the concept of "playing with your food" to a whole new level.

"What am *I* doing here? What are *you* doing here?" Noah put back on her.

She could do the whole "I asked you first" thing, but

that would just be childish. "I came here to tell you that I have absolutely nothing to say to you," she told him.

"You're saying something now," he reminded her.

"That's beside the point. After the weird way you behaved at the dance tonight, I want to make it crystal clear that I want absolutely nothing to do with you from now until the end of time."

"Okay . . . ," he said. "Then why are you still just standing there?"

"I'm not!" she yelled. *"I'm storming away!"*

"Uh . . . no, you're actually not . . ."

And then another sound filled the freezer. It was neither a *thud!* nor a *whomp!* It was more like a *ka-chung!* A very heavy, and unpleasant, *ka-chung!* It was the kind of sound beyond which no others mattered.

"Ogden?" said Noah. "Ogden!"

But Ogden was not in the freezer. He was on the other side of the massive stainless steel door. The one he had just closed on Noah and Sahara.

• ● •

At first, Ogden thought that Sahara's arrival was an unfortunate complication, but he quickly realized that it was precisely the distraction he needed. Without her, Noah would most definitely have seen him sneaking out of the freezer after Ogden knocked down that side of beef, and he would have most definitely tried to stop Ogden before he closed the door.

Ogden knew that in addition to protection against predators, animals had built-in defenses against their environments. Musk ox evolved a thick coat of hollow hair that provided excellent insulation. Wood frogs could stay frozen solid for months, then be fine when they thawed. And if Ogden's thesis was correct, Noah would exhibit some animalistic survival trait when faced with the prospect of freezing to death.

The plan was to leave Noah sealed in there for about half an hour—which should have been long enough for his body to kick into survival mode, but not quite long enough to induce lethal hypothermia if it didn't. Sahara's presence in the freezer, though an unanticipated variable, just might add enough stress to the situation to trigger Noah's unique genetic soup to brew up some truly exciting responses.

There was, of course, the expected pounding on the door, followed by the traditional "Ogden, I'm going to kill you" that came with this sort of scientific stress test, but the sounds were so muffled by the thickness of the door that they weren't too distracting, and eventually they stopped.

There was, however, one variable that Ogden should have expected but didn't.

"What are you doing back here? You have to leave—we're closed," said Fresh and Funky's night manager, a man so beefy that the meat in the freezer had nothing on him.

"But my friend—"

"I am not your friend, and you have to leave." Then

he grabbed Ogden and dragged him out of the meat department.

"No, you don't understand!"

"Oh, I understand plenty! You think I don't know what you kids do? Turn all the items upside down on the shelves? Rearrange the produce in provocative patterns? I will not allow our store to be the subject of yet another offensive video meme!"

And he practically hurled Ogden out the front door, locking it behind him.

8

Stop Your Blubbering

INSIDE THE FREEZER, THE POUNDING, AND THE CURSING, AND the unrepeatable threats against Ogden did nothing to get that door open.

"Phones!" said Sahara.

They both pulled out their phones, but the freezer walls were too thick to get even a single bar. That's when they realized how cold it was. They already knew it was cold, it being a freezer, but it wasn't until they stopped moving that they began to feel the true bone chill of the place.

"Okay," said Noah. "Well, the good news is that there's no windchill factor."

Sahara stared at him, shaking her head in amazement. "Seriously?"

"Lemonade, Sahara," he said. "I'm just trying to make lemonade, okay?"

"Yeah, well, it's already turning into a slushie."

· ● ·

"Nine-one-one, what's your emergency?"

"I'd like to report a serious industrial freezer situation."

"Ogden? Is that you?"

He thought, at first, the fact that Arbuckle's 911 operator knew him by name would be a good thing. Perhaps he'd get more personalized service.

"Yes, it's Ogden," he answered. "I need you to send a rescue team down to the Fresh and Funky."

"Oh, really," said the operator. He could hear her smirk like some sort of audio emoji.

"Yes, really—this is an emergency!"

"That's what you said last time, when you called in to report a herd of ocelots approaching the town."

"That's ridiculous," Ogden said, snorting. "Ocelots don't travel in herds; they're solitary hunters."

"I know, that's what we found out!"

"I never said it was a herd, I said it was an *infiltration* of ocelots—since they don't travel in packs, I had to come up with a collective noun for them. But if you'd been following your own police scanner, then you would know about the increase in unusual roadkill in our area since they raised the speed limit. Most notably, armadillos—which happen to be a primary food source for medium-sized wildcats—so

92

where there are *fezzes* of armadillos, *infiltrations* of ocelots will not be far behind!"

Ogden knew this was beside the point now, but he simply couldn't stand an uneducated police force. He realized he had to get back on track, because time was running out. "Listen to me, there are two kids locked in a freezer—"

"Is this a riddle? I know the answer—the poison was frozen in the ice cubes!"

"You're not hearing me," Ogden said more urgently. "This is a matter of life or death!"

Then a deputy suddenly came on the line. "Like that time you insisted a shadow government was running the world from the back room of the 7-Eleven on Arbuckle Highway?"

"I never said shadow government," Ogden pointed out. "I said 'shadowy governmental types.'"

"And at last year's FossilFest, when you accused the mayor of cannibalism?"

"That so-called turkey drumstick was *huge*!"

"Believe it or not, Ogden," said the deputy, "we do occasionally have actual emergencies, so please stop wasting our time." And they hung up on him.

Ogden climbed on his bike and pedaled home. His first thought was to tell his parents—but he knew they'd be just as dismissive as the police. It was a true burden to be a bearer of light in a world so steeped in denial.

But he wasn't upset—just resigned. And on the bright

side, this was actually the perfect test—because it was a *true* life-or-death situation. Ogden was confident Noah would either develop the strength to tear open the freezer door or find some other defense mechanism to save himself and Sahara. And that would be a good thing, right? Because Noah would then be a hero in Sahara's eyes, which is what he wanted anyway.

On the other hand, Ogden could be wrong, and they'd both die. But Ogden was never wrong.

Well, almost never.

• ● •

Noah had a meager hoodie; Sahara had a light windbreaker. Neither item did a thing to keep out the cold.

"Noah, this is serious," said Sahara. "You see this kind of thing in the news every day."

"Clickbait," Noah told her. "The headlines are misleading. People don't usually die in freezers."

"People don't usually have a friend who locks them in for fun."

"It wasn't for fun, but I see your point."

Noah was sure that Ogden would let them out, but after fifteen minutes, it became clear that neither he nor anyone else was coming to their rescue.

Sahara huddled in a corner, and Noah went over to her. "Stay away from the steel wall," he said. "It will drain your heat faster."

"Don't you think I know that?"

He stayed beside her, and it occurred to him what they needed to do. "I know this sounds like a line...but we should huddle to conserve body heat."

In truth, Sahara was thinking the same thing, but she didn't want to be the one to suggest it. How sad if they froze to death because neither of them was willing to make the first move.

"Fine," she said. "But this doesn't mean anything."

Noah didn't respond, but he wrapped his arms around her and pulled her as close as he could. It wasn't the worst thing in the world. But what was she thinking? Everything about this was terrible.

She reassessed the room. In addition to the hanging meat, there were cardboard boxes of prepackaged stuff. "We could put the cardboard beneath our clothes for insulation," she suggested.

"Good idea," Noah said. But he made no move to get up. And although she wanted to spring into action, the shared body-warmth thing was hard to give up. She had been on the verge of major shivering before, but at least for the moment, she was okay. She knew, however, that it wouldn't last. For either of them.

Noah knew it, too. He could feel his nose and ears becoming increasingly numb. But inside, there was a tingling from his core. At first, he thought it was just because he had his arms around Sahara, but to be honest, in the moment, that felt more awkward than anything else. And that tingling . . . he had felt it before. When he was up on the rings and thought he was going to make an absolute fool of himself. When he was on the dance floor and *did* make an absolute fool of himself. The tingling resolved into an odd warmth. And his clothes began to feel very uncomfortable.

Sahara looked at him strangely.

"Are you okay?" she asked. Which was a stupid question, because the two of them were most definitely not okay. "You look funny."

Not surprising, because he felt funny. He looked at his hands: His fingers looked thicker. His skin looked stretched. And his clothes—they didn't just feel uncomfortable. They felt painful. They were cutting into his skin.

Sahara didn't notice that, because she was so fixated on his face. He didn't seem like the same boy he was a moment ago. The shape of his face actually changed. She had seen this before. She knew exactly what was happening.

"You're having an allergic reaction," she told him. "What are you allergic to? Do you have an Epi-Pen?"

"I . . . I don't think that's it," said Noah.

And then the seams on his hoodie burst.

Noah knew this was going to get worse before it got better. His T-shirt held, but now, as he swelled, he knew the shirt wouldn't hold much longer, and the fabric was hurting him so much he didn't want it to. There was a tiny hole in the shirt just to the right of his navel. He dug

96

a finger into the hole and tugged at it. That's all it took to make the T-shirt shred, and out from it burst a gelatinous wave of fat.

Sahara pulled away from him, staring in disbelief. "Noah! My God, what's wrong? What's happening to you?"

And he knew. He knew because Ogden's crazy theory wasn't so crazy after all.

"Don't be scared," he said, in a voice that sounded like his, but played at a much slower speed. "But I think I have a blubber problem."

Sahara did not know what to say to that. This was not a phrase commonly spoken in any language under any circumstances. Yet as she watched Noah's expanding gut spill out over the taut elastic of his sweatpants, she realized that there was no other way to describe it.

"Does it hurt?" she asked, and she immediately felt stupid for asking it.

"No," he said. "It just feels . . . odd."

Sahara knew that there had to be an explanation for this. There were explanations for everything, and once you knew it, whatever was so strange, so disturbing, didn't seem that way anymore. Perhaps this was a hallucination brought on by hypothermia. Or perhaps he was turning into a—

"Walrus," said Noah, in that strange, rubbery voice. "I feel very . . . walrus-y."

Sahara could not stop staring at him. Folds and folds of

the stuff. What had been six-pack abs when he was on the rings were now lost beneath a bulbous landscape of rolling fleshy hills.

"Yeah," he said. "Definitely walrus."

Noah decided that he should never, ever again, for the rest of his life, say the phrase "This could not get any worse." Because the world always found a way to prove that assessment wrong. Here he was, bloated with blubber, in an industrial freezer, under the gaze of Sahara Solis, who looked as if she might hurl at any instant, although if she did, it would probably freeze halfway out of her mouth and become a vomit ice sculpture. One more thought you can't unthink.

But she didn't throw up. She didn't scream. Instead, she took a long look at him and said, "Maybe we don't need those cardboard boxes after all."

• ● •

There is something to be said for wrapping a girl in your blubber. Because after you get past that, the rest is easy.

"It's . . . really warm," Sahara commented as she pressed herself against him. Noah didn't feel the cold anymore. He felt tired and content—like you feel after eating a big Thanksgiving meal.

"Pull some more around you," Noah offered. "Really, I don't mind."

She shifted and let the layer of blubber envelop her like

a blanket. To Noah, it kind of felt as if he was absorbing her. Like the Blob. He didn't know if that was good or bad.

Sahara, on the other hand, didn't feel as if she was being absorbed. It was more like Noah had molded himself to make room for her. And that wasn't a terrible thing.

"I know this is gross," he said. "I'm sorry it has to be this way."

"It's not so bad," she told him. "It's like in *The Empire Strikes Back*, when Han saves Luke by shoving him inside the guts of the tauntaun."

"I can't believe you know what a tauntaun is," he said. They both laughed a little at that.

He told her a little about Ogden's theory.

"So...let me get this straight," she said. "You were a possum in the stairwell, a chimpanzee on the rings, and a penguin at the dance?"

"Sort of. I don't actually become them; I just take on their key traits."

"Well, obviously. I mean, if you actually turned into a penguin on the dance floor, I think I would have drawn the line."

"I wouldn't blame you."

"Hey," said Sahara, "I'll bet you were channeling a gibbon, or something like that, when you fell on me from the trees."

"I...never thought of that."

She pulled a bit more of Noah's blubber over her to

keep out the cold. Although it wasn't really about keeping out the cold, was it? Blubber was all about keeping in the warm.

"Do you think there's anyone else in the world who can do what you do?" she asked.

"Probably not," said Noah.

"Good," said Sahara. Because if there was anything that Sahara liked, it was people who were one of a kind.

9

Capsule Thirteen

MEANWHILE, ACROSS THE ATLANTIC OCEAN, WHERE IT WAS already morning, another boy who, not coincidentally, was also named Noah hopped into a crowded capsule of the London Eye—one of the largest cantilevered observation wheels in the world. Noah, who hailed from Norwich, near England's eastern shore, had never been to London. He had never been anywhere. His parents were stay-at-home types who feared crowded places, and they never ventured more than twenty miles from their town. They had no intention of letting him go on this field trip, which is why he never told them about it and forged his mother's signature on the permission slip. As far as they knew, he was safe and sound at Moriarty Magnet School, and they were none the wiser.

Capsule thirteen began to ascend as the wheel slowly revolved. It was fairly crowded—at least twenty people—but as he looked around, he realized he somehow had gotten separated from his classmates. Not one of them was in this pod with him. Through the floor-to-ceiling glass, he could see them in the capsule ahead, and the one behind, but none with him. Great. According to the brochure, the Eye took half an hour to do a full revolution, which meant he'd be stuck in here with strangers. Oddly, all of them were stern-looking men in bowler hats, except for one woman wearing a pearl necklace, who was smiling kindly at him.

"Young man, are you here by yourself?" the woman asked.

Noah turned to her. "I'm on a school outing," he said. "But all my mates abandoned me." He glanced at the row of stern men in bowler hats. There was something strange about them that he couldn't quite place. Also something strange about the woman's eyes.

"Oh, that's too bad," she said, but her smile never left her face. "I'll bet you can see forever at the top."

"They say you can see forty kilometers." Noah looked toward the top of the giant revolving wheel and squinted. Their capsule still had a while to go before it got there.

"Well, that's almost forever," said the woman with a giggle.

Her laugh was infectious, and Noah found himself giggling along with her. He also felt a bit dizzy. He must have begun to sway a bit, because the woman asked, "Are you all right?"

"Just a little woozy," he told her.

"That'll be the altitude," she said, although they really weren't all that high yet. Still, there weren't many tall buildings in Norwich, and Noah had never been to the top of one, so perhaps a little bit of altitude went a long way.

It was then that he remembered an odd little warning his paranoid parents gave him when he was little. *"Beware of smiling people with strange eyes."* They had only said it once, but it had stuck with him.

"I . . . I just need to sit down," Noah said, and he stumbled toward a seat. "Excuse me," he said to the man in the bowler hat standing in his way. That's when he realized the strange thing about these men—they weren't casting shadows. Not a single one of them. And the weird-eyed woman just smiled.

"Oxygen deprivation," she told him. "Don't fight it, just let it come."

"Let . . . what . . . come?" he gasped.

"Why, your end, of course."

Beware of smiling people with strange eyes. Strange, like no eyelids?

"H . . . H . . . Help!" he rasped to the men around him, but they ignored him.

"They won't assist you," the woman said. "I needed them here to make the capsule appear full, but they've done their job."

And just like that, they vanished. Now it was just the woman and an astonished Noah.

"Holograms!" she said with a delighted clap of her hands.

"You're . . . draining . . . the air . . . out of . . . the capsule," Noah managed to gasp.

"Yes."

"But why?" he asked, straining to breathe. "You'll die . . . with me."

But the woman shook her head. "No," she said, "because I'm a hologram, too."

And just like that, she vanished as well.

"Sit," her voice continued. "You'll be more comfortable."

Noah tumbled over the seat, missing it completely and ending up on the floor.

"You'll want to die quickly," she advised him. "Trust me—you don't want to be alive for what comes next."

"Wh . . . ? Wh . . . ?" He couldn't even get out the word. But she knew where the question was going.

"Next, we open a portal to the sun, and you'll be incinerated by a flash that's over five thousand degrees Kelvin. No mess, no bother. Well, maybe a little bit of mess, but you get the point."

Squiggles began to fill his vision, followed by black spots that turned the bright sky at the apex of the wheel dark. And the darkness remained.

"Goodbye, Noah Secundus" was the last thing he heard the woman say. "It was a pleasure knowing you."

A few moments later came the flash. It only lasted for an instant, and when it was done, nothing remained of this N.O.A.H. but ash. And no one ever found that ash, because, as anyone who works at the London Eye can tell you, although there are thirty-two capsules, there is no capsule thirteen.

10

Not a Squonk

CHUCKY CLEAVER WAS BORN TO BE A BUTCHER. IT WAS RIGHT there in his name. He couldn't avoid it if he tried, so he embraced it. From the time he was little, it was evident. As a baby, he cut his own meat. He had a full collection of knives by his tenth birthday, and he knew how to use each and every one of them and all their specific purposes. By thirteen, he had taken first place in half a dozen meat-cutting competitions in local fairs, and by twenty, he held the world record for reducing an entire cow into small, cellophane-wrapped packages in less than three minutes. He often thanked the good Lord that there was a profession for him in which he could put his passion to work, for who knew what he might have been doing with his time otherwise.

Then hard times came when automation took over the big food chains, leaving meat maestros like Chucky with few options. Thank goodness for the Arbuckle Fresh and Funky, where automation was still a thing of the distant future.

His day would start before the store opened. He'd chop apart a side of beef to get his blood flowing, then quarter a dozen chickens or so for good measure. But on this particular morning, when he opened the freezer, he found something that made him drop his cleaver. Right on his foot. Causing him to lose yet another toe in a senseless butcher-related accident.

· ● ·

Noah awoke to find a police officer poking him. When he opened his eyes, the officer screamed and hopped back, surprised to see the shapeless blob that Noah had become was alive.

"Are . . . are you all right?"

"Yeah," Noah groaned, barely recognizing the morning thickness of his own voice. "A little warm, but yeah, I'm fine."

"Warm?"

As he looked around, it all came back to him, and he remembered where he was. "Sahara!" he said. "Where's Sahara?"

Then the massive folds of blubber spilling out over his waistband, like the mother of all muffin tops, began to ripple and undulate. And out from under the largest fold emerged Sahara.

The cop screamed and jumped back again, practically falling into the store manager behind him, who practically fell into the butcher, who already seemed to be in some amount of pain.

"I can explain," said Noah. But then realized that he couldn't...so he just started...well...blubbering. "It's like this: It was late, and we needed some meat...yeah, meat, but the door closed...and I had...uh...an allergic reaction...to the meat."

Then Sahara jumped up. "Do you have any idea how dangerous anaphylactic shock can be?" She burned an accusatory glare at the gawking manager hiding behind the grimacing butcher, who was hiding behind the stunned police officer. "How could you be so irresponsible as to have a freezer without an emergency release? We should sue! Your store should be shut down! Officer—arrest this man!"

Now it was the manager's turn to blubber.

Noah heaved himself upright, feeling gravity in a way he had never experienced it before. And while the officer made no attempt to arrest the manager of Fresh and Funky, he was disoriented enough for Noah and Sahara to push past them—and by the time they were out of the store, Noah's body had reabsorbed all the blubber it had produced overnight. The paramedics, who had just arrived, raced past them and into the store, pushing a gurney—but the only thing they found worthy of medical attention was the butcher and his toe.

• ● •

Noah arrived home and slipped in through his bedroom window just as his alarm began ringing. He hit snooze and collapsed on his bed—but found that he wasn't tired. Apparently, walruses slept very well.

Sahara, on the other hand, was exhausted when she got home. Noah's blubber had kept her warm, but she was too freaked out to sleep. And it wasn't exactly comfortable. More like spending the night wrapped in tofu.

Her parents were on the verge of sending the National Guard out to search for her, and she had to defuse their anger/panic.

"My friend April had a sleepover after the dance. Don't you remember?" Sahara said. She had learned that "Don't you remember?" was a very useful phrase to use with her parents, because they always had a million things on their minds, so it was reasonable to assume they might miss something she said.

"But we saw you come home. . . ."

"Well, duh—I had to get my pj's."

And since it was such a rare thing for Sahara to lie to them, they didn't question it. Thus, the situation was defused. In truth, Sahara didn't have a friend named April. It stood for "All Purpose Response If Late." She had invented April years ago but never actually had to invoke her before; however, as Sahara's life was now taking a strange twist, she suspected April would soon become her best friend.

• ● •

Ogden paced anxiously in the vicinity of Noah's locker, nervously downing grape PEZ one after another out of a vintage Spider-Man dispenser. He watched kids file past him—kids who were entirely oblivious to the announcement that the principal might soon be making about two of their classmates who may or may not have frozen to death in the Fresh and Funky, which would most likely go out of business because of it, and then where would they be? No one wanted to shop at Cheap and Chewy—its produce was garbage—but after the various lawsuits that would inevitably shut down Arbuckle's only grocery alternative, people wouldn't have a choice.

Ogden tipped back Spider-Man's head yet again and ate the next PEZ right out of the infamous web-slinger's neck. He had to stop this negative thinking! When he got caught in spiraling thoughts, it never did anyone any good. He imagined whole communities could be devastated by the force of that whirlwind.

When Noah finally entered the school, looking okay, Ogden's burst of relief resolved into embarrassment that he had been worried at all. Of course Noah was okay! And so was the Fresh and Funky. Or at until the next freak accident—which was bound to happen, since the market clearly didn't have effective safety protocols.

Ogden hurried toward him. "So, the stress-induction experiment was successful! Tell me what happened, and don't leave out any details! Did you grow a dense layer of underfur, like a polar bear? Did you develop antifreeze in your blood, like the Antarctic icefish? Or did you just headbutt the door down like a bighorn ram, thereby saving not just yourself but whatserface as well? How is whatserface anyway? Did she live, or did you weep over her frozen body like a squonk—which is mythical, but who knows, you may have mythical DNA also—which means you could have breathed dragon fire, and warmed the freezer up, too." Ogden took a moment to catch his breath. "So, which was it?"

Noah held up his hand to Ogden like a "halt" signal. "You know what?" he said. "I'm not going to tell you." Then he swung open his locker, nearly hitting Ogden in the face.

"But . . . but you *have* to tell me!"

"No I don't," said Noah, busying himself with locker business.

"But I need data!"

Noah slammed his locker and turned to face Ogden. "Then you shouldn't have tried to kill us!"

Ogden refused to back down. "Great breakthroughs in science always come at great risk. Look at all the astronauts who died in our attempts to escape the bounds of our puny planet. McNair, McAuliffe, McCool. And besides, the fact that you survived proves I was right all along!"

"Fine," Noah said. "As much as I hate to admit anything to you, you were right. But it doesn't explain *what*

I am. It doesn't explain *why* I do these things. I don't even know *who* I am anymore!"

"Noted," said Ogden. "Now that we know what you can do, we have to figure out why." Ogden did a quick calculation. "Four possibilities: It's an accident, evolution, a secret government project, or a foreign conspiracy," he declared. "Let's begin by analyzing the types of accidents that could have turned you into a quasi-human freak show."

But Ogden stopped, because he saw a look in Noah's eyes that concerned him, and that made him think maybe Noah was going to express the traits of the female praying mantis and bite off his head. Although that generally only happened during mating, so he was okay. He hoped.

And then another voice entered the conversation.

"There's a fifth possibility," said Sahara, very much alive, and eavesdropping behind them. "That you're an imbecile, and the manager just opened the door before we froze to death."

Ogden sighed. "(A) my IQ is off the charts, and (B) I don't think so. The point is that we all need to be on the same page if we want to figure this out, so I will gladly forgive you for your abrasive personality if you get with the program."

"*My* abrasive personality?" said Sahara, incredulous.

"Yes—and speaking of pages, you might want to keep this." Then Ogden pulled out a few sheets of paper from his backpack and handed them to Noah.

"What is it?" Noah asked.

"I wrote a eulogy for your funeral. Just in case."

Noah reviewed it. "Wow. Uh...thanks?"

Then Ogden handed an index card to Sahara. "I wrote one for you, too, but it's kind of short, since I don't know you very well. You should probably get someone who knows you better to write your eulogy."

The sentiment was then punctuated by the tardy bell, which brought them all one step closer to Saturday school with Mr. Kratz.

• ● •

As it happened, Kratz was lurking in the classroom that Noah and his friends were standing next to. He didn't intend to lurk—he had just left a history teacher a scathing note for daring to bring up a science-related topic (climate change) in her class without clearing it with him first (as if a *social studies* teacher could have anything worthwhile to say about science).

As he was reaching for the doorknob, he thought of the perfect parting shot to add to his note—something about the atmosphere not being the only thing full of hot air—when he recognized the voices of Noah and his co-conspirators in the hallway outside the room. Kratz put his ear to the door and listened intently, but the only words he was able to make out clearly were "foreign," "astronaut," and "funeral."

It made Kratz laugh. As if three fourteen-year-olds could plan the murder of a foreign astronaut. Such a mission would take an entire team of deep-cover operatives, not a triad of middle schoolers. Perhaps they were discussing a movie. Or maybe the objective of a new video game. If it were the latter, it sounded intriguing enough for Kratz to want to play. Especially if he could find some cheat codes so he could get right to murdering the astronaut. But wait—he was getting off topic. He had to remind himself to stay focused on the real issue: the fact that Noah Prime could camouflage himself at will.

It was time for him to put his own plan into motion to prove it—which would restore him to his position of power and influence in the military-industrial complex.

Of course, the problem with a plan is that one had to actually have one. Right now, all Kratz had was his own eyewitness account of the phenomenon. But he did have a military spy drone with a high-resolution camera that he had taken with him as an "unauthorized parting gift" when he was so unfairly ejected from his high-level position. It was sleek, stealthy, and powerful. With it, he could secretly observe every moment of Noah Prime's life. That wasn't a plan, but it was very definitely the beginnings of a scheme.

And schemes were undeniably Kratz's specialty.

• ● •

Memes and GIFs, and posts and pics, and hashtags and viral videos. They all go to the same place: nowhere.

The cloud doesn't exist. It's just a series of ones and zeros stored on microprocessors in warehouses and office buildings around the world that require a ridiculous amount of air-conditioning, because that many ones and zeros generate enough heat to boil a small ocean.

And yet, once you upload something into that nowhere place, it somehow exists everywhere. A painful pratfall in Pittsburgh is, within seconds, being ROTFL'd in Rotterdam. A Stupid Pet Trick in Patagonia is being shared by siblings in Siberia. Because once you cast your fate to the cloud, it can be viewed by anyone, anywhere.

Some people find that scary.

It was the reason why Noah's parents were so adamant that he stay off social media. Many times, he had tried to create profiles for himself, but he never got away with it. His parents would find out and lecture him about data breaches, privacy invasion, and corporate greed. "Social media is melting people's minds!" they would proclaim. "And single-handedly melting the ice caps." After a while, Noah found it wasn't worth the fight.

But in this day and age, even without a personal presence online, it was impossible not to have some kind of digital footprint. The cloud found you everywhere, from traffic camera footage to school pictures. And sometimes people posted you in videos. And sometimes those videos went viral. Like the one that showed some random kid, in some random school, suddenly growing hair on his arms while doing amazing gymnastics. That kind of video would be seen by many eyes. Some of them unblinking.

"We found him!" the mission assistant said to his commander, who was a woman of many disguises, having played everything from a nurse in Argentina to a tourist in London.

She watched the video several times, allowing herself to enjoy the swelling sense of victory. The other N.O.A.H.s were dead. Only one remained. And now they knew exactly where he was!

"Good work," she said, her mind already gearing up for this final undertaking. "And to celebrate the end of our mission . . . let's make this one spectacular!"

11

Roadkill, Ugly Babies, and One Crunchy Taco

NOAH DID **NOT** INVITE SAHARA OVER FOR DINNER. IT JUST KIND of happened.

"If you really want to help Ogden and me figure this out, we should have a real meeting of the minds that won't get interrupted by school bells," he said, when their midday discussion was interrupted by yet another bell.

"Good idea," she said. "What time should I come over?"

"Wait," said Ogden. "You're asking her over for dinner? What about me?"

And just like that, it was a done deal.

"Great," said Noah's mom when he told her. "I just bought a roast for the weekend, but I'll defrost it and make it tonight."

"Uh...," said Noah, "did you get it from Fresh and Funky?"

"Yes, why?"

"Sahara's vegan."

Actually, she wasn't. Noah had witnessed her devouring a hot dog at lunch with a carnivorous ferocity that would make a lion hang its tail in defeat. But after last night, the thought of eating anything from the Fresh and Funky meat department just felt, well, unappetizing.

• ● •

When Sahara arrived that evening, punctual to the second, Noah made as un-awkward an introduction as one could make between your mother and a girl you've recently spent the night in a freezer with.

"It's a pleasure to meet you, Sahara," she said, and Noah was greatly relieved that his mom, unlike him, got her name right the first time.

As for Sahara, she had no idea how this evening would go. Honestly, after last night's strange and surreal blubber-extravaganza, she didn't know what to expect from Noah's family. But Noah's mom seemed friendly and normal. Part of Sahara was relieved, while another part was mildly disappointed.

Sahara wondered if his parents had the slightest clue about what was going on with Noah. From Sahara's experience, it often seemed that parents knew a lot more than they let on . . . but on the other hand, they were often overconfident in their powers of observation. They might catch a whole lot of little things, but the occasional big thing can slip through the cracks.

Noah's mom, however, seemed to pay a lot of attention to details. The skillful floral arrangement on the dining table, for instance.

"The flowers are beautiful, Mrs. Prime," Sahara said.

"Why, thank you!"

"She grew them herself," Noah informed her.

"For reals?" said Sahara, and she was immediately horrified that she actually said "For reals."

"Yeah, out in our greenhouse," Noah said.

"You have a greenhouse?"

"We do!" said Noah, and then he smirked. "For reals."

Sahara glared at him, but then Noah laughed in such a way that made her laugh, too, in spite of herself.

"C'mon," said Noah, "I'll show you."

Noah led her out the kitchen door, through an expansive yard with no boundaries but the woods. They passed a barn where someone inside was hammering to classic rock tunes.

"What's going on in there?" Sahara asked.

"Oh, that? It's my father's workshop. He's...uh...a cabinetmaker."

"You have a creative family."

"Yeah. Guess I didn't get those genes."

Sahara found herself going just the tiniest bit sour.

119

"No, you just got the genes that will make you the star of the gymnastics team."

She could tell that Noah caught her tone, because he stopped to gauge her. Then he grinned, and she swore she caught a twinkle in his eye. "The star of the *guys'* gymnastics team. The girls' team already has a star."

Sahara laughed. "You should go for it! In this life, we've got to use what we're given, and you've been given some . . . interesting stuff."

" 'Interesting.' " Noah chuckled. "Yeah, you could call it that."

Past the barn was a wild meadow slowly being overtaken by the forest, and in the middle was a circular glass greenhouse.

"This used to be a farm back in the day," Noah told her as he led her down a path to the greenhouse. "But the land grows whatever it feels like now."

Sahara looked out over the field. "Well, there's lots of wildflowers."

"I'm sure the manslaughter hornets helped pollinate them."

"The what?"

"Sorry—Ogden-speak. We had a bee problem, but Ogden was convinced they weren't bees. Anyway, my dad got rid of them."

"Good—because I'm allergic," said Sahara. "One sting, and my face would blow up like yours did last night."

Noah grimaced. "Did I really look that bad?"

"Unrecognizable."

"I guess we should talk about that," Noah said.

Sahara considered it, but finally she said, "I think I'd rather just look at flowers right now."

Noah did not want to talk about it, either. He didn't even want to think about it. Not when the world was currently making so much sense. But talking about it was why he, Sahara, and Ogden were getting together tonight. Noah didn't even know what talking could yield other than more questions. Like, why was he this way? And what should he do about it?

Think about it later, Noah told himself, allowing the greenhouse and Sahara to be welcome distractions.

They reached the greenhouse door. The windows were fogged, so you couldn't see what was inside. Noah paused for effect.

"The wildflowers are nice—but wait till you see the ones my mom grows on purpose!" Then he opened the door, and they stepped inside.

Sahara had been in a greenhouse before. A fourth-grade trip to the botanical garden in Portland—and yes, that glass atrium was big, and full of all kinds of plants, but it had nothing on the Primes' little greenhouse. Flowers of every color and variety filled the space all around them. Multiple shades of tulips, roses, and carnations, as well as more exotic ones that Sahara didn't know the names of. It was breathtaking.

"My mom cultivates flowers from all over the world," Noah explained as he guided her through it. "This is her Asian section. Over here are African plants—she has a different section for every continent."

"It's bigger than it seems on the outside," Sahara commented.

"Yeah, funny how that works."

He led her to the middle, where a large pot was filled with withered stalks.

"Aw," said Noah, "you missed it! It was blooming last week."

"What was it?"

"An orchid she was growing. She crossbred a whole bunch of flowers to make it—so it was special. A little bit of everything."

Sahara offered him a sly grin. "Kind of like you."

Noah didn't know what to make of that. It bothered him, but not necessarily in a bad way. "Well, everyone's a little bit of a whole lot of things."

"Yes," Sahara agreed. "But most of those things are human."

Noah had no response to that. So, before things could get truly awkward, Sahara changed the subject.

"Your parents really should rent this place out for weddings. I mean, it's kind of romantic."

"Romantic?"

"Don't you think?"

And that left the two of them just standing there, staring at each other.

If the moment was awkward before, it had gone off the cliff now. Noah felt his cheeks begin to flush. The thought of being with Sahara in a place that was substantially more romantic than a meat-filled industrial freezer was triggering a response.

"Oh no!" said Noah, beginning to panic. "Not now!"

"What's wrong?" And then Sahara realized. "Is it another animal reaction?"

Noah nodded, then paced, trying to make the feeling go away, but his freak-out only succeeded in accelerating it.

"Is it a possum again?"

"No."

"Penguin?"

"No."

"What, then?"

"It's not like it tells me ahead of time!"

Then Sahara gave him a long, strange look and said, "Ooh..."

Noah did not like the sound of that. "Is that a *good* 'ooh,' or a *bad* 'ooh'?"

"It's just an *ooh*, ooh."

"Tell me!"

"Well...it's your hair."

"Is it falling out?"

"No, but it's changing color."

"What color is it?"

"Uh . . . all of them?"

Sahara found it really hard to describe at first. Noah's hair had gone a sort of dark turquoise with spots of rich blue, as well as feathery tendrils of red and green. Odd, but familiar. All at once, she got it!

"Noah, your hair has gone full peacock!"

"What? Show me!"

And so Sahara pulled out her phone, turned on the camera, and let him see the selfie screen.

Noah yelped at the sight of himself.

"It's not so terrible," said Sahara. "Actually, it's kind of pretty."

"You're not helping!"

"There's nothing wrong with wanting to be pretty, Noah."

"I know," he told her. "But I'm not that guy!"

"Are you sure? Because your hair has a different opinion."

The only thing he was sure about was that he couldn't let his parents see him like this. They'd ask too many questions that he wouldn't be able to answer. Noah tried to flatten his hair, but it kept standing back on end like a preening peacock. He had to think. This was just like the penguin dance, right? Peacocks strut and show their feathers to impress peahens.

"Quick," said Noah. "Think of the most unromantic things you can think of!"

"Okay ... Give me a sec ..."

"Hurry!"

"Uh ... Roadkill. Moldy bread. Ugly babies."

"Good! Keep going."

"Midterms. Toenail clippings. My aunt's hairy neck mole."

"Seriously?"

"Ugh, don't ask."

After a few more unpleasant examples, Noah felt the flush in his cheeks fading and the urge to strut his stuff going away.

"It's working—your hair isn't as peacocky anymore," Sahara told him. "The colors are almost gone."

Noah took a deep breath and another, and finally he felt normal shades return within as well.

"All better now?" asked Sahara.

Noah nodded, then said something he never thought he'd say. "Let's not say or do anything romantic again," he told Sahara. "Because what if next time I take on the mating ritual of a shark or something?"

"Why? What do sharks do?"

"I have no idea, but do you really want to find out?"

• ● •

When they got back to the house, Ogden was there waiting, and he could not be dissuaded from the belief that Noah and Sahara were making out in the greenhouse.

125

"It's not like that, Ogden," Noah said, even though he kind of wished it were. But until he got himself under control, that was a nonstarter.

"It's the truth, Ogden," seconded Sahara. "We were just out there...admiring the colors."

Noah threw her the briefest of glances, but he decided to just let it go.

"Whatever," said Ogden. "It's not my business anyway."

For dinner, to accommodate the dietary restrictions Sahara didn't know she had, Noah's mom made tofu tacos, and they weren't bad. Or, as Ogden put it, "These are disappointingly delicious," because they could not be made fun of.

Noah's dad came in from his workshop as everyone sat down, bringing with him a strong wooden scent.

"Smells like Christmas!" Sahara commented.

"Yep, that's our dad!" Andi said.

"I was just deep into a pine coffin," he explained.

"Oh," said Sahara. "I'm...sorry?"

Noah sighed. "The cabinets my dad makes are actually..."

"People cabinets!" Andi chimed in.

"Oh...I see," said Sahara, both horrified and thrilled.

Noah went on, "Anyway, he wasn't actually 'in' it."

"No, I was," his dad corrected. "The client is about my size, so I was testing it out."

"Wow," said Sahara. "That's...dedication."

"He's got a cedar one out there," Andi told her, "if you want to try it out after dinner."

"And," pointed out Ogden, "the cedar will keep moths from eating your clothes while you're in there—dead or alive."

"Can we please change the subject?" moaned Noah.

"So, tell us about yourself, Sahara," his mom said as she passed the plate of entirely unfunny tacos.

"You never ask *me* about *myself*," said Ogden.

"That's because we already know more about you than we really want to know," said Noah's father jovially.

"Point taken," said Ogden.

"Well . . . I'm a gymnast," Sahara began. But before she could say anything else, the roof exploded.

• ● •

They say most accidents happen at home. But when they say this, they generally mean someone slips off a ladder or falls down the stairs. Roofs may leak, or even collapse, but they rarely explode. Gas tanks explode. Boilers are known to explode. But not entire roofs.

The last documented accidental roof explosion occurred in Lyon, France, when a university was undergoing routine maintenance, which turned out to be not quite so routine after all. Naturally, some comically inclined *imbéciles* immediately applied the expression *"Ils ont fait sauter le toit,"* or "They blew the roof off," simply because the phrase is hardly ever used literally—only metaphorically, such as at a concert when a band pulls out all the stops— which is also a metaphor, having something to do with the pipes on church organs. Which are rarely at concerts that blow the roof off.

But with regards to Noah's house, it was very definitely literal. And this time, it wasn't an accident.

Ogden was taking a bite of his taco at the instant of the explosion. For a moment, and just a moment before rational thought kicked in, his mind said, *Wow, that's one crunchy taco*, but when a roof beam came down, demolishing the table and laying waste to every last one of the sadly un-mockable tacos, he knew something larger was going on. In Ogden's experience, it was never a good sign when things started exploding.

Sahara had the quickest reflexes and sprang away from the table as if dismounting from a gymnastics routine. She was quick to notice the terrible stench that came with the explosion. A stench that seemed to encase her just as thoroughly as the coffin she hadn't tested but now wished she had, because the smell of cedar would have been much preferable to this.

Noah responded to the explosion as Noah responded to many stressful situations these days: He exhibited a very specific defense mechanism. In this case, he responded like a startled skunk, spraying a foul funk from a scent gland in the small of his back that hadn't been there a moment before. And due to the angle he was sitting at the moment of the blast, the spray's trajectory was in the general direction of Sahara.

And then things really started to get weird.

"Evasive Protocol One!" shouted Andi.

"What?" said Noah. *"What?"*

"Escalate!" said Noah's father, suddenly wielding a massive, futuristic-looking weapon.

"Fine," said Andi with a shrug, "have it your way. Evasive Protocol Two!"

She looked up at the gaping hole in the roof—and laser beams shot from her eyes.

"Andi???" said Noah.

She turned at his voice, and her eyes cut a flaming path across the wall.

"Stop distracting me, jerk, I'm busy." Then she turned her laser eyes upward again, targeting something large and metallic that hovered above the house, raining down destruction.

Around them, the entire kitchen was on fire, and Noah, trying to get his priorities in order, realized that the blaster in his father's hand, the fact that his mother was now levitating, and the small missiles that were now launching out of his sister's mouth were all less important than making sure Sahara and Ogden were still alive.

They were. Ogden was trying to protect himself by crawling beneath sofa cushions like loose change, and

Sahara was looking at Noah's family in horror while simultaneously grimacing from the awful stench that now clung to her.

"Why do I smell like skunk?" she cried.

"Get him out of here!" Noah's dad shouted to Andi. "Take him to the ship!"

"We have a ship?" said Noah.

But before anyone could answer, Andi took a direct hit from an ion cannon or something, and her head flew off, ricocheting off the wall and landing in their fish tank, which, amazingly, was still intact, although the fish inside had clear suspicions that something was up.

Sahara screamed. Ogden squealed. Then the headless Andi reached into the fish tank and picked up her head by the hair. She turned it to face the three other kids; it coughed out a goldfish, then it spoke.

"Come with me if you want to live," she said in a deep monotone with a slight Germanic accent. "Kidding not kidding! Come on!"

While Noah's parents, in various anti-gravitational positions, fired blasters at the huge hovering craft, Andi ran toward the door, with Noah, Sahara, and Ogden close behind.

"Andi," Ogden pleaded, "please tell me there's a logical explanation for all of this."

"Yes, Ogden, of course there is," Andi said. "We're

under attack, duh. Now please open the door—my hands are full."

Ogden opened the door, revealing two humanoid figures in silver suits.

"Silver suits? Ugh! You're such clichés!" said Andi's decapitated head; then it fired lasers at them, and the figures disappeared in a flash of light, leaving glowing after-images on Noah's retinas.

"This way!" Andi shouted, running toward the woods.

Noah and the others followed, but more silver-clad figures streamed out of the woods, too many for Andi to blast all at once. Two grabbed Ogden as Sahara leaped away. Noah backpedaled as Andi did her best to pick off the aliens, or whatever they were.

Then, apparently, his mom's and dad's blasters found their mark. The massive floating disk started to wobble and whine, and finally it crashed down on the house, splintering it and sending debris flying in all directions.

Noah turned to watch—and at just that moment, something small and hard, with four little titanium propellers, fell out of the sky and hit him on the head, knocking him out cold.

• ● •

Kratz, in his apartment a few miles away, saw the whole thing on his laptop—which he was using to control the spy drone he had sent to observe Noah. Now he watched in growing shock as timbers fell, furniture shattered, and things blew up. He knew the military-grade drone was powerful and sturdy, but had it also been weaponized? Was it truly capable of doing so much damage?

Just before, he had it hovering outside the kitchen window. Nothing seemed unusual—merely six people having dinner. But apparently, he must have hit a wrong button and sent it some sort of attack command, because the window suddenly shattered. He tried to quickly back the drone out, but he must have severed a gas line, because there was an explosion and the roof caved in. The drone went flying, and now Kratz was panicked. Bright flashes everywhere, smoke, fire—and then the drone's fish-eye lens showed the strangest things. For a moment, it caught something that looked like a giant glowing steel disk above the house, but clearly it was just that his perspective was off, and it was merely a falling frying pan, for what else could it be?

Again he tried to maneuver the drone away from the house—and saw, to his horror, that one of the drone's razor-sharp titanium propellers had decapitated a little girl. This was a first, even for him.

Full retreat was in order, but as he tried to call the drone home, it hit something, and the image was lost.

Horrified and reeling, Kratz leaned back in his armchair. He wondered if destroying a home and decapitating a minor would be considered a capital offense. All the more reason, he concluded, to prove that Noah Prime was a human chameleon. Because once he proved that, he was sure all would be forgiven.

• ● •

As anyone who has ever been sprayed by a skunk knows, the foul smell is almost impossible to remove, especially once it sits on your skin for more than a few minutes. And while recommendations for home remedies abound, they are about as useful as spraying Axe on certain middle school boys. It makes you smell like a skunk wearing cologne.

When Sahara arrived home after the attack on Noah's house, the choking fumes surrounding her nearly drove away any thought of alien battles. She had but one imperative: *Get rid of the smell!*

She stumbled in through her front door, choking, eyes watering, but before she could even inhale the air to ask for help, her mother had already sprung off the couch.

"Whoo, girl," said her mom, taking a few steps toward her. Then she took a step back and waved her hand in front of her nose. "You smell like death on a hot Tuesday."

Sahara nodded. "I got skunked," she said, realizing the fewer details she gave about the evening, the better.

Her father came in from the kitchen and seemed about to swoon from the reek.

"Oh man, that skunk must have had superpowers!" he said. "Don't touch anything."

Sahara's mom glared at him. "Instead of making your daughter feel worse, be useful and get some baking soda.

"Baking soda. Right," said Sahara's dad, happy to leave the room. "And what about tomato juice?" he called.

"Made up by some tomato juice company," her mom yelled, quickly googling on her phone. "Stick to the baking soda—oh, and it says grease-cutting dishwashing liquid!" Then she softened her voice and spoke to Sahara. "Come on, honey, let's get you into the shower. Quick, now!"

Sahara stomped up the stairs and into the bathroom, followed by her mom. "Hope you don't love that outfit— these clothes are a casualty of war."

"I'll survive," said Sahara, getting into the shower.

"Where did it happen?"

"Noah's house," Sahara answered.

"Before or after dinner?"

She was about to say "during," but that would have begged too many questions. "I really don't want to talk about it," Sahara said.

There was a knock on the bathroom door, and as it opened a crack, her mom reached out and took the box of baking soda and the dishwashing liquid from Sahara's father.

"Only half a box?" her mom asked, shaking the baking soda.

"That's all we had in the pantry" came her dad's

muffled voice. "Should I go to Fresh and Funky to get the industrial size?"

"Good idea. I'll text you if there's anything else we need."

While Sahara slathered herself with blue dish soap, her mom shook some of the baking soda onto the scrubbing brush, then reached the brush into the shower and started scrubbing. Hard.

"Ow! Give me that!" Sahara demanded, grabbing the brush.

Her mom handed it over. "It has to be firm if you want to get rid of the smell. You gotta take off whole layers of skin."

"I *know* how to *exfoliate*!" Sahara said, more miffed by the second. Not by her mother but by the whole situation. In reality, this horrible, gut-wrenching smell was small rotten potatoes compared to everything else that had happened that night. She hadn't even begun to process it all—and, to be honest, she was actually grateful that the smell was strong enough to knock out all alien thoughts. But as she showered and scrubbed, the smell began to lessen, and the memory of the alien attack, if that's what it was, began to fill the stench-free spaces in her mind.

After the first wave of the attack, Andi, holding her head in her hands like a lantern, had led them outside. More attackers in silver onesies tried to grab Sahara, but she leaped up and took hold of a tree branch. It wasn't as smooth as the wooden bars she was used to swinging from, but it worked. She swung out, over their heads, and dropped a few feet away. Ogden managed to kick one of them in the knee, causing the being to drop in pain (at least alien kneecaps were just as vulnerable as human ones), and Andi's head zapped the others.

Then she saw Noah on the ground. At first, she thought he had been hit, but there was no blood, no blast wound. Instead, there was a drone with a bent propeller whirring uselessly on the ground near his head. It looked like a fancier, heavier version of one she had once gotten her dad for Father's Day from Best Buy. Her first thought was that if these aliens shopped at Best Buy, humans really didn't have anything to worry about. But then she realized the drone likely had nothing to do with the attack.

"Go!" Andi's head had said. "I'll take care of Noah. Just go."

Well, if Andi could shoot aliens while holding her head in her armpit, Sahara felt confident she could also protect Noah—and the best thing she and Ogden could do would be to take themselves out of the equation, so Andi wouldn't have to protect them as well.

"Split up!" Ogden told her. "Harder to catch us that way. And serpentine! Harder to shoot a swerving target."

Which might have worked for Ogden, but Sahara had always been about making a fast beeline to Anywhere But

Here. She kept on running and didn't look back again until she was on her porch—when her sense of smell overcame her flight response, and she realized just how horrible the stench of skunk was.

Half an hour and several skin layers later, Sahara collapsed on her bed in exhaustion.

"It's not as bad now," her mother told her. "I'm sure it'll be just a bad memory by morning."

Once her mother was gone, Sahara closed the door to her room and slid under her covers to hide, which she hadn't done since she was a little girl. *It's okay to hide under the covers*, she thought, *when monsters are real*.

12

The Facts of Life-as-We-Know-It

NOAH WOKE UP IN HIS BED.

Just like any other morning.

He sat up and looked around. His blinds were drawn, but he could tell from the light seeping through the cracks that it was early morning. He looked up. The roof was completely intact. In fact, his entire room seemed in order, except of course for his desk, which was its usual mess.

He got out of bed, his legs a little wobbly as he crossed the room to the door. It looked normal. And he was freaking out.

Because he *knew* last night wasn't a dream.

Oh, he wanted it to be. More than anything, he wanted his exploding house, headless robotic sister, and levitating, laser-toting parents to be part of some exhaustion-induced nightmare. And although he had to admit there had been a number of occasions when he'd wanted to knock Andi's head off himself, what he saw last night was not just the manifestation of some subconscious desire. It happened.

And yet . . . everything was back to normal. How could that be?

He opened the door to his room and walked down the hall to the kitchen. Everything was exactly the way it had been before "the attack," as Andi had called it, before vaporizing a pair of SYFY channel alien baddies at their front door. The same family photos were on the hallway wall, slightly crooked in the exact same way—no scratches, no scorch marks. Not a single thing around him hinted at the fiery battle.

His mom was making sack lunches for him and his sister. "Good morning, honey," she said, without a care in the world.

Noah sat down at the table, too disturbed to even speak. Andi was there, her head back on her shoulders, her usual bowl of cornflakes before her, full of more milk than flakes, like always.

"Hurry up and eat, sweetie," his mom said. "You have to get to school."

"Not hungry," Noah said.

"Well, at least have some juice," said his mom. She poured a glass and brought it to him at the table.

He stared at it. A glass of juice. A box of Froot Loops on the table waiting for him. All so normal, and yet . . . *"Froot Loops are all the same flavor!"* Ogden had told him. Proof that the world we think we know is wrong at every level.

"No," Noah said, pushing the juice back toward his mom. "No, I'm not going to just go along with this, like nothing happened last night. No. Just NO!"

His mom looked at him strangely, as if this were the first she was hearing of it, but her smile didn't fade. There was something a little off about her. Something . . . *askew*, if that word could be used for a person. But everything about everything was completely askew right now. Then his father walked into the kitchen.

"What are you talking about, son?" his dad asked. "What happened last night?"

Noah stood up and faced him. "Don't!" he said. "I know it's an act. Stop lying to me."

His parents were still smiling at him, but he could now see the concern in their eyes. He looked at the floor to avoid their gazes, and to try to get his thoughts in some kind of order. Then he glanced toward the living room—and froze.

The living room window framed a scene he had never seen before.

For his entire life, that window had faced the woods, but now he saw a cornfield that seemed to go on for miles under a clear blue sky.

Noah felt an unfamiliar tickle on his scalp, goose-flesh so tight it was tugging the hair on his head on end. He touched his hair. It felt sharp and thick. Like porcupine quills. He raised his arm and pointed at the window. "Wh-wh-where are we? What's going on?" It was one thing to *believe* last night wasn't a dream, but it was another thing altogether to face actual proof.

Noah's father turned to his wife. "I thought you erased his memory."

"No," she said, "*you* were supposed to erase his memory."

"I distinctly remember you saying that you were going to do it."

"Oh, so now this is *my* fault?"

Noah spun back and looked from one to the other, then to Andi, who sighed. "Parents," she said to him. "Fine in concept, but in reality? Not so much."

"Hey, Noah!" his father said, "Got something to show you in my workshop. I think you'll really like it." His dad took him by the arm and tried to gently guide him to the door, but Noah shook him off and backed away.

"No! Do you think I'm stupid? I'm not letting you erase my memory!"

His father sighed, then looked at him, finally offering a moment of honesty. "Son, believe me, if we tell you what's going on, you're going to wish you *did* have your memory erased."

"So do it after you tell me," Noah said. "Because then I'll know what it is I'm better off not knowing, and I'll cooperate when you make me un-know it."

Andi stood up. "That's actually a good idea," she said. "And trying to grab him with that porcupine hair is going to be an unpleasant experience for everyone."

Noah's mother and father looked at each other, and his mom gestured for him to sit down with them at the kitchen table.

"It's like this, Noah," said his dad. "In this universe, there are bright stars that give their light to everyone, and there are black holes, which just suck everything in and destroy it—"

"No, no, no," said his mother. "That's not how to approach this. Keep it simple." She smiled at Noah. "Honey, every basic building block is made up of opposites. Take the atom: electrons and protons, which in turn are made of quarks and neutrinos and so on and so forth—you see?"

"How is that any better?" said his father. "I already feel like I need a textbook."

"Nope," said Andi, "I'm not opening my textbook app. It's not worth the trouble."

Noah could tell this was going nowhere, and he wasn't about to sit still for a "facts of life" talk, even if it wasn't the facts of life as he knew it. He held up a hand. "Okay, you know what? I don't think this is helping."

His father sighed. "I'm sorry, Noah. None of us ever expected we'd have to have this conversation."

Then his mom reached out and took his hand. "The point is, we love you, Noah, and we're not going to let anything happen to you. That's the only truth that matters."

Noah felt her hand, soft and warm, and he gave it a gentle squeeze. "I know, Mom."

And then he realized—"But what about Ogden and Sahara?"

Then Andi spoke up. "When that drone fell out of the trees and knocked you out, they were running pretty fast. And besides, they weren't the target, you were. I would say the chances are somewhere around 93.7 percent that they got away."

"Listen," said his dad, "maybe you shouldn't go to school today. Just stay home, take it easy."

"School?" Noah said, as a thought occurred to him. "But how could you swing that? I mean, clearly this isn't Arbuckle. No one here will know who I am. Or did you tweak everyone's memory to account for me?"

They just looked at him, and then his father said, "Well, we did have all night."

"Why don't you just go rest," his mom said softly.

"Okay," said Noah, trying not to think about it. "I'm going to go lie down now, in that room that looks just like mine."

"It *is* your room. It really is," said his mom.

"Of course it is," confirmed his dad. "This backup house is an exact replica, right down to the moldy sandwich under your bed."

Noah headed down the hall in a daze, not sure which was worse: the fact that he had a replica backup home in case of alien attack or that his entire family was perfectly okay with this. He wanted his friends back. Ogden and

143

Sahara didn't have backup lives, and he was sure that they were just as freaked out by all of this as he was.

And even if they escaped, now the enemy—whoever or whatever they were—knew his friends were a part of this.

• ● •

Mission Luminary Vectoria Centra—Vecca for short—had found that for every two glorious triumphs, there was one colossal failure. Perhaps that's why she was allowed to maintain the leadership position of Mission Luminary, and the power that came with it—because headquarters knew that her successes outnumbered her catastrophes.

The failure to apprehend and kill Noah Prime was definitely a catastrophic event—which meant a big win was surely on its way. But first, they had to find the troublesome boy again.

Her second-in-command was on the other side of the mostly empty warehouse that was their current base of operations, staring at a screen, studying the results of the latest planet-wide scan. His name was Rom, short for Norom, though no one called him that but his mother—which meant no one at all, since their species technically didn't have mothers.

"Anything?" she asked, trying to hide her impatience, but not doing a very good job of it.

"Not yet," Rom said. "His biometric signature is difficult to discern . . . but we believe he's still on this continent."

"Narrowing it down to one-seventh of the planet's landmasses is not very helpful," she said, her voice rising with each syllable. She took a cleansing breath to relax herself, but it just made her cough. It was this Earth air. What species in its right mind needed that much oxygen? "He was last seen with a protective android, wasn't he? Expand your search parameters to look for its energy signature."

"Good thinking," said Rom.

"That's why I'm mission luminary," said Vecca. Although if she didn't get this N.O.A.H. terminated soon, she might not be the luminary of anyone's mission anymore.

• ● •

"The last thing you need right now are idle hands," Noah's father told him later that morning, then put him to work sanding down a half-finished cedar coffin in the barn, while his father studied and organized tools on a shelf, as if he'd never seen them before. He seemed to put a temporary hold on erasing Noah's memory, although Noah was constantly on guard, because he didn't know what a memory eraser looked like, which meant it could be any tool his father took in hand. But perhaps they had decided that bringing him in on this—whatever it was—was easier than hiding it all from him. After a while, Noah began to relax. Still, he couldn't help but ask a few key questions here and there.

"Hey, Dad, am I human?"

His father hesitated before answering.

"Yes and no."

"Are you and mom human?"

He paused before responding.

"No . . . and yes."

"What about Andi? Is she human?"

"Oh, absolutely not."

"Hmm," said Noah. "That explains a lot."

"You have no idea."

His dad stood back to admire Noah's work. "I think that is as smooth as anything I've ever seen," he said. "You did a good job, Noah."

Somehow, Noah wasn't too enthused. If anything had gone wrong back home, that coffin could have been his. It might still be. He didn't even know the forces that were after them. Or was it just him they were after? That was a question he was too scared to ask.

"You know," his dad began, as he hung a wood file back in its place, "I have to tell you, you impressed me today."

"I did?"

"Sure." His dad stopped and looked straight at Noah. "You know, in every person's life, there comes a moment when their world turns upside down in its own way. Not everyone can handle it. You did."

"Well," said Noah, "I kind of had no choice."

"You didn't choose the moment, but there's an infinite number of ways you could have responded. You faced the situation head-on."

146

"I still don't know what the situation is."

"It's complicated," his father said.

"That much I get."

"The point is, you confronted it. You didn't run away from it."

"Not my style," he said.

"Which is why I'm so proud of you."

Noah offered him a slim, pained smile, which was the best he could muster under the circumstances. "Thanks, Dad."

But for some reason, that made his father uncomfortable. He took a deep breath. "One more thing I think you should know," he said. "We...that is, your mother and I...aren't exactly the same people who were with you when your house was attacked."

"Wh-what do you mean, 'aren't exactly the same people'?"

"Well...your *actual* parents were captured." Then he squared his shoulders proudly. "We're your backup parents!"

"Oh. Uh...okay."

"So, you're good with that?" his backup father asked.

"Sure," said Noah. "I think I'll go to my room now."

Noah left the workshop. Ten minutes later, he was running as fast as his legs could carry him to the nearest bus station.

• ● •

Albion, Iowa, which was where Noah's backup house was located, was like the Midwest version of Arbuckle, Oregon.

147

And like Arbuckle, there were buses passing through town like clockwork, because there were always plenty of people trying to escape, as well as plenty of people returning after their escape failed.

The bus station was in the center of town, and even though there was no attendant present, Noah used the available schedules to plot a route back to Arbuckle.

A bus was leaving for Omaha, Nebraska, in about ten minutes, and from there he could take a train to Portland— a two-day trip. After that, he knew it would be fairly easy to find a way back to Arbuckle. He had pulled together enough cash in the small bank he kept on his desk— identical to the one in his destroyed house, down to the penny—for the bus ride to Omaha, but after that he'd have to get resourceful.

The bus arrived. He could smell the bitter scent of exhaust, and once he boarded, and the bus pulled out, the engine made such an unsettling rattle as it got up to speed that Noah wasn't sure it would make it to the next town, much less all the way to Omaha. Then, just a couple of minutes into the trip, he heard a familiar voice behind him.

"Took you long enough."

He whipped around and saw Andi sitting there. Noah stood up so fast he bumped his head on the luggage rack.

"Settle down," she said. "Come sit with me."

"No! I don't want to have anything to do with you!"

"Trust me," she told him calmly. "The toddler who was

sitting in your seat from Waterloo to Albion had bladder issues. You don't want to sit there."

Noah, knowing he was caught, and that there was nothing he could do about it, moved back a row and sat down next to her. "How did you get on the bus before I did?"

"Do you really want me to get into temporal shifts and rural micro-wormholes?"

"Not really."

"Good, because it'll make your brain blow up anyway, and that wouldn't help anyone, would it?"

"Do our 'backup' parents know I left?"

Andi rolled her eyes. For a moment, Noah thought lasers might shoot out again. "Of course they know."

"And they're letting me go?"

"They've got their own headache right now," she told him. "Their supervisors are pretty upset that they told you as much as they did."

"They barely told me anything!"

"Even that was too much. So our backup parents are being brought in for disciplinary action."

"Is that bad?"

"Think Saturday school, but on the surface of the sun."

"Youch."

"Don't worry, they can take it," said Andi, "but while they sort stuff out, I've been put in charge of protecting you. We've moved up from Evasive Protocol Two to Evasive Protocol Three."

"Is that worse than Two?"

"Way worse. Usually involves the kind of stuff you see in really high-budget movies about the end of the world. Scorched Canadian cities, liquefied extras, a dog that some little kid tries to save—it's not pretty."

"Are you going to drag me back to our fake home now?"

"Can't," said Andi. "Evasive Protocol Three means I have to protect and assist you by any means necessary. Which means I can't *make* you do anything, unless it's to save your life."

"Sounds like a program glitch."

Andi sighed. "Tell me about it."

"So . . . what now?"

Andi shrugged. "Up to you. Safest thing right now is to stay mobile, traveling to unpredictable places. My algorithms tell me that Rapid City, South Dakota, is the single most unpredictable place we could currently go."

Noah considered it, then shook his head. "No. I'm going back to Arbuckle. If Mom and Dad—our *real* mom and dad—have been captured, we have to find them. And we need to make sure that Sahara and Ogden are all right."

"Finding Mom and Dad won't be easy—and the last thing they'd want us to do is look for them, because it puts you in danger . . ." Then Andi sighed. "But I will admit that I'm worried about them, too. I'm even worried about Sahara and Ogden—but if you repeat that, I'll deny it."

Noah couldn't help but smile just a little bit. Which made Andi frown.

"Why are you grinning like that?"

Noah shrugged. "It's not every day you find out that your sister is an insanely cool killer robot."

"*Android*," she said. "Andi as in Android—but not the phone. Although I *am* a phone, but not an Android. I'm more like an iPhone—but if you call me Siri, I will rip your heart out and feed it to the annoying kid behind me because *I am NOT Siri*. I have much better voice-to-text capability."

Noah made a mental note not to irritate his sister anymore.

"Well, we have a long trip ahead of us. Maybe you could tell me what our backup parents wouldn't."

But Andi shook her head. "You don't have high-enough security clearance for me to tell you about yourself. Except to say that you were named 'Noah' for a reason. The rest you're going to have to figure out on your own."

13

The Cowboy, the Samurai, and Mr. Quiche

THAT MORNING, AROUND THE TIME THAT NOAH WAS BAILING from a strange house, or rather, a *familiar* house in a strange place, Sahara was staring at her bedroom ceiling, not wanting to be awake, but having no choice in the matter. She had been staring for at least an hour, using the blank ceiling as a canvas for her thoughts. She hadn't gotten out of bed since crawling into it the previous night, after her little chemical shower.

"So, you never told me," her mom asked when she finally ventured downstairs, "other than getting skunked, how was dinner at Noah's?"

"Nuts!" was all Sahara said, and her mom just nodded.

After what she had experienced last night, it seemed odd to find everything so normal this morning. But then, what did she expect? It wasn't *her* parents shooting blasters at aliens. She wasn't the one with a headless robotic sibling. Even so, her whole world—her whole universe—had changed overnight. Somehow, she felt that her own personal reality needed to, in some small way at least, reflect that.

"Buying lunch, or should I pack you something?" her mom asked, so oblivious to the larger issues of human existence that it was painful to witness.

"Actually, I'm not going to school today."

Not today, not tomorrow, not ever again was what she wanted to say. What was the point of sitting in math class and solving for X, when X is *a freaking ship of three-headed aliens from Alpha-freaking-Centauri?*

Well, okay, they weren't three-headed—but they might as well have been. And chances are they weren't from Alpha Centauri, what with billions of possible star systems, *and my God, I'm starting to think like Ogden, which means this truly is the end of the world.*

"What's wrong, baby? Is it the skunk smell? It's almost gone now, so no one'll notice." Which, of course, wasn't true. Even with the best remedies available, skunk was still skunk. At best, she would smell like an old rubber tire for a few more days—but that was the very least of her problems.

"No, it's not that. It's something I ate. It must have been what the Primes had for dinner last night."

To that, her mom nodded knowingly, accepting the sad and universal truth of Other People's Cooking. She went off to work, leaving Sahara with a bucket by her bed and a bottle of Pepto Bismol on her nightstand, along with the dishwashing liquid and the giant economy-size baking soda her father had bought, in case a second treatment was required.

Once her mother was gone, Sahara retreated under her mildly musky covers, determined to disappear into her alternate dimension of one—but try as she might, she couldn't stop reliving the trauma that was dinner with the Primes.

The morning was half over when Sahara found it in herself to throw back her covers. There was too much she didn't know—and it was more than just curiosity. She had to find out if Noah was okay. She had to see for herself what was left of his home. To prove to herself that it actually happened. *Face your fears*, she had always been told. What she feared most was last night's alien attack. And so she forced herself to go back, determined to pick through the wreckage for clues as to what the hell was going on.

• ● •

She rode her bike to Noah's house—which was isolated enough down a woodsy road that there were no neighbors. Still, people must have heard the blasts and explosions for miles.

She left the main road and headed down the dirt path, but as she approached the clearing where Noah's house had stood, she didn't see hints of the wreckage. Instead, she saw flickers of something tall and gray through the trees. When she came around the last few trees, she finally recognized what she was looking at.

Stonehenge.

The ruins of Noah's house had been replaced by Stonehenge.

She dropped her bike, then slowly walked to the center of the stone circle, beginning to think that maybe she was the subject of an extremely elaborate, extremely expensive practical joke.

"Impressive, yes?"

She spun at the voice and saw a man in a suit strolling out from behind one of the massive vertical stones. He wasn't all that tall—perhaps about Noah's size.

"Who do you think would build something like this?" he continued. "Besides ancient Druids, that is."

"Stay back!" she said, reaching into her backpack. "I have pepper spray!" Which was true. She had come prepared for any contingency. Although for all she knew, these aliens breathed caustic, peppery air.

The man stopped, a dozen yards away and nodded.

"Good for you," he said. "These days a person can never be too cautious. Tell me, what were you expecting to find here?"

"None of your business!" Sahara said.

"Well," said the man, "my business isn't yours,

either—but I'll tell you why *I'm* here. I was looking for the Prime residence. Mr. Prime was working on a bespoke casket for me, and I was coming to check on it. Imagine my surprise when I found *this* here instead. Unless, of course, my GPS is off, and I wound up in Wiltshire, England."

"If that's true, and you're not one of them, then how did you get here?"

"One of *who*?" he asked.

"Answer the question!"

The man sighed. "I wasn't about to have my car come down a dirt road and get stuck in the mud. So I sent my driver off to get gas, and I walked the rest of the way on foot. Simple as that. He should be back shortly."

The man seemed genuine, but Sahara wasn't about to trust anyone. It was hard enough to trust her own eyes... but the fact that there was someone to corroborate what she saw before her relieved at least some of her anxiety. Sahara sized him up. He was Southeast Asian, and the suit was nicely tailored and screamed wealth—and it occurred to her who this must be.

"Are you that guy who built the Arbuckle town square? Mr. Quiche?"

"It's Ksh, with a 'K,' no vowels."

Clearly, he wanted her to tell him whatever she knew. She didn't want to give him more than he needed to know, but it wasn't in her nature to be entirely dismissive.

"Well, you're in the right place," she told him. "But

something happened. There was...an accident here last night," she said. "The house kinda sorta burned down."

"Kinda sorta," repeated Mr. Ksh.

Sahara looked around again. The clearing around the towering stones looked as if it had been untouched for years. "There should be ruins..."

"Well, technically speaking, these *are* ruins," the man pointed out. "Just not the ruins of a farmhouse." Then he clapped his hands together. "I do love a mystery!"

But mysteries left clues. There wasn't a single clue as to how this place came to be. Until Sahara took a closer look at one of the stones—where a small chunk of what appeared to be skin was stuck to the surface. "There!" she said. "Do you see it? Dangling flesh!"

Mr. Ksh walked over, squinting as he took a closer look.

"Actually," he said, "it looks more like tofu."

Before Sahara could respond, she heard voices approaching. She ran behind the closest stone and pulled Mr. Ksh with her.

"Why are we hiding?" he asked.

"Because," she said, "after last night, there's no coffin for you if you die."

That got him to shut up.

Peeking out from the side of the rock, Sahara watched two men come out of the woods, into the clearing, and into the circle of stones. These two were even more out of place than Stonehenge. One was dressed like a samurai warrior and the other like Buffalo Bill, all leather fringe and cheap rhinestones.

"After the mess our attack force left last night, it's important that nothing look amiss," said the man dressed as the samurai. "This structure is roughly the same size as the one that was here. According to our research staff, this is a classic example of Earth architecture." He nodded in approval. "No one will notice the difference."

So these two were part of the alien squad who attacked last night! Apparently, they weren't limited to silver flight suits—although if these were supposed to be human disguises, they had seriously missed the mark.

The rhinestone cowboy shook his head. "Maybe it's just me, but this doesn't look like the buildings we've come across in the area."

The samurai gave his companion the smug smile of a person so sure of his own intelligence that he's a fool.

"You know *nothing* about this planet. I guarantee you, this structure is from the same era, give or take a few thousand years," he said.

"And what about that?" the cowboy asked, pointing at Sahara's bike, which was lying just outside the circle of stones.

"A common human transportation device," the samurai said, "no doubt placed there by our construction staff to give the place a lived-in look."

Mr. Ksh glanced at Sahara with sparkling, intrigued eyes. "Aliens! Now it all begins to make sense."

Sahara shushed him, and they returned their attention to the samurai, who was having trouble with the sash on his kimono, and the cowboy, who couldn't seem to get the hang of walking with spurs.

Then a third person entered the circle, this one dressed as a chauffeur.

"Oh wow," he said. "It looks just like Stonehenge—but without the graffiti."

The samurai pulled his sword and took a stance. "Come no closer!" he said. "I know how to use this!"

"No you don't," said the cowboy.

"Hey," said the chauffeur, "is this some sort of role-playing game? Because I'm down for that."

The samurai held his stance for a moment longer, then just gave up and turned to the cowboy. "Take care of him."

The cowboy started looking through his many pockets, then pulled out a marble. "Biomass bomb?"

"If that's the best you can do, fine."

"If you're going to attack me," said the chauffeur, "at least let me roll some defensive dice."

The cowboy ignored him, threw the marble—and the chauffeur instantly dissolved into a crumbling mound of six hundred thousand red ants, which had the exact same biomass as the chauffeur.

"There. One less prisoner we have to deal with," said the cowboy.

Sahara could only gape at the mound of ants, wondering if that had also been Noah's fate. Or was he one of the prisoners they were talking about?

Mr. Ksh shook his head in disbelief.

The samurai and the cowboy strode back down the driveway, arguing about whether a step pyramid would have been a more appropriate structure, and giving a wide berth to the pile of ants swarming in understandable confusion.

Sahara closed her eyes and let out her breath slowly, releasing all of her tension.

"I've changed my mind," said Mr. Ksh. "Some mysteries I *don't* love."

And he turned to leave.

"Wait!" said Sahara. "We have to follow them."

"Not necessarily the best course of action," he said. "Assuming they haven't turned my car into a pile of LEGOs, I plan to drive to work, hire someone to build an ant farm for my poor chauffeur, and continue preparation for the Fossil Day Festival—which, I assure you, will be the most memorable one yet."

"FossilFest? With all this going on, you're worried about FossilFest?"

Mr. Ksh sighed. "Life must go on, in spite of alien encounters," he told her. "I suggest you get back to living *your* life until we know more. And perhaps we *will* know more when we next encounter each other, hmm?"

Sahara was furious. Here was clearly a man with the money and resources to do something about this, but he would rather just wait and see what happens. Well, if Ksh wouldn't help her, she was determined to do this on her own.

"Fine. If you're not going to help me, get out of my way," she said as she pushed past him, got on her bike, and pedaled off after the oddly dressed aliens.

At the main road, she hid for a moment behind Ksh's chauffeur-less Cadillac, watching the cowboy and samurai as they hopped into a small blue car—a classic T-Bird that was also from a different time period, but accidentally cool.

Although she pedaled as hard as she could, the car was fast disappearing in the distance. But the road ahead, she knew, would soon end at a sharp right turn past the rail-road tracks—so she made a right turn into the woods, to cut a diagonal that could put her ahead of them.

When she heard the train horn blasting in the distance and the crossing bells, she knew this was her chance. If the T-Bird got stuck at the crossing, she could get across the tracks and be in front of them, provided she could beat the train herself.

When she reached the tracks, she looked down the line and saw that the train was still some distance away. She had almost hoped she could make a death-defying leap and just miss the train's leading edge. But she had defied death enough in the past twenty-four hours. No need to risk it again if she didn't have to.

She crossed the tracks, reached the main road, and waited there, hoping the T-Bird was still on the other side of the train, and that it would take the main road into the heart of town instead of turning immediately onto the freeway.

Finally, the last car of the train went by, and she saw the blue T-Bird waiting patiently for the long arm of the crossing gate to go up. When it did, the T-Bird continued down the road, heading toward the center of town, instead of taking the on-ramp for the freeway. When it passed Sahara, she followed, hoping they didn't recognize her bike.

A block later, the car pulled into the parking lot of a convenience store. From across the street, Sahara watched the samurai and cowboy go inside, and they didn't come back out.

She decided it was a little too obvious to just stand there gawking—it was clear she was "casing the joint," as they said in old gangster movies, so she crossed the street and casually walked into the store, as if she was there for nothing more than Doritos and a Red Bull.

The cowboy and samurai weren't there. Strange. As she continued around the store, pretending to browse, she wondered where they could have gone. She noticed a door marked EMPLOYEES ONLY. Could they have gone in there? Sahara stopped in the candy aisle and picked up a pack of gum, then took it to the bored, uniformed clerk at the counter.

"Just this," she said. Then, as the clerk rang it up, she asked, idly, "By the way, did you see those two weirdly dressed men come in here?"

The clerk scanned the barcode of the gum and slapped it down on the counter in front of her. "Cash or credit?" he asked.

She handed him some money and waited for her change, wondering if he hadn't heard her and was just robotically repeating his script. Or maybe he actually *was* a robot, as such things were no longer beyond the realm of possibility.

"Excuse me—I asked if you saw two weirdly dressed men come in here. One was a cowboy, the other a samurai."

"Couldn't say," he told her flatly. "Cowboys come in here all the time. Samurai not so much." Then he handed her the change. "Have a nice day."

Well, if Noah, or Ogden, or anyone else were being held prisoner, then they were behind that door. And there had to be other ways to get in.

Outside, Sahara made her way around to the back of the building—a plain brick wall with a locked steel door. No possible way in. She was almost ready to give up when she caught sight of a tiny purple object on the ground near the back door. She bent down to pick it up.

A single grape PEZ candy.

She'd seen Ogden eating these—and they weren't the kind of common candy one found just lying around. Did Ogden drop it on purpose? Perhaps he had left a trail of them like bread crumbs to this door.

This meant that Ogden had to be in there! But with no way in, there was nothing she could do at the moment. She'd have to come back later, with a plan.

Incredible, she thought. *Who knew that the back rooms of 7-Elevens would be hotbeds of alien activity?*

The answer, of course, was Ogden.

14

Squirming Beneath Her Skin

IN SPITE OF OGDEN'S GENERAL TERROR OF BEING CAPTURED BY aliens, he couldn't help but feel vindicated in his belief about the back rooms of 7-Elevens. His instincts had, as always, been correct—there actually *was* a conspiracy centered around the back room of the local 7-Eleven. And if *that* was true, what else might prove to be valid?

He had always assumed that the back rooms of these sorts of places must be larger than they appeared from the outside—but he was not expecting this. The back room of the 7-Eleven was a vast warehouse space the size of an airplane hangar—but empty, since the alien ship that it would have contained had been destroyed in the attack. Well, yes, there were some cases of snacks, soft drinks, and Slurpee mix stacked in the corner, but other than that, nothing.

Ogden had suspected that this sort of dimensional stretching was possible, but it was something he imagined would show up in some NASA facility, not his neighborhood convenience store. It was, to say the least, very convenient.

The aliens had put him in a cage and left him there. The cage was in the middle of the hangar—precisely equidistant from every wall, ceiling, and floor, suspended, he assumed, magnetically, since there were no ropes or chains holding it up. It resembled a hovering birdcage more than anything, with a small dispenser for water and food. The food was Corn Nuts, likely culled from the 7-Eleven stock. He had eaten them all while he waited for the aliens to show up, and now he had a bit of a stomachache.

Finally, two of them came in through the door. One was a man who wore a purple pinstripe suit and yellow fedora out of some color-blind version of the 1930s. The fedora had a green feather in it, which completely clashed with everything else. The woman wore an orange-and-pink paisley dress straight out of the '60s. She wore white lipstick and a string of pearls, and her hair was done up in a beehive hairdo. Ogden had to admit that his curiosity about all this was beginning to outweigh his fear.

"Nice outfits," he said. "But you do know that people don't dress like that, don't you?"

"Of course they do," said the woman, who appeared to be the one in charge. "We did an extensive study of your visual culture."

"You mean movies?" Ogden asked.

"Yes. Which is how we know they're accurate."

"Right. Good thinking," said Ogden. "But here's a tip: If you want to be taken seriously as an alien presence, you should, at the very least, be wearing dark, intimidating suits."

The two otherworldly emissaries looked at themselves, and each other, but suspended judgment.

"You do realize that one or both of my parents are probably looking for me."

To that, the woman smiled and said, "Last night, we took the liberty of sending one or both of your parents a textual message using your black-mirrored communication device. I believe it read, 'I shall be overnighting with the Family Prime, and shall return anon.'"

Wow, thought Ogden, *it sounded just like something I might text*.

"So ... what are you going to do with me?"

"That depends on what you do for us," said the woman. Then she gestured to the man, who put on a pair of dark glasses, sat in a chair, opened a laptop, and began tapping away. The problem with this picture was that (a) there was no chair, and (b) there was no laptop. The man just seemed to be typing on empty air.

"Don't mind my associate," said the woman. "It's his job to keep a record of our ... conversation."

Just then, someone came in from the 7-Eleven—a guy dressed in a generic polyester uniform common to all

167

convenience store employees. Well, at least the uniform seemed to be from the current decade.

"Excuse me," he said. "Sorry to bother you—but there's a man out here with a rudimentary ballistic weapon, and he is asking for all the money in the register. Should I give it to him?"

The woman let out a gust of exasperation. "Did you at least put him in time-stasis?"

"Of course."

"Then why couldn't you figure out that the human in question is perpetrating a crime?" she said, and waved her hand dismissively "Send him to penal colony 487-22-Z. They can always use another triiodide miner."

"But he only has two arms."

"He'll manage."

The store employee left, and the woman turned back to Ogden. "Now, then," she said.

"Now? Or then?" Ogden asked.

"Excuse me?"

"I hate that expression. It's an oxymoron. Is it 'now' or is it 'then'? I'd appreciate it if you could be precise in your temporal references."

The man with the imaginary laptop laughed. "Got you there!" he said.

She threw him an icy glare, then returned her attention to Ogden.

"Let's talk about your friend. Noah Prime."

"Sure, but what I'd really like to talk about are *your* friend's shades," Ogden said, pointing at her associate. "Are those Vantablack lenses? Because I can't see the tiniest reflection from them at all, and there's no darker substance on Earth. But I've never heard of Vantablack sunglasses."

"Yes, they are," said the man, duly impressed, "coated with dimensionally shifted polycarbonate."

"Then I assume your chair and laptop are made of dark matter, which is why I can't see them. Is it the dimensional shift that keeps them from coming in contact with regular matter?"

"Enough!" said the woman. "*We* ask the questions."

"Fine," said Ogden. "Ask away."

"What do you know about Noah Prime?" she demanded.

"Lots of stuff. He likes motocross. He's good at whatever he tries to be good at. Oh, and he seems to have enhanced multispecies DNA." Ogden figured there was no problem telling them that, because clearly they already knew or they wouldn't have come after Noah. It gave the illusion of him being agreeable, without providing them with any critical information.

"So you are aware of his abilities..."

"They're hard to miss if you're looking closely, but luckily most people don't. Or at least 'people' in the local definition of 'people.' I mean no disrespect to *you*, of course."

169

"None taken," said the guy in the Vantablack shades.

"Stop answering him!" The woman demanded.

"Quid pro quo," said Ogden. "Quid pro quo. 'You scratch my back, I'll scratch yours.' Another expression I don't like, by the way. But if you want my cooperation, trading answers is the best way."

The woman crossed her arms. "Fine," she said. "But it's still our turn." She took a step closer to his cage. "As I'm sure you're aware, your friend escaped. And *I* think you know where he went."

Ogden considered this. The fact was, Noah never *went* anywhere. His family didn't leave Arbuckle, not even on vacation. It made sense now—if their whole purpose was to keep a low profile, Arbuckle was the place to do it. Bottom line, Ogden had no idea where Noah was, but he couldn't tell these two that, or they might send Ogden to penal colony 487-22-Z, and although triiodide mining sounded intriguing, something told him it would get old real fast.

"I'm waiting," said the woman. "I can see you know something. It will be better for you—and everyone you know—if you tell me."

There was really only one way to deal with this: the same way he dealt with his parents whenever they attempted to press him for information. He would turn it back around on them.

"You know what really disappoints me," Ogden said. "The fact that you even have to ask. You act like you know

170

what you're doing, and yet you failed to do the simple, obvious trick of tagging Noah with a tracking beacon. Why not? You had plenty of time during the attack. And if you watch Earth movies, as you say you do, you must know that obvious trope! But no—you had to blow up his house and lose him."

Now the two of them weren't even willing to meet his eye. He had them!

"You are unaware of the complexity of the situation," the woman said, but clearly she was just making excuses.

"Well, next time, I hope you'll think things through a little bit better." Ogden said. "These Corn Nuts, for instance. I mean, seriously—couldn't you have at least gotten me some of those warm convenience store taquitos?"

• ● •

"I think he's one of us."

Vecca nervously fiddled with her pearls as she paced in a hidden corner of the extra-dimensional hangar—a spot that Ogden couldn't see.

"He doesn't look like one of us," Rom pointed out.

Vecca sighed in what had come to be perpetual exasperation. "*We* don't look like us," she reminded him. "It's easy enough to put an agent in a human skin—and if Objective Management wanted to check up on our mission, I'll bet they'd send an undercover operative disguised as a human."

171

"If that's true, it's a better skin than ours. His has eyelids."

"And his questions were pinpointed—like someone who knew exactly what they were talking about," said Vecca. "And he also called us out on our errors."

The fact that Noah Prime had escaped irked Vecca to no end. He should have been easy to catch and kill. And yes, even if they couldn't catch him, they should have managed to track him, just as Ogden had suggested. It was the bumbling hands of others that had let him escape, but she was in charge of the mission, which meant the blame fell squarely on her shoulders. Or would have, had her species had such things as shoulders.

"Remember," she pointed out, "we're still under investigation after that business with the Andromedan ambassador. Of course they'll be watching us."

"That wasn't our fault," Rom insisted. "Shaking hands is a universal gesture. How were we supposed to know it would make the ambassador's skull explode?"

The fact was, they should have known that the Andromedan's grasping appendage was also its biological defense mechanism. Because any attacker that grasped it would also be killed in the explosion. Half of Vecca's team had been taken out, as was most of the arriving diplomatic party. Once the Andromeda Galaxy found out, there'd be war—but since Andromeda was 2.5 million light-years away, it would be quite some time before they got solar wind of the disaster and could launch an attack. Still, the thought of eventually having an entire galaxy angry at her in some future eon was not a pleasant prospect.

It was the Office of Interstellar Research that was supposed to warn them of such things. Well, at least they had gotten Earth right.

"So what should we do?" Rom asked.

Vecca considered the situation, squirming a bit beneath her artificial skin. "We need to be careful, just in case he *is* a spy from HQ," she told him. "We have to handle this so-called human with kid gloves."

Rom furrowed his eyebrows. "I'm thinking that making gloves out of a kid could be a violation of local laws and customs. Unless, of course, nobody likes the kid. Do you have one in mind?"

" 'Kid' as in baby goat. It's a human expression. Probably another one that our subject would hate."

To which Rom said, "What's a goat?"

Vecca threw up her fists in long-suffering fury. "I don't know! I haven't seen one yet, but gloves are apparently made from its babies, and all of that is entirely beside the point!"

"Got it," said Rom. "So what should we do?"

Vecca looked at him as if she might detonate like the Andromedan ambassador. "Get him taquitos!"

15

Thirteen Hours to Kill or Be Killed

THE WEST GALACTIC OFFICE OF INTERSTELLAR RESEARCH WAS not incompetent, merely overworked to the point that its researchers only had time to learn about 10 percent of any planet's biological and cultural facts. It never got anything wrong ... but its reports delivered quite a few half-truths. Or tenth-truths, to be more accurate.

When the researchers discovered the vast array of "visual records" of Earth, otherwise known as movies, they were delighted, because it made their job easy. And since they were from a culture that had remained exactly the same for over thirty thousand of their years, they naturally assumed that Earth would be the same as well. The concept of changing fashions and period architecture was so foreign to them that it never crossed their minds. They simply assumed that togas and turtlenecks coexisted peacefully. On the ground, however, the mission operatives couldn't help but notice that they were often stared at.

With regards to extra-dimensional spaces hidden in back rooms, that was easy enough to accomplish. Old technology. And it wasn't just convenience store back rooms. Noah's mother's greenhouse had been another such space—although the effect was much subtler there.

But now that greenhouse was gone. Only the backup greenhouse remained, far off on a farm in Iowa—and that one did not have an extra-dimensional component, because (a) Mrs. Backup Prime had no further use for it, as she was in "Saturday school...on the surface of the sun," as Andi had so eloquently put it, and (b) the greenhouse had already fulfilled its function.

As for the actual Mrs. Prime, she was still with Noah's father, both being held prisoner by Vecca. And, as anyone who knew Mission Luminary Vectoria Centra could tell you, she always kept her prisoners close. Which meant Noah's instinct that his parents were still somewhere in Arbuckle was right on target. But getting back to Arbuckle was not going to be easy.

"Usually, I could create a portal," Andi told Noah, "but that would take more battery power than I currently have."

And so they were at the antiquated mercy of human ground transportation.

Elsewhere in the world, that might not have been a problem. In much of Europe, for instance, trains run like precision gear works. But unlike those rail systems,

American long-distance trains are a brilliant advertising campaign for staying home.

They are convenient for no one, their schedules are mere suggestions—and even when they do manage to hit the bull's-eye with a schedule, it's usually some surreal time that doesn't actually exist on the clock, like the ungodly hour of Z, or half past the square root of two in the morning. Even worse, transcontinental trains and buses have absolutely no tolerance for each other. Thus, trying to transfer from bus to train, or vice versa, is like trying to land a helicopter on a submarine.

With that in mind, it was no surprise that when Noah and Andi's bus arrived in Omaha at 2:21 PM, there wasn't a connection to a westbound train until nearly thirteen hours later, at 3:14 AM.

• ● •

Noah sat with his so-called sister on a worn wooden bench in the station, trying to figure out what to do with himself during the thirteen-hour layover. He watched a pigeon that had molted all the feathers on its left side like a fashion statement, as it meandered the ground at his feet, pecking at cigarette butts. It paused in its labors and looked up at Noah with an expression that clearly said, "You can wait here in the station, but I wouldn't advise it."

"This is ridiculous," said Noah. "Aren't there other buses or trains we can take?"

"Not headed in our direction," Andi said calmly.

"I've got an idea—you managed to book us train tickets with that Wi-Fi connection in your head, right?"

"Actually," said Andi, "it's in my left shoulder blade, but yes."

"Then just book us plane tickets! I'm sure there are flights out of Omaha tonight."

"Not without changing planes in Dallas, Chicago, or Salt Lake City."

"I can live with that."

"No," said Andi. "That's the problem—you won't. First of all, I will never make it through security. And second, airports will be full of aliens looking for you."

Lying low was going to be a challenge—and it occurred to Noah that his whole life had been about lying low. His parents forbidding social media. Living practically off-grid in a small nowhere town. It was all about keeping him as invisible as possible. But it's hard to stay invisible when a gymnastics routine you did is well on its way to becoming an internet meme.

Noah looked around him. Omaha's downtown train station was a bit of a mausoleum, though a grand one. Tall windows and heavy chandeliers harkened back to a time when train travel was luxurious. Now the place was just ghostly. He kept expecting to see someone in a bellhop's uniform beckoning him toward a Death Train, saying, *"Room for one more..."*

Noah balled his hands into fists and turned his eyes up, cursing at the high ceiling. "I can't stand this!"

"Get angry enough," said Andi, "and maybe you can run all the way to Oregon like a cheetah on steroids."

"You're not funny."

Andi sighed. "Give me a second," she said. She blinked twice, then turned to Noah. "There. I just booked us a hotel room. We can rest there until we have to catch our train."

Meanwhile, the pigeon was joined by half a dozen friends, and they proceeded to attack a fast-food bag, pecking it apart. Noah found himself wanting to know what was in the bag, and it immediately made him wonder if he had some pigeon in him as well. The sooner they got out of that station, the better.

• ● •

Andi hacked the hotel's computer so that it showed them already checked in as "the Harrington family," and since the key was electronic, Andi was able to unlock the door with her palm.

"Are you a can opener, too?" Noah asked.

Andi glared at him. "And a scalpel. So you'd better shut up unless you want some brain surgery in your sleep."

The room was adequate, the beds functional, and the TV, like all hotel TVs, had aspect ratio issues, stretching faces so everyone looked moonlike. They called for room service, which turned out to be so unmemorable that they forgot what they were eating while they were still eating it.

Noah stretched out on his bed and closed his eyes. If

someone had told him the day before yesterday that he would be holed up in a hotel room in Omaha, Nebraska, under an assumed name, with an android . . . but he couldn't even finish the thought, because to be perfectly honest, no one would have told him that.

"There's a *Twilight Zone* marathon on TNT," Andi said brightly, which really didn't help things.

"Why would I want to watch a *Twilight Zone* marathon?" demanded Noah. "I'm *living* a *Twilight Zone* marathon!"

"Stop being so dramatic," Andi told him. "You're alive, and the Anusians don't know where you are."

He sat up. "Anusians? Is that what they're called?"

"Well, I wouldn't call them that to their face." Andi was silent for a moment. "I'm really not supposed to be telling you anything."

"You're supposed to be protecting me, right? Wouldn't it help if I knew what I've gotten myself into?"

"You haven't *gotten* yourself into anything, because you were already in it the moment you were born."

"Stop giving me riddles!" Noah shouted. He stood up, wondering if strangling her would still be considered homicide—or would it be "androcide"? But if her head flying off didn't leave her with any ill effects, there was nothing he could do to her that would be remotely satisfying. Noah doubled over and groaned, as if his stomach hurt— but a stomachache would be easy compared to this. Each doorway seemed to bring them to yet another fresh hell, of which there were more levels than Noah could count. And *Twilight Zone*s never ended well for anyone.

"Why don't you just relax and watch TV with me? Look, Talky Tina is about to kill the bald guy."

Noah stormed across the room in exasperation and collapsed in the desk chair, almost but not quite hard enough to break it. There was a little plastic display on the desk labeled THINGS TO DO IN OMAHA. It was full of various brochures. Noah idly leafed through them. *"Visit Robber's Cave!" "Come See the Revolving Jail!" "Here It Is: The World's Largest Ball of Stamps!"*

But there was one in particular that caught his attention.

"Look at this," Noah said, turning to his sister. "Omaha has a world-class zoo."

"Tell me something I don't know," said Andi, unimpressed. "Oh wait, you can't!"

But when Noah flipped over the brochure to the map on the other side, Andi got worried "Noah," she said with the sort of voice one uses to coax someone in from a ledge, "what are you thinking?"

"I'm thinking that if I've got a bunch of animals inside me, I ought to go visit my brethren."

"I don't think that's a good idea."

"Then stop me," said Noah, strolling casually to the door. "Oh wait, you can't."

16

A Serving of Ribs

OMAHA'S HENRY DOORLY ZOO, AT 160 ACRES AND MORE THAN seventeen thousand animals, could certainly be considered world-class. And aside from a pesky orangutan, who became notorious for repeatedly escaping through air vents and picking locks with a piece of wire, the animals were fairly content with their digs.

Noah and Andi arrived at 4:00 PM, an hour before the zoo closed.

"This can only end in tears," Andi said. "Not mine, because I don't have tear ducts. But certainly yours."

Which, come to think of it, made sense now, because while Noah knew Andi would often whine and complain, he had never seen her actually cry.

"It's a zoo," said Noah. "What could possibly go wrong?"

They were advised many times—first by the ticket

seller, next by the ticket taker, and then by the security guard inside the gate—that they had only an hour to view the animals, before the proverbial hounds were released and everyone was chased out.

Noah headed straight for the zoo's centerpiece: a massive, glass-paneled geodesic dome, which the brochure promised enclosed the largest indoor desert in the world.

"Pretty impressive, huh?" said Noah.

"Yeah," said Andi, running to keep up with him. "It reminds me of the biosphere on Rigel 3."

"Is that also a zoo?"

"No, a prison," Andi said. "But advanced organisms do pay to see the inmates in their natural environment."

They wandered through the dome's exhibits: venomous desert snakes, a pair of disinterested tortoises, rubbernecking meerkats.

Oddly enough, Noah was never much for zoos. That was Ogden's thing. Going to the zoo was fun only because he got to watch Ogden in *his* natural habitat. But now he didn't even know if Ogden was okay. All the more reason to get back to Arbuckle.

Noah hoped that being here among these creatures might spark something in him. A memory, a feeling, a sense of why he was the way he was. But he felt like nothing more than a kid at a zoo. One who had arrived too late to see much of anything.

By a quarter to five, areas of the dome were being roped off in a synchronized effort to herd everyone toward the front entrance and the gift shop, the only place that stayed open until every visitor's last penny was spent.

But Noah noticed that the various desertscapes under the dome had nooks and crannies along the winding paths that were easy to hide in.

"What do you think you're doing?" Andi asked, when Noah squeezed himself into one of those crannies.

If Ogden were here, he would have come up with a long list of experiments that would help Noah understand his abilities. Granted, half of those experiments might kill him, but that didn't mean they weren't worth trying. And so Noah had to ask himself, *What would Ogden do?*

• ● •

"I can't believe we hid out in the zoo and stayed after closing," Andi said, "and didn't get caught." She looked around. "Where is security in this place anyway? Shouldn't zoos have better security?"

"You'd think," said Noah.

"Well, it explains how that woman got in after hours a few years ago and tried to pet the three-legged tiger."

"What happened to her?" Noah asked.

Andi gave him a deadpan stare. "They became the very bestest of friends and took selfies together. What do you think happened to her?"

"Right. I'll make sure to steer clear of three-legged tigers."

There were, of course, security guards after closing. But in a 160-acre zoo, they were spread pretty thin. As long as Noah and Andi avoided security camera sight-lines, they were fine. No one came to investigate something they didn't even know was there.

"I have half a mind to trip the alarm," Andi told Noah. But she said it in a whisper, making it clear the other half of her mind wasn't going to let her do it. He knew she was just as curious as he was about what might be learned from an unauthorized animal encounter.

The lights in the dome were dim enough to just see the paths, and they cast long shadows. About an hour after closing, Noah ventured out, with Andi close behind. He had already clocked that a guard only came by once every half hour. That gave him plenty of time.

"What creature do you intend to unnecessarily disturb?" Andi asked.

Noah didn't answer, because he knew she would just try to talk him out of it. But he had his plan already set. When Ogden had locked him and Sahara in the freezer, it was because he knew the only way to trigger Noah's animalistic response was extreme duress. And while there were many different creatures under the Desert Dome, the freshwater crocodiles were the ones he had his eye on.

There were six of them in an open pit that, during the day, was constantly monitored by a zookeeper to keep people from jumping in on a dare, or because they wanted to pet the three-legged crocodile—its similarity to the three-legged tiger being entirely coincidental.

When Andi saw where he was headed, she stopped short. "Don't. Even. Think about it."

"You want me to stop?" said Noah. "Fine. Then tell me what you know."

Andi grunted in frustration. "I can't."

"Can't? Or won't?"

"CAN'T," said Andi. "My programming won't allow me to divulge anything to you."

"Even if it saves my life?"

"Noah, I swear, if you send me into a logic feedback loop that fries my processor, I'm telling Mom and Dad!"

That made Noah laugh. "Always the little sister."

Then he jumped into the pit.

He landed on his feet, crouching, with one hand on the ground to steady himself. Although he'd made some noise when he landed, the crocs were still sleeping.

"Get out of there now!" Andi warned in a loud whisper. "While you still can!"

Noah ignored her and moved closer to the sleeping crocs, clapping his hands to wake them. One of the animals half opened its sleepy eyes. When the eyes focused on Noah, its lids sprang open all the way, and the animal raised itself on its haunches while opening its enormous mouth.

"Oh yeah," said Noah to the crocodile, "I must be delicious, huh? Come and get me!"

The crocodile took a step forward. Noah felt the impulse to back up, but he stood his ground. It would take a serious defense mechanism to ward off the enormous croc, and he could already feel his adrenaline starting to rocket him toward fight-or-flight, the very state where the magic happened.

Of course, Ogden would insist it was science, not magic. That was one of the things Noah had to find out. But as the croc came closer, Noah's body did nothing.

Any minute now, Noah said to himself.

He waited, confident that he would kick into defensive mode, and he believed it right until the moment the croc launched at him and clamped its mouth shut on his arm.

• ● •

The pressure from the jaw of a crocodile is approximately 3,700 pounds per square inch. About one thousand people are killed every year by crocodiles, and, since crocodiles usually swallow their prey whole, victims have been cut fully intact from their bellies. Never alive, though. While, theoretically, one might survive being swallowed whole by a crocodile, there's not much to breathe down there in its stomach.

• ● •

The croc had Noah's arm, which had begun to gush blood, and still Noah's body hadn't responded with a single defense mechanism, except for wetting himself like a tortoise, although, granted, it might not have been a tortoise response at all, but that was his story and he was sticking to it.

"Andi!" he shouted. "Help me! Shoot lasers out of your eyes!"

"You're not the boss of me!"

"You're supposed to be protecting me!"

"Sorry, program glitch: I can't save you from yourself."

Trying to get a better grip, the crocodile released his arm briefly, and Noah used the sudden freedom to scramble backward. But before he could get far, another beast lunged at him and seized him around the waist. With its jagged teeth digging in, it started to drag him toward the water.

The pain was intense, but Noah became aware of a different kind of pressure in his chest, and he looked down just in time to see his own ribs suddenly bursting through his sides like daggers, in a nasty spray of blood and gristle.

"Aahhhh!" he screamed. "What's happening to me?"

Like a sprung trap, his sharp ribs stabbed the crocodile in the mouth, and it must have hurt. A lot. Because the beast suddenly twisted violently and let him go.

• ● •

Being a zoo security guard was like being an anesthesiologist. The job was 99 percent boredom and 1 percent panic.

And for senior zoo-cop, Joe Spangenberg, tonight was of the panic variety. He had just done a patrol of the park, where he had found nothing unusual. He was sitting in the office monitoring various cameras, having just finished the last bite of a particularly tasty meatball hero, when he looked up to see a kid being eaten by a crocodile while a little girl stood by watching like it was, well, a day at the zoo.

He quickly alerted the other guards and made a beeline for the Desert Dome as fast as he could go. Half of him was worried about that poor kid, the other half about his poor job. Because this happened on his watch. Regardless of the outcome, it was his head that would roll.

When he arrived, the boy was no longer with the crocs but was lying on the path beside the enclosure, being attended to by the little girl.

"My God!" Officer Spangenberg said. "Are you all right? What are you two even doing in here?"

"Leave us alone," said the girl. "This is not your problem."

But it most certainly was his problem. "I'll call an ambulance," he said. "Everything will be okay."

But as he got closer, he saw that the boy didn't look like your ordinary crocodile-chomped victim. His clothes were bloody—that was expected—but there were also sharp, bony spikes sticking out through the sides of his shirt. Then they slowly withdrew back into his body, with a terrible bone-grinding sound, as he grimaced and groaned.

188

Officer Spangenberg had seen many strange things, but he had never seen anything like this. He opened his mouth to speak, but then he realized that his body had other plans. He turned his head, and his entire meatball hero paid a second visit.

Then, when he was finally done heaving, he turned back to the two kids. But they were gone.

• ● •

Andi, who had a built-in Uber app, got them a car to the hotel. The driver asked no questions but did offer them cold water and a phone charger.

"Seen worse than blood in this car, believe you me!" he said, then gave them a happy litany of all the things that had been in his back seat, some of which, in fact, might still be there. "Long story short, we never found that last scorpion, but it's gotta be dead by now, you think?"

Once they were back safe at the hotel, Andi dabbed Noah's wounds with some antiseptic she had gotten from the hotel's sundry shop.

"It hurts!" Noah wailed.

"And it *will* hurt," Andi said. "Pain is a natural reminder of the things a person should not do." Then a hypodermic needle extended from her right index finger, and she jabbed it into his arm. "But this should help."

"I almost died!"

"Hardly," Andi scoffed. "And if you hadn't exhibited

189

a suitable defense mechanism in time, I would have intervened. You know that, right?"

At first Noah didn't answer, and then he finally said, "What happened to me back there?"

"The Spanish ribbed newt turns its ribs into weapons when attacked," Andi told him. "I can say with a fair amount of certainty that was the defense mechanism you exhibited." She leaned back, taking an overview of his wounds, which had already stopped bleeding. "The Spanish ribbed newt heals remarkably quickly, and therefore so should you."

And, in fact, Noah noticed that the wounds, which had been gaping, had pulled together, as if by invisible sutures.

"So have you learned anything, besides the fact that crocodiles bite?"

"Leave me alone," Noah groaned.

"Listen," said Andi, more gently, "I can tell you this much. You're thinking about this ability wrong. These aren't superpowers that you have—they're more like side effects."

"Side effects of *what*?"

"I can't tell you that—only that you have a greater purpose than performing tricks. But trust me: If you throw yourself in front of a speeding train, you will die. If you put your head in the mouth of a lion, you will die. Understand?"

Noah nodded.

"Get some rest," Andi said. "I'll go dredge up some clothes for you from the hotel's lost and found. And then we have a train to catch."

190

17

Confusion Is My Superpower

LATE THAT SAME AFTERNOON, SAHARA WENT BACK TO THE 7-Eleven. There was no easy way into that back room—but a quick check on Google Earth showed a nice big air duct on the roof. A duct meant a vent, and a vent was doable.

A quick check inside the store showed business as usual: hot dogs, energy drinks, and lottery tickets served by the same clerk, who looked a little too ordinary to be ordinary. He was being harangued by someone complaining about the complete lack of taquitos on the heat rollers, so he never saw Sahara peering in. Before the clerk could take notice, Sahara slipped out and around the side of the building. Then she climbed up on a trash bin and used it to vault up. Her gymnastics training gave her an assist, but she couldn't help wishing she had some of Noah's abilities in that moment. Gecko cling, or something. She didn't make it all the way up, but she did manage to get a grip on the edge of the roof, then was able to flip herself up. Once there, sure enough, there was a duct with a vent just large enough for her to fit inside. She removed the grate and climbed in.

Shimmying down air ducts always seemed a more spacious affair in the movies, and not nearly as dusty. She sneezed several times, and she was sure that someone below must have heard her.

Finally, she reached a hinged grate beneath her and peered through. She thought she'd be above a simple 7-Eleven storeroom, but instead of a nine-foot drop, she was at least thirty feet above the concrete floor of a massive warehouse that couldn't possibly be there.

She didn't even try to wrap her mind around it, because she worried that, after all she'd already seen, her mind might snap like an old rubber band. Right in the middle of the concrete floor was a space full of plush furniture on a fancy rug. And there was Ogden, luxuriating in his own personal lounge.

Then the grate fell, and Sahara tumbled out of the vent. She reached out just in time to grab the edge—which left her hanging by one hand above a deadly drop. Down below, the grate landed on the ground, startling Ogden.

"Sahara?" he said, incredulous, as he looked up. "What are you doing up there?"

"I'm here to rescue you," she said. *"Help!!!!"*

Ogden quickly pushed all the pillows and soft furniture to a spot directly beneath her. She lost her grip and fell from the duct, feeling like the performer at the circus who dives into a barrel. But she hit her mark—and the pillows did manage to break her fall. She tumbled off of them, landing gracelessly at Ogden's feet with a thud and an "oof."

"What an entrance," said Ogden. "Lucky for you they replaced my cage with this seventies living room set. Beanbags are better than bars for a thirty-foot drop." Then he held out a plate to her. "Here, help yourself to dinner."

That's when Sahara noticed that there was a table filled with all sorts of food in warming trays, like a fancy wedding buffet.

"We have to get you out of here!" she said in a panic.

"Thank you, but no," Ogden told her calmly. "I'm perfectly happy to stay where I am."

"But . . . but . . . you've been captured by aliens."

"And," added Ogden, "they're treating me extremely well." He sat back down in an overstuffed armchair. "I like them. They're my kind of people."

Sahara balled her hands into fists. "They're NOT people!"

"Technicalities." Ogden picked up a meat skewer from the buffet table and took a bite. "You might think I'm a captive, but I see myself more as a guest."

Sahara took a good look at the elaborate spread of food, then turned back to Ogden, pointing at the meat skewer in his hand. "Aha! What if they're just fattening you up to eat you? For all you know, that skewer is human meat!"

"That's ridiculous," Ogden said. "It tastes like chicken." Which made Ogden pause for thought. He took a long look at the meat on the skewer, then gently put it down. "I dislike you immensely right now."

"Good, then we're finally on the same page."

"Okay, so even if you're correct and they're fattening me up for some alien Thanksgiving, I'm pretty lean at the moment. Which means it will be *months* before I'm ready to be stuffed and baked. I'll be happy to escape after I put on a few pounds."

"Have you forgotten what they did last night? They tried to kill us!"

"I'm sure they had their reasons."

"For all we know, Noah is dead!"

"Actually, no," said Ogden, studying his choices on the table, avoiding the trays of meat. "He got away, and they're still looking for him."

That was the first good news Sahara had heard all day. She relaxed a bit. "What else did you find out?"

"Oh, lots of things," Ogden said. "Area 51 began as an alien practical joke. And while our moon isn't made of cheese, there are *other* moons that actually do have a dairy component."

"Did you find out why they want to kill Noah?"

194

"We have no proof they want to kill him," Ogden said. "Maybe they just want to talk to him."

Sahara kicked his chair. "You don't blow up someone's house and replace it with Stonehenge if you just want to have a chat!"

That got Ogden's attention. "Stonehenge? Really?"

"Yep, down to the last monolith."

"Can I see?"

"Only if we escape," Sahara pointed out.

Ogden considered it, and Sahara looked at the buffet. "Unless you're ready to be served on a skewer as an Ogden-kabob..."

Finally, he caved, with a heavy sigh.

"Fine," he said, grabbing a shrimp fork from the buffet table. "I'll pick the lock and go with you. But if it turns out they weren't planning to eat me, I'm going to be very annoyed."

• ● •

The moment they pushed open the back door, the entire town's alarm system began to blare as if someone had triggered the end of the world.

"Oops—they must have that door set to trip Arbuckle's Early Warning System," said Ogden.

"Or we're all about to die," offered Sahara.

"I choose to believe option A," said Ogden.

195

The Early Warning System was set up should Mount Hood ever erupt, melt its snowcap, and cause a massive mudslide that would wipe out Arbuckle. It was tested twice a year—and went off accidentally about as often, resulting in somebody somewhere being fired.

"We have to get out of here, before the aliens find us and vaporize us!" said Sahara, pulling Ogden down the alley to the narrow strand of trees between the 7-Eleven and the street behind it.

"Stop stressing out," Ogden said. "The only person they really care about is Noah, and since I don't know where he is—and since they *know* I don't know, they won't spend much time looking for us."

"How much time is 'not much time'?" Sahara asked.

Ogden shrugged. "Half a day at most. Then I'm sure they'll be on to more important things. Like finding and maybe killing Noah—which I'll agree is a fifty-fifty proposition. But either way, the best thing we can do for him is to hide out in an unlikely location and keep them looking for us until they lose interest."

But hiding out meant they couldn't go to their respective homes, because those would be the first places the aliens would look. Thinking of home twanged a very unpleasant chord in Sahara. "My parents!" She pulled out her cell phone as she ran, tapped her mom's number, and flooded with relief when she answered.

"Mom!" she said. "Uh . . . how are . . . things?"

"Hi, baby. How come you sound so stressed? Your stomach still giving you trouble?"

"Tell her nothing!" whispered Ogden. "She'll have plausible deniability if the aliens interrogate her."

"No, my stomach's fine now," Sahara said. *Half a day*, Ogden had told her. Could she stand half a day hiding out with Ogden? Did she have a choice?

"I...uh...just wanted to tell you that I'm spending the night at April's," Sahara said. "By the way...has anyone come by asking about me?"

"No," said her mother. "Who you expecting?"

Then Ogden tapped her on her shoulder, flustering her. "Um...hold on a sec." She muted her phone and turned to him. "What?"

"Unless your parents are standing between the aliens and Noah, I think they're fine. The less they know, the safer they are, I think."

"That's a lot of 'I thinks' in there."

Ogden shrugged. "Well, if I'm wrong, there's nothing you can do anyway."

Sahara unmuted her phone. "Hi, Mom, I'm here."

"Baby, give me April's address. If you're staying there, I should know it."

"Yes. Yes, you should. Hold on a sec." She muted her phone again. Sahara was terrible with this sort of spontaneity. Anything she thought of sounded made up, like "123 Avenue Road," and it gummed up her mental works so much that nothing else got through. So she turned to Ogden.

"She wants April's address."

"Who's April?"

"She doesn't exist!"

"You have an imaginary friend, too?"

"Never mind that—I need an address that sounds real."

"Hmm . . . how about 368 Thirty-Eighth Street?" Ogden suggested.

Sahara unmuted her phone and repeated the address to her mother.

"Great, now give me her number," her mother said.

"Phone's dying," Sahara said. "Gotta go—but I'll call as soon as—" And then she hung up abruptly, breathing a sigh of relief. "Whose address was that?" Sahara asked Ogden.

"It's the house from *The Goonies*," Ogden said with a shrug. "In Astoria."

"Astoria? That's like two hours away!"

"You needed an address to give your mom—and who knows if the aliens were listening in, so the farther the better," he pointed out. "Besides, I don't think these particular extraterrestrials have a concept of human distances. If you said you were having lunch in Paris tomorrow, they wouldn't bat an eye. Assuming they have eyelids to bat, which I don't think they do." Then he strode off. "Come on, I know the perfect place we can hide out."

• ● •

Arbuckle's old water tower had been swapped out for a newer, shinier model some years earlier, but when the town council discovered how much it would cost to demolish the old one, they decided to leave it standing. The drum of the old tank soon became a free billboard for anyone daring enough to climb the ancient ladder so they could slap up advertisements, tag it with graffiti, or just draw something rude. But Sahara and Ogden were the only ones messing with it today.

"Is this really a good idea?" Sahara asked as she followed Ogden up the tower's old ladder. "Anyone looking up will see us climbing."

"You're thinking like a human, not an alien."

"How do *you* know how aliens think?"

"Practice."

They reached the platform that supported the water tank, and Ogden led Sahara around the tank to a hatch secured by an extremely rusted padlock.

"Great," said Sahara. "How are we supposed to get in?"

"Like this." Ogden took off his left shoe and smashed it against the rusted lock over and over until the lock broke off.

"Ferrous oxide!" he said, flicking away some of the rust. "Gotta love it!" Then he opened the hatch and stepped in as if he was walking in his own front door.

"I get the feeling you've been here before," Sahara said as she followed him in.

"Yeah," Ogden said. "When I was little, I ran away from home and hid out here for three days." He kicked a fast-food bag near his feet. "And I think this was mine, so I doubt anyone has been in here since."

"That was you?" Sahara said. "I remember that—it was all over the news."

"I know! My fifteen minutes of fame lasted a whole three days!" Ogden said with a bit of pride in his voice. "Which reminds me—give me your phone."

Sahara hesitated, then reluctantly gave it to him, and she watched over his shoulder as he entered a phone number and sent a text.

Mom. Prime. Phone died. CU2morrow

"What's that supposed to mean?" Sahara had to ask.

"Exactly!" said Ogden. "Confusion is my superpower." And he handed her back the phone.

Sahara took an uneasy breath. Even though they were now concealed in an unlikely place, she didn't feel any better about their situation.

"I still don't feel safe here, Ogden. I don't know if we'll be safe anywhere!"

"Okay, okay." Ogden pressed his forehead into his hands and started breathing deeply.

"What are you doing?"

"Quiet! I'm tapping into the universe."

Ogden took one more deep, snuffling breath, then said, "Got it!" and opened his eyes. He went back out to the rusted ladder. Sahara stared in disbelief as Ogden kicked it over and over until it broke free and arced gracefully away from the water tower, like a gantry falling back from a rocket about to launch, then landed with a muffled crash against a stand of trees.

"Ogden!" Sahara shouted. "What did you do that for?"

"Think about it!" Ogden said. "Now this is the *last* place the aliens will look for us! They won't think that we're up here because, with no ladder, clearly there's no way we could have gotten up here!"

Ogden's logic was like a snake eating its own tail. It formed a perfect loop, but not without a certain amount of pain and cannibalism.

"Okay, that does sort of make sense . . . but how will we get down?"

Ogden just shrugged and headed back inside. "I'm sure the universe will present us with an answer in the morning."

"Morning? You expect me to stay here with you all night? While the aliens could be out there vaporizing Noah?"

"Listen," said Ogden. "It might not sound like it, but I'm just as freaked out as you. But Noah would want us to be safe, wouldn't he? And right here, right now, we *are* safe."

Sahara heaved a heavy sigh. A snake eating its own tail.

Until it completely devoured itself, and there was nothing more to fight about. "Morning...," she said, resigned.

"Like my grandpa used to say, 'Things always look clearer in the morning light,'" Ogden said. "Of course, he was legally blind, but the metaphor still holds."

18

If He Were Dead, We Wouldn't Be Here

BACK IN THE YEAR 2017, A VERY STRANGE OBJECT PASSED through our solar system.

As it was discovered by astronomers in Hawaii, it was given the Hawaiian name "Oumuamua." Interstellar object Oumuamua was 2,600 feet long and 260 feet wide. It was a bit too far away to get anything more than a fuzzy picture that looked like a giant cigar. No one knew where it came from, or what it actually was; all astronomers knew was that it looped around our sun with strange acceleration in a way that didn't fit with gravitational norms, then slingshotted into deep interstellar space, never to be seen in our galactic neighborhood again.

Astrophysicists puzzled and theorized, then finally decided that its odd appearance meant that it must be a shard of a shattered planet. And that its odd movement could be explained by the expulsion of gas, much the way a comet gives off a glowing tail. It was filed away by science as "one of those things" and left at that.

While sometimes a cosmic cigar is simply a cosmic cigar, in this particular instance, Oumuamua was, in fact, a spaceship. It was built and populated by a species of highly intelligent bacteria, who were attempting to colonize the one hospitable planet of our solar system. Earth.

However, through a series of incredibly inept calculations by the germ in charge—and a cover-up by that same germ, in a desperate attempt to cover its own waste-elimination duct—Oumuamua, with its trillions of bacterial colonists, missed the mark and was doomed to a tragic eternity lost forever in deep space.

All this to point out that while every being, large and small, has a perfect match somewhere, they don't always appear on the same planet. Thus, only the mysterious mind of the universe knew that the incompetent, self-important bacterium that botched its species colonization effort... had an equally incompetent and self-important counterpart on Earth... named Q. Theodore Kratz.

• ● •

Kratz was lying as low as a snake in a sandstorm. He kept expecting the authorities to show up at his door to arrest him for destroying Noah Prime's house and killing everyone in it. The police, the FBI, Interpol—some official agency was coming for him; it was only a matter of time. Every sound in the night was a SWAT team raid; every distant siren was his doom approaching; and every thunderous crash from his absurdly loud upstairs neighbors was a commando team coming through the ceiling. His sleep, when he did manage to sleep, was troubled and full of nightmares featuring explosions and headless little girls.

How could this have happened to him? He always saw himself as so methodical, so careful. The fault clearly lay with the drone. The military-industrial complex had no business creating something so dangerous! Someone should go to jail for this. Just not him.

Aside from complaints about fireworks in the woods, there was no news of the disaster the following morning. The only hint that anything was amiss was Noah Prime's absence in class—and there was nothing remarkable about that. Teenage boys shirked their educational responsibility on a regular basis. They had barely bothered to show up to his online classes during the year-that-must-not-be-mentioned. And when they came back, he could swear that all their eyes were set slightly deeper into their heads, as if the puny brains behind them had atrophied, having spent months doing nothing but playing video games and eating Cheetos.

His classes went on that day with the same dreary monotony as always. Putting on videos so he didn't have to interact with his students. Reciting dull lessons by rote. The usual. But today, even when he confiscated a ringing cell phone and dropped it into the classroom fish tank, the act held none of its usual pleasure.

All he could do was wait for the authorities to show up and arrest him for the murder of the Primes.

His doorbell rang at about seven that evening, right in the middle of a *Halo* battle and a bowl of Cheetos—and when it did, Kratz knew his end was at hand. The man and woman at the door were dressed in dark, intimidating suits. What could they be but the Feds?

"Can I help you?" Kratz said, trying to sound as innocent of multiple homicide as he possibly could.

"Dr. Quantavius Theodore Kratz?"

"Yes?"

"We have some questions for you. May we come in?"

Kratz felt his knees turn to Jell-O. He wanted to slam the door in their faces, slip out a window, and escape. But his apartment was on the third floor. And even if he could get out without any broken bones, where could he run? There were certainly places he could effectively disappear. He had always wanted to go to Argentina. A pity he didn't speak Spanish. The only other language he was fluent in was Klingon, a triumphant remnant of his youth. He was highly skilled in conjugation and usage—and, in fact, had won the official Oregon State Klingon Spelling Bee. Alas, it would not help him in Argentina, except possibly in small circles at certain conventions.

"Yes, of course, come in," he said. "Is something

wrong? I've been laboring over my students' assignments for days, so I'm not aware of anything at all going on in the outside world. It's just home, and school, home and school, with nothing in between."

Then, as soon as they were inside, they cut through all small talk, with an object that they pulled from a sack, which they slammed down on Kratz's dining table. It was the damaged drone.

"Does this belong to you?" the woman asked.

"Of course not!" he told her, trying to keep his voice from quivering. "Why would a simple science teacher like myself own such a device?"

Then her associate heaved it over, flipping it belly-up. Written neatly on the scorched and dented surface, in bright silver Sharpie, were the words "Property of Q. T. Kratz."

Aargh! He feared his propensity for labeling all his belongings would someday cause him grief. But how could he help himself in a world so ridden with crime?

"I'm sure there are plenty of Q. T. Kratzes," he offered.

"Actually, there's not," said the woman.

"There's a G. T. Kravitz in New York," said the man, "but I doubt she would have misspelled her name. Besides, she's been dead for thirty-eight years—long before there were aerial drones. Or, for that matter, silver Sharpies."

Kratz swallowed hard. He knew where this went from here. Now would come the handcuffs, and the perp walk, and a trial with a boneheaded, knuckle-dragging jury, all inevitably leading to prison, and a hardened pack of sneering, jeering inmates who would not at all respect his personal space.

"You were surveilling Noah Prime," the woman put to him. "Why?"

And when he didn't answer, she tried to narrow her oddly wide eyes at him.

"Who are you, Dr. Kratz?" she demanded. "And what do you know?"

• ● •

Mission Luminary Vectoria Centra absolutely detested having to involve humans in her search for Noah Prime. The mission was already behind schedule, and from what she knew of humans, they had an almost supernatural ability to foul up the simplest of things. Take space travel, for instance. These wasteful humans build noisy chemical rockets to hurl heavy machinery into space, when all they need do is harness the smallest amount of dark energy to counteract the force of gravity. It's not like dark energy blows up planets. Much.

Unfortunately, with Noah missing, and with Ogden, their one possible lead, having escaped, there was no trail to follow. Of course, if Ogden was, as they had suspected, a mole sent by headquarters, he was already writing up a negative report about Vecca's performance. All the more reason to finish the mission successfully and as soon as possible. That being the case, Vecca had no choice but to question the man with the drone.

"Who are you, Dr. Kratz?" demanded Vecca. "And what do you know?"

"I'm nobody! I know nothing!" he responded, which was truer than Kratz knew, but Vecca and Rom were not buying it.

"We can do this the hard way . . . ," said Rom.

"Or the easy way?" asked Kratz, which seemed to confuse Rom.

"No, it's all varying degrees of hard."

"Which is why," added Vecca, "there are specialists like us, to take care of business. And today, our business is extracting information by any means necessary."

One of those methods involved sucking out Kratz's memories so they could systematically pick through them—but they preferred not to do that if they didn't have to. Searching through downloaded memories for whatever one happens to be looking for took forever. *Literally* forever in certain more advanced species. In a human, it would probably take about a week, and they didn't have the time.

She glanced at the pocket portal projector clipped on Rom's belt, cleverly disguised as a laser pointer. She could open a portal to some terrible place and threaten to hurl Kratz through it. But looking around, she couldn't imagine a more terrible place than his apartment.

She pulled out her travel levitator, cleverly disguised as a human writing instrument, and pondered it for a moment. Perhaps she could use it to smash Kratz against the ceiling and floor repeatedly until he begged for mercy. But that would be messy, as well as noisy. Possibly even noisier than the family in the apartment upstairs.

Maybe gaining Kratz's cooperation through gentler means was the best course of action.

"What is that?" Kratz asked, looking at the travel levitator. She quickly put it away.

"What does it look like? It's a writing device."

"Well, yes," agreed Kratz, "it does look like an antique fountain pen; however, a fountain pen doesn't normally warp space around it . . ."

"Depends on the ink," offered Rom.

"Listen to me," said Kratz, pleading. "You don't have to do this! I'm one of you!"

That made Rom smirk. "I sincerely doubt that."

"It's true!" he insisted. "I worked for the government, just as you do! And by the looks of that 'pen,' I imagine it's a very special arm of the government. The kind most people don't know exists—just like the kind I worked for!"

"A very special arm . . . ," repeated Vecca.

"Yes, in more ways than one—I ran the Federal Office of Biological Experimentation (FOBE) . . . until an unfortunate appendage growth incident—which was not entirely my fault, by the way, but they had to blame someone." He cleared his throat with distaste at the memory. "Back in those days, I went by Dr. Quantavius—surely you've heard that name!"

"Dr. Quantavius . . . ah—of course," said Vecca, playing to his ego and assumptions, which would most certainly grease the gears. "Who doesn't know Dr. Quantavius?"

Kratz breathed a deep sigh of relief. "Now that you realize who I am, I'm sure there must be an agreement we can come to. No need to 'detain' me, or to bring me in for 'questioning.'"

"We're not here to 'detain' you, Dr. Kratz."

"You're not?"

"And cooperation is so much more pleasant than interrogation."

"Sometimes," pointed out Rom.

"What you do with your time and your drone is your business, Dr. Kratz. But your interest in Noah Prime is of interest to us."

"Why?" Kratz asked, suspicious. "What do you know about him?"

"We know he's missing," Vecca said.

"You mean . . . he's not dead?"

"If he were dead," said Rom, "we wouldn't be here."

Kratz considered this. "And so you came to seek my help?"

"Since he was clearly the subject of your ongoing surveillance, we suspect you have key insights," said Vecca.

211

"Now that you know he's still alive, you might be able to give us a lead on where he's gone."

"Where he's gone?'

"Yes."

"Noah Prime."

"Yes."

Suddenly, Kratz's eyes widened. "Of course! As a matter of fact, I do know where he would have gone! Yes! I'm a hundred percent certain! How could I have missed it?"

"We're listening," said Vecca, with what little patience she had left.

"Hmm . . . Telling you won't be a good idea," Kratz said. "I'm sure he knows you're after him—he'll see you coming from miles away. But I can bring him to you! We're close! He trusts me. Yes! Yes, that's it! I'll bring him to you! Serve him right up on a silver platter."

"Tempting," said Rom, "but we really don't have time for a large meal."

"I agree," said Vecca, "but if you are willing to bring him to us without any culinary preparation, that would be sufficient."

"And . . . what do I get out of it?" Kratz asked.

Your continued existence, Vecca thought, but she had to play the game Kratz thought they were playing if she wanted his cooperation, so instead she said, "What is it you want?"

Q. T. Kratz was not a man who ignored opportunity. Especially when that door swung wide open and hit him in the face. Of course, he had absolutely no idea where Noah might be, but he couldn't let a small detail like that stand in the way of him making himself a very sweet deal.

"I want a fully functioning, fully staffed laboratory to study him," he told the two agents.

"That can be arranged," the woman said.

"And a modest share of profits from the military applications of Noah Prime's biological peculiarity."

"I'll have to make a few calls," she said, "but I'm sure we can work something out."

"And," added Kratz, "I want to own the patent on any consumer products derived from his DNA."

She thought about it and shrugged. "Fine. Anything else?"

Kratz thought for a moment. "And last, but not least, I wish to have something named after me."

"I see. Would you prefer a building? A ship? A syndrome?"

"Your choice. I'm not particular."

She then gestured to her associate, who opened a briefcase Kratz hadn't seen him holding and pulled out a folder.

"Here's the contract," he said. "You'll find everything you requested is right there."

"A contract? How is that possible—I just gave you my demands . . . uh . . . that is to say, my *'reasonable requests'*?"

The woman sighed. "If you must know, this briefcase has a secret time-traveling compartment."

"Yes," added her associate. "Our lawyers wrote up the contract next Tuesday."

Kratz couldn't help but be impressed. "Wow, you folks sure made some advances since I was there!"

"So do we have a deal?" the woman asked.

Did they have a deal? Kratz knew the alternative all too well. If he didn't agree, they would turn him over, and he'd face the consequences of having killed the rest of Noah's family. This was a no-brainer. Kratz flipped the document to the signature page, then reached for a pen—but found that a pen would not be necessary. He had already signed the contract at some point in the future.

• ● •

"Do you really think he can be trusted?" Rom asked as they drove off.

"Not at all," Vecca admitted. "But when you promise a lesser being something they want, your interests miraculously become theirs. Trust is no longer in the equation."

Rom chuckled. "If only he knew he'll never get any of those things."

Vecca turned to him, scowling. "Of course he will," she said. "I am a woman of my word, Norom. A contract is a contract—and if he delivers Noah Prime to us, arranging the things he requests won't take more than five minutes of our time. Of course, with the boy incinerated, there won't be much to study or profit from—but we'll still be keeping up our side of the bargain."

"True enough," said Rom. "Isn't it nice when everybody wins?"

The two drove into the night, satisfied that their mission was back on track.

It would be a long time before they realized that their travel levitator, pocket portal projector, and even their memory-extraction hypercube had been stolen by Kratz.

19

The Miserable Mystery Tour

EVEN THOUGH THERE WASN'T MUCH NOAH COULD SEE OUT THE windows at night, he liked sitting in the train's observation car. He didn't spend a lot of time watching the passing darkness, but whenever he looked through the glass, he felt reassured by the occasional light gleaming from a window or from a headlight on a lonely road. It meant the real world was still out there, even though his world had taken a turn to the surreal.

Andi sat next to him, absently flipping pages in a magazine. He knew she could flip through those pages at blazing speed and still pick up all the information, but she must have been aware that that would be suspicious.

"In case you're interested, I just downloaded all global communication for the past twenty-four hours."

"Why would I be interested?"

"Because I've detected phone activity for both Sahara and Ogden—so they're probably okay."

It gave Noah a surge of relief, but a guarded one. They might be safe for the moment, but that moment might not last. All the more reason to get back to Arbuckle.

Noah slowly scrolled through animal-related websites on his phone. The hagfish, he discovered, released a toxic, slimy substance when threatened. He closed his eyes and thought about that. Did it resonate with him at all? No. He opened his eyes and scrolled on.

The Malaysian exploding ant, he read, has a large gland in its body filled with poison. When predators attack, the ant contracts its muscles, making the gland explode, spraying the predator with the poison. Again he closed his eyes, and again he was aware of no feeling that he was capable of such a thing. He clicked on another link.

The pistol shrimp, when threatened, can snap its claws with so much force it creates a tiny sonic boom that stuns its predator. Noah looked at his hand but felt nothing.

"Hmm," Andi said, looking up from her magazine, her face scrunched a little too tightly, as if maybe she had to go to the bathroom, which Noah had no idea whether androids actually had to do. But if not, it might explain why the two of them never got into fights about their shared bathroom at home.

"What's wrong?" Noah asked.

"I don't want to freak you out or anything, but my power is low, and I may go into power-saver mode."

"What? You what?" Noah said.

"Yeah, I should have been paying closer attention to my battery icon. I'm at less than one percent."

"Uh...okay. There's an outlet here, under the window..."

She glared at him. "As if."

"So what do you want me to do?"

"You'll need to get me a beryllium sphere, a small one. Size triple-Z."

Noah just stared at her. "I have no idea what that is."

"You've seen one before—I had a spare one in my room. It looked like an orange softball."

"I thought that was an orange softball."

"Exactly. Think about it. Have you ever actually seen anyone playing with an orange softball?"

"Uh, no."

"That's because they're *all* beryllium spheres!"

"Well, where do I get one?"

"They're easy enough to find, you just—uh-oh—" Then she compacted down into a small pink suitcase.

• ● •

Since the human race first understood the concept of "stuff," and the desire arose to take it with them, luggage has been an issue. Cloth bundles came undone, or tore at the slightest graze of a branch, so more solid containers

218

emerged. First came sturdy wooden trunks that were more like furniture than objects designed to move from place to place. The modern suitcase didn't appear until the twentieth century, and yet, with all of humanity's advances, it wasn't until 1970 that someone thought to give it wheels.

The rolling suitcase formerly known as Andi was of the hard plastic variety. Even though there was a latch on the case, it refused to open, no matter how hard Noah pressed it—and if Andi had a key, it was now on the inside. But even if he could open it, Noah wasn't sure he really wanted to. What would he find inside? Semiconductors and gears and motherboards? Or some weird pseudo-biological goo? He didn't want a glimpse of his sister's guts in any form.

No one had noticed Andi's sudden transformation, and Noah realized that yelling at a perfectly ordinary-looking suitcase, while perhaps not unusual behavior for people on trains, would most definitely draw unwanted attention. Even so, the unassuming pink suitcase did attract the attention of a conductor doing his rounds.

"Is this yours?" asked the conductor, pointing to the suitcase, which was now wedged into the aisle seat next to Noah.

"It's my sister..." Noah hesitated, then added, "...'s. Yeah, it's my sister's."

"It can't stay there—it's gotta go on the overhead rack."

"Uh...I don't think she'll like that..."

"Where is she?"

"She's, um, in the bathroom," Noah said.

"I'll help you with it." The conductor tried to lift the suitcase, but he was clearly not expecting the weight. "Holy cow, kid, what do you have in here, bricks?"

"My sister doesn't travel light," Noah said as he stood up to help the conductor. They lifted the suitcase, their arms trembling from the weight as they raised it over their heads to the rack—but as is always the case, it was exactly half an inch too large to fit. They gave up and let the case tumble back down to the seat. Defeated, the conductor looked at the bag and said, "I'll make an exception this time." And he let Noah and his compacted sister be.

Noah leaned back in his seat. He draped his arm over his sister the suitcase, then closed his eyes. This was going to be a long trip.

• ● •

Dr. Quantavius Kratz knew that the history of technology was all about theft. Google stealing from Microsoft, Microsoft stealing from Apple, and Apple stealing from Google to complete the sacred tech circle.

So, when it came to the curious objects Kratz had taken from his visitors, it was just business as usual as far as he was concerned.

He achieved the items through careful sleight of hand—because in his youth, he had dabbled in magic. Not actual magic, but the stagecraft of illusion. He could make things appear to levitate by using a microfiber thread. He could shake your hand and remove your watch without you ever noticing, then make it magically appear in your best friend's pocket, thereby ending the friendship.

The skill came in handy once he realized that the only people who wore watches anymore were those who wanted to show off extremely expensive timepieces. As a young man, he had paid his entire college tuition by selling Rolexes that magically appeared in his pocket.

The name "Dr. Quantavius" was originally a stage name before he actually got his PhD—which was perhaps the one thing in his life that was a legitimate accomplishment. As for his days as an amateur magician, it all came crashing down—literally—when one of his audience volunteers took part in a guillotine trick that turned out poorly.

Although Kratz never performed publicly again, he kept up his sleight-of-hand skills because they occasionally came in handy—as they had today.

After the two operatives, who he believed were government agents, had left, he considered the objects he had taken. He saw them as an advance payment for his services. Now he simply had to figure out what they were and how to make them work.

The first, as he previously noted, appeared to be an antique fountain pen, but having worked for a secret government agency, he knew that a pen is never just a pen. On close inspection, he could see a series of strange symbols on the barrel. There was also a button. He aimed the pen toward the ceiling, then pressed the button to see what it would do.

The device powered up, and he waved it like a wand. Immediately, his hair seemed to stand on end, while up above, the aforementioned noisy neighbors made new noises. They gave off exclamations and gasps and terrified pleas to whatever God it was they worshipped. But things became really interesting when he hit the button a second time, which turned the device off.

Now came a massive *thud!* from above, so powerful that it cracked his ceiling and sent a light fixture crashing to the floor—and from the upstairs apartment, he could hear wails of distress and crying children.

Hmm. Interesting.

He went over to a window and aimed the device outside, at a couple who were sitting on a bench making out. He hit the button, and they were both instantly catapulted skyward. *Ah—so this was a levitation device!* He held the device steady and slowly lowered his aim. As he did, the catapulted couple were gently returned to their bench, dazed by the experience—but not dazed enough to stop smooching.

Having confirmed what the "pen" did, he placed it into his shirt pocket and took a look at the second object: the laser pointer. It was deceptively heavy and had multiple buttons. When he pressed one, it didn't project a light.

Instead, it opened a small hole in midair, out of which dropped a single chess piece—a rook, to be exact—which landed in his bowl of Cheetos with a puff of orange dust.

Kratz retrieved it, put it on a shelf, and made a note that further experimentation on the "laser pointer" would be required.

The third object was something Kratz had slipped out of the briefcase after the male agent opened it. This one was a bit harder to figure out. It was an articulated cube—better known as a Rubik's cube—that had been fully solved, with solid colors on every face, matching the colors of the spectrum: red, orange, yellow, green, blue, indigo, and violet. Aside from being made of titanium, it appeared ordinary in every way.

He gave it a single twist to test it out—and suddenly felt odd in a way he could not quite explain. It was as if the object had just shaken his hand and stolen his watch. The feeling of being robbed was so unpleasant that Kratz decided to put the cube down . . . And although Kratz considered himself an observant person, it never occurred to him that he had just been holding a seven-sided cube.

• ● •

A standard three-row-by-three-column Rubik's Cube has more than forty-three quintillion possible combinations. But add a seventh side, and things become tricky.

It's not simply a matter of adding a fourth dimension.

That, as any four-dimensional being can tell you, would be easy. Instead, it's squeezing a previously nonexistent dimension in between the existing ones. It would be like having a coin where one side is heads, the other side is tails, and the third side is all the internal organs between head and tail splattered on more than forty-three quintillion walls. Thus, a seven-sided articulated cube can be a perfect data storage device, because not only can it hold an infinite amount of data, it can hold an *infinite amount* of infinite data. In other words, one could input everything from every possible parallel dimension into the cube, and it would still be less than a single grain of sand on an infinite number of infinitely large beaches.

The storage cube in Kratz's possession had a very specific purpose—as evidenced by the feeling he had of being "robbed." In this case, all that was stolen from him was the memory of his aunt Agnes, who he never thought about anyway. But had he given the object a few more turns, it could have been a whole lot worse. Because that particular hypercube had been formatted for the storage, duplication, and destruction of stolen memories.

20

Deadbeat in a Cheap Skin

NOAH OPENED HIS EYES, AND HIS HAND SHOT UP REFLEXIVELY TO shield them from the morning sun. He looked around, registering where he was, and it all came back. He was on the train back to Oregon. Although he had dozed in and out all night, he didn't feel the slightest bit rested. No wonder people on trains got cranky. Like the wizened, white-haired woman who now eyed him from across the aisle.

"Aren't you even the slightest bit concerned?"

Noah yawned and stretched. "Huh?"

"The little girl you were with! She could be lost, or kidnapped, and you're acting like nothing's wrong."

Noah's brain was nowhere near up to speed, and not ready to handle this. He just stared at her, blinking.

"Do you have any idea where she is? Or don't you care?"

Noah reflexively glanced at the suitcase, which drew

the woman's eyes to the suitcase as well, before turning back to him. "For all you know, she could have fallen off the train and been cut in half by the wheels! Her crushed, lifeless body could be caught between train cars! And you're just going to sit there?"

There were multiple ways to handle this. He could escape to a different car and hide out there. He could make excuses, like saying that their parents picked her up at the previous station. But he took a good look at the woman's veiny, wild eyes and decided that if he remained calm, he'd be much more believable than she was. He crossed his arms and said, "I don't know what you're talking about."

The woman gasped, her gaze never softening. "Liar!" she said. "Liar, liar, liar!" And she wagged a finger at him.

A conductor arrived, drawn by the commotion.

"Is there a problem?" he asked.

Noah made sure he responded first. "Yeah, this lady won't leave me alone."

The conductor turned to her. "Ma'am, I'll have to ask you to take a seat."

"Why don't you ask him about the girl!" she yelled. "He did something to her, I tell you! She was here, and now poof! She's gone!"

But this wasn't the same conductor Noah had encountered last night. This one had no idea Noah had a travel companion. It would be just his word against the nosey woman's.

The conductor sighed, clearly on Noah's side. "Son, I'd be happy to reseat you . . ."

Noah thought he had it all handled. Until someone two rows behind him said, "I saw her, too."

"So did I," said someone else.

"I heard them arguing last night," yet another person said. "And now she's gone!"

The nosey woman pointed her crooked finger at Noah again. "You see! You see!"

And then the conductor noticed, in the little seat-back compartment, two tickets. Suddenly, he was eyeing Noah with a very different expression than a moment ago.

"I can explain," Noah said.

The conductor crossed his arms. "I'm listening."

But Noah had nothing.

"He did something to her!" the woman said. "I feel it in my bones!"

"Aw, come on!" said Noah, as more and more eyes turned to him. "If I did anything, someone would have seen!"

"Nobody saw the Muskogee Bus Butcher, either!" yet another person said. "He killed his victims in bus bathrooms and hid them in a duffel bag!"

"In little pieces!" a small child in the next row added.

"That's true!" someone agreed. "And train bathrooms are even bigger!"

The conductor crossed his arms. "All right, out with it, son. Where is she?"

And again, Noah's eyes darted to the suitcase. That singular glance was not lost on the nosey woman. "She's in there!" she proclaimed. "He's hidden her body in the suitcase."

"In little pieces!" the small child said.

"Come to think of it, that suitcase was pretty darn heavy . . . ," said the other conductor, who just arrived.

"Why would I put my own sister into a suitcase?"

To which the old woman replied, "People are very strange."

"I think we can clear this up easily enough," the conductor said. "Why don't you just open the suitcase and let us see what's inside."

Noah let out a nervous little giggle. "Open the suitcase?"

"That's what I said."

"You want me to open it?"

"Is that a problem?"

"Well . . . it's just that . . . I can't . . . I don't have the key!"

"Then who does?" the conductor asked.

The train began to slow down. Noah glanced out of the window to see they were pulling into the next station.

"Arrest him!" shouted the nosey woman. "Arrest him before he kills again!"

The conductor reached down and grabbed Andi's retractable handle. "We've got tools in the back; we'll break it open."

"No, wait!" said Noah, his heart pounding. "Maybe I can open it after all."

He was only stalling, but it gave him enough time to think—and for his adrenaline to build. He felt the familiar tingling sensation that he always felt before his body did something very, very strange. Andi had told him not to use his power . . . No, that's not what she said, exactly. She said his powers were a kind of side effect of something else. He didn't know what that something else was, but he knew one thing for sure: Side effects were very powerful things.

Pistol shrimp, Noah thought, and he snapped his fingers.

The resulting sonic boom knocked the conductor off his feet, blasted the nosey lady all the way down the aisle, and blew out a few of the observation car's windows.

Noah looked down at his hand in wonder. He did it! He summoned the defense mechanism he wanted, when he needed it!

He wasted no more time. While the conductor and the stunned passengers were still strewn on the floor, Noah grabbed the handle of the suitcase and quickly left the train, just as it came to a stop.

He ran across the platform, through the station, and out into the street, pulling the suitcase behind him without once looking back. He had no idea what city he was in, or how far he still had to go to get home. All he knew for sure

229

was that he needed Andi's help. And he wasn't going to get that unless he could find a triple-Z beryllium sphere.

• ● •

While any advanced race could easily find a source of clean, renewable energy to power its androids, like solar or wind energy, there were more serious obstacles than one might imagine. Such as a species of living light that existed on the surface of white dwarf stars, and a species of wind that lived on giant gas planets. For countless eons, they had raged against the idea of wind and light being exploited for the selfish energy needs of material beings. Because of that, using such renewable forms of energy was banned from the civilized universe.

However, while Earth movies such as *The Matrix* might suggest otherwise, there has never been a species of *battery* that has come forth claiming to be alive and professing its right not to be exploited. Thus, beryllium power cells became the power source of choice.

Noah neither knew nor cared about the troubled history of energy in the universe as he escaped into what turned out to be Rapid City, South Dakota. He had no idea if the conductors had decided that he and his missing sister were somebody else's problem or if the Rapid City police were rapidly determining his whereabouts.

He had to get Andi working again.

She had said that beryllium spheres were easy enough to find before she had contracted into her current state. Odd, because if they were easy to find, wouldn't Noah have come across them somewhere other than in her room?

Then it occurred to him that perhaps he was overlooking the obvious . . .

• ● •

There was a mall in Rapid City's small downtown, and that mall had a SportsNation—one of those big-box sporting goods stores that carried everything from basketballs to crossbows. He strolled in with his roll-aboard sister, which brought forth a quick glance from an employee creating a running-shoe pyramid. There was probably a store policy against bringing in suitcases, but no one seemed too eager to enforce it.

Noah found what he was looking for down the baseball aisle: a small bin of orange softballs on the bottom shelf. Easy to miss if one wasn't specifically looking for them. He picked one up and hefted it. Was it his imagination, or was there something odd about it? Not so much its weight or the way it looked, but how it felt. As if it was more than just cork and leather.

He brought it to the checkout counter, but the UPC sticker wouldn't scan.

"That's odd," said the cashier, and after the third try,

231

she called over another cashier, as if the machine might behave better for someone else. But the second cashier could only confirm that, even though they sold orange softballs, they didn't actually sell orange softballs.

"How about you pick out a regular one," the second cashier suggested, "or if you need it for a night game, we have Optic Yellow, too."

"No," Noah insisted, more certain than ever that he had made the right call. "This is the one I want."

And so they called over a manager, who was equally perplexed. "Tell you what," he said. "Come to my office, and if we can't find it in our product database, you can have it for free."

However, once in the manager's office, everything changed. The manager sat down, typed a bit on his computer, then turned back to Noah, folding his hands on his desk, and offered up a smile.

"So, what model is it?" the manager asked.

"Uh . . . what model is what?"

"Your android," he said, indicating the suitcase. "Not many manufacturers design them to fold into Earth objects. Is it standard, or did you have it custom-made? I'll bet it's custom-made!"

"Mister, I don't know what you're talking about," Noah said. "I'm just here to buy a softball."

"C'mon, kid, who do you think you're fooling? Who buys an orange softball? It's obvious that you came here for a beryllium sphere, so drop the charade so I can sell it to you, and you can be on your way to wherever it is you're going. My guess is that you're on some sort of interstellar wilderness adventure vacation. Although I must say, you should have purchased a better skin. Human teenagers tend to be viewed with suspicion, and that disguise will limit you to age-appropriate activities. Besides, it doesn't seem all that well made."

Noah sighed. "Listen, I don't want any trouble."

"Of course you don't. Will this be cash or charge?"

"How much is it?" asked Noah, pulling out his wallet, but the moment the "manager" saw his bills, he laughed.

"Oh, no, no, no—you can't buy a beryllium sphere with Earth currency."

"It's all I've got right now."

"You expect me to believe that? I wasn't born yesterday. Technically."

"How about this," said Noah. "We power up my android, and once she's up and running, I'm sure she'll be able to pay whatever it costs."

But the man wasn't buying it. "How do I know you won't instruct her to vaporize me the moment she powers up?"

"Do I look like the kind of person who would do that?"

"You look like a deadbeat in a cheap skin."

Just then, there was a knock at the door, and when it opened, a buff security guard entered. His face was substantially lopsided in a way that was impossible for human faces to be. Clearly, the manager's moment of typing had summoned this security being, which meant that Noah was in serious trouble now—but the only thing that he could think to say was "Now, *that's* a cheap skin."

"He's definitely the one we're looking for," the guard said, although his voice sounded more like a chorus of hundreds. "Thanks for letting us know. Here's the reward. A high-end, multifunctional, fully programmable alternate universe." Then he handed the manager something that looked like a small black pyramid.

"Always happy to do my civic responsibility," the manager answered, before turning to Noah. "You're quite the fugitive, Mr. Prime—considering the reward being offered for your capture. Nothing personal, of course."

Noah felt a familiar rise of adrenaline and tried to direct it to his fingertips, figuring he could do a repeat performance of the pistol shrimp sonic boom, but the guard blasted him with a weapon that turned his veins to ice and his flesh to stone. The last thing he heard before he lost consciousness was the store manager complaining about his reward.

"What? This alternate universe is an off-brand knock-off. What are you trying to pull?"

21

Not Only Don't I THINK I Can, I Resent Being Asked

Nine hundred miles west of Rapid City, the morning sun began to warm the steel drum of the old water tank. The day before had been overcast, sparing Sahara and Ogden the swelter that would have made their hiding place unbearable. But today was one of those rare things: a sunny day in Arbuckle. Which meant Sahara and Ogden couldn't stay there long, or they'd risk being parboiled.

Sahara had barely slept all night, between her fading confidence in Ogden's broken-ladder solution and the extra-terrestrial thoughts flitting through her mind. She finally fell into an uneasy sleep around midnight, after changing her coat from blanket to pillow, then woke, thinking it must be morning, only to discover it was just 3:00 AM. It didn't help that Ogden's snores echoed around the steel drum, making him sound like a sleeping giant. But even worse was his peculiar trait of sleeping with his eyes open, which she discovered when she shined her phone light at him, only to nearly jump out of her skin when she saw him staring blankly in her direction. If it wasn't for the snoring, she'd have thought he was dead.

Sometime around seven, she finally lost consciousness again, only to be woken up by Ogden minutes later. He had opened the hatch, and light was streaming in, illuminating the drum. In the dark, it had seemed so much larger, and so much less spider-infested.

"Not a morning person, are ya," said Ogden, sounding annoyingly chipper. "Now's not the time to be sleeping in."

Sahara yawned and silently wished she had kicked Ogden during the night to stop him from snoring. Or just for the sake of kicking him. If Ogden was right, the aliens would have given up looking for them by now and focused their attention on finding Noah. And if Ogden was wrong, it didn't matter, because she wasn't staying up here a minute longer.

She joined him at the hatch and looked at the fallen ladder. "So how are we supposed to get down?"

"I've got one word for you," Ogden said, proud of whatever bright idea had bitten him during the night. He smiled at Sahara and said, "Gymnastics!"

The silence could probably be heard for miles.

"That's it?" Sahara said. "That's the wisdom the universe shed on you?"

But even as she said it, she looked down at the girders supporting the water tower and considered. It really wouldn't be impossible for her to use her skills to get to the ground. Ogden's half-baked idea was more baked than she wanted it to be. How aggravating.

Ogden stretched. "When you reach the bottom," he said, "tilt the ladder back this way so I can get down, too."

"I'll think about it," she said. Then she tentatively climbed over the rail. Dangling from the edge of the platform for a moment, she put her feet on the steel girder. *Just like the high bar*, she thought. Of course, that was only about nine feet above the mat.

The mat. That made Sahara glance down. As she suspected, there was nothing blocking a straight drop to the concrete foundation far, far below. A hundred feet, she estimated, which made this the *very* high bar.

Shutting the distance to the ground out of her mind, she let her training take over. She took one careful step, then another. As she feared, the girder was slippery, still wet from morning dew. It would dry off in the next hour or so as the sun rose higher, but she didn't have time to wait, so she planted her feet firmly to make sure they didn't slide. A steady breeze was blowing in her face, so she leaned out a bit to counterbalance it, then slowly made her way down the sharply angled crossbeam to the relative safety of the horizontal support strut. Then, moving with growing confidence, she shimmied down the next set of crossbeams—until the breeze suddenly cut out, and she felt herself tipping forward. She jerked backward too far, her arms pinwheeling as she tried to regain her balance. Then she slid down the rest of the crossbeam, leaping off a few feet before she reached the ground. *Not bad*, she thought, wiping her rust-covered hands against each other. She walked over to the ladder, which now leaned crookedly against some trees, grabbed a couple of rungs, and pulled as hard as she could. It barely budged.

"Come on!" Ogden shouted down. "What's taking so long?"

"It's heavy!" Sahara shouted back.

"Need I remind you of *The Little Engine That Could*?"

Ogden's patronizing tone infuriated Sahara—but she used that fury to her benefit. She got underneath the ladder and pushed. She remembered seeing weightlifters in the Olympics, and how they didn't lift randomly but coordinated their muscles, and she tried to do the same. Finally, the ladder rose from the trees, reaching the top of its arc, and Sahara let gravity swing it back the rest of the way to the tower.

Ogden stepped back as the top of the ladder slammed against the platform with a loud *clang!* and bounced a few times. Then he climbed down with such casual ease, Sahara just had to knock him to the ground the second he arrived.

Rather than complaining, Ogden just laughed and popped back up.

"It worked!" he said. "Making you angry released just enough adrenaline for you to lift the ladder!"

Which just made her angrier. "Don't talk to me," she said.

"As you wish," he responded.

"That's talking."

They walked through the woods together, but when they got to the street, Ogden made a left turn while Sahara turned right.

"Where are you going?" Sahara asked.

"I'm going to see Stonehenge," Ogden said. "Wanna come?"

"I've seen it," she said. Then she headed toward home without giving Ogden another glance. Was it evil to imagine him squished beneath a fallen Stonehenge slab? Probably, but she imagined it anyway.

• ● •

Sahara kept to the edge of the woods, just off the road, as she headed home, and when the trees along the street became sparse, she went behind the houses, beyond the backyards, where the fences stood guard against the woods—and anything that dwelt within.

As Sahara skirted the back fence line, she wished she could be on the other side of the protective barriers, safe from an alien she was certain would step out from behind a tree at any moment.

But that didn't happen. Taking a circuitous path to stay under cover of the woods, she got home in one piece, and she eyed her house from the trees across the road. She looked up and down the street, then overhead, and studied the roof of her house. Nothing looked out of place.

She took a chance and made a dash for it, across the street and up her steps, the key already in her hand, now in the lock—when the door was suddenly pulled open by someone inside, who stepped into the doorway.

An alien!

But no, it was just her mom, leaving for work.

"Baby, you surprised me," her mom said, stepping out of the way to let her in. "I thought you'd go straight to school from April's. There's tuna in the fridge, if you want to make a sandwich for lunch." Sahara nodded and yawned. "Poor thing," her mom continued, touching Sahara's cheek. "Did you get any sleep last night?"

Sahara yawned again. "Not much."

Her mom hustled down the driveway. "Gotta get to work, baby. I'll see you when I get home!"

Sahara watched her mom get in the car and drive away, giving her a small wave as she went. Then Sahara shut the front door and looked both ways down the hall. Her mom was acting normal enough, but she couldn't be too careful.

She gave the house a wary once-over. Nothing was out of place. Her dad had already left for work, too, and there were no aliens hiding in any of the closets or under the beds. She made sure.

Which meant one thing: She had frozen her butt off all night in the water tower for nothing! Nothing!

But more irritatingly, it meant Ogden was right once again. The aliens didn't care about her. That should have left her relieved, but instead she was deeply disappointed. Not that she wished to be disintegrated or experimented on, but it was *SO* unfair that they didn't even *want* to!

What's wrong with me? She went to her bedroom and hurled herself headfirst into bed, nearly giving herself a concussion on the headboard. *I should be happy that I'm alive, and ignored by deadly aliens. I should be content that they have absolutely not the slightest interest in me whatsoever.* And yet she was anything but content. She stewed and simmered trying to understand the mysteries of the universe, but more so the mysteries of her own troubled thoughts, until she finally fell asleep, exhausted in every possible way.

• ● •

Ogden found the replica of Stonehenge to be a disappointment. First of all, the original monoliths were sandstone, and these were granite. Second, they weren't angled properly to line up with celestial happenings. That might not seem important now, but to an ancient Druid, a stone temple that did not properly reflect the solstices could mean the difference between abundant life and being stomped flat by Arianrhod, the goddess of the sky. One would think that an advanced alien species would be a bit more detail-oriented and think twice before ticking off imaginary gods.

There had been no sign of the aliens at all since he and Sahara left the water tower. Perhaps it had been an over-abundance of caution to hide out there, but it was kind of fun to relive his childhood runaway adventure. But if, on the other hand, they were still actively looking for him, he'd know soon enough, because one does have to go home eventually. And if he was still a person of alien interest, he'd rather know sooner than later. So, after his visit to Stonehenge, he headed home, pausing only for a moment in the street to remember the date, so he knew whether to go left to his mom's or right to his dad's. He could not recall the date at all, but he went to his mom's, since their prime number custody arrangement left him there about two-thirds of the time, so the odds were better.

"Mom, I'm home," he called as he entered, but got no response—neither from her, nor from any alien that might have been in hiding, disguised as anything, even an arm-chair for all he knew. Everything was quiet. Ogden realized that his mom was already gone for the day—but she had left him a note on the kitchen table:

> Ogden, honey, if you're going to stay with the
> Primes on a non-prime night, you need to let me
> know. Unless your text meant you were at your

father's thinking the night was numerically prime,
but either way, Prime or prime, you must be more
communicative because I cooked a whole prime rib
with no one here to eat it.

    Love,
    Your Mom

Good—his text yesterday had the exact befuddling effect he had intended. He knew she wouldn't check with his father, because, aside from the occasional shouting match in the street, she "would rather eat my own eyeballs" than initiate a conversation with him. And if she tried to call any of the Primes, it was definitely going to voice mail. Still, the note irked him. *Why on earth would she write, "Your Mom"?* he thought. *I mean, who else's mom would leave me a note like that?*

It was a school day, but Ogden decided he had more pressing concerns today than institutionalized education. He was determined to find out what happened to Noah.

He went to his room, fired up his computer, and performed an in-depth internet search, looking for anomalies, impossibilities, or unusual goings-on over the past twenty-four hours that might point to Noah.

He found a couple of items of interest. One, newly posted, was a mysterious sonic boom that had shattered the windows of a train car in South Dakota, and another was a mysterious attack last night at a zoo in Nebraska.

But when he dug into the sonic boom story, he found it included rumors of a missing girl in a suitcase and grisly comparisons to the Muskogee Bus Butcher. That didn't sound like Noah at all. And the zoo story, despite some blurry video footage, seemed to be more about the security guard making stuff up in an attempt to save his job than anything that did or didn't take place in the crocodile pit.

There was also an odd story about a war that had unexpectedly been started, all because a Bulgarian chess champion was accused of cheating by his Albanian opponent, when a rook disappeared from the table. But as curious as it was, Ogden couldn't see how Noah could be involved.

Ogden concluded that Noah couldn't possibly be connected to any of those events. He sighed. If only life could be that easy. Further research would be necessary if he were to figure out where in the world Noah Prime could be.

22

Are We There Yeti?

Noah awoke to the sun peeking through his blinds and right into his eyes. He rolled over, turning to the wall, hoping to sleep a bit more before his alarm went off—which is what he might have done on any normal morning. But as his senses returned to him, he realized that this should not be a normal morning at all.

He sat up and looked around with an almost painful sense of déjà vu. He was in his room, and it looked exactly the way it was supposed to—with the single exception that when he opened his blinds, he was faced with a range of jagged, snowcapped mountains stretching as far as the eye could see.

Oh no, thought Noah, *not again*.

He quickly dressed and ventured out of his room, into whatever awaited him.

Andi was at the kitchen table, eating cornflakes with

too much milk. "Worst bed head ever," she observed on seeing him, then went back to her soggy breakfast.

Noah's backup mother was emptying the dishwasher of last night's dishes—except that there hadn't been dinner dishes to clean last night, because last night's dinner never happened.

"Good morning, honey," she said with a smile. Now that Noah knew it wasn't really his mother, the signs were much more obvious. Yes, she looked like his mother, but not entirely. Her eyebrows, for instance, were a little too high, making her seem to be in a constant state of surprise, and her lips were a little stretched, as if someone had pinched her cheeks and her face had stayed that way.

Noah said nothing. He knew better than to speak before he could fully assess the situation. Instead, he sat down silently across from Andi—who leaned toward him and whispered, "Play along."

Noah sighed. *Play along*. Easy for her to say. This was a game Noah had no interest in playing, but what choice did he have? So he poured himself a bowl of cereal, with less milk than Andi, as he might on any pre-home-detonation morning—but his first spoonful tasted so outrageously awful, he gagged and splattered Andi with half-chewed Froot Loops and milk. She dropped her spoon and glared.

"Mom! Noah just projectile-spat at me!"

His backup mother's surprised eyebrows raised even

farther, making her forehead all but disappear. "What is it, Noah? Is there something wrong with the yak milk?"

Then Noah's backup father entered. "Couldn't be," he said. "I milked the yak just last night."

Noah, who was entirely unprepared for yak milk, realized he was on the verge of vomiting forth all of his internal organs like a sea squirt, which would not have been fun for anyone, but he wrangled in his gag reflex and got it under control just in time.

"No," he rasped, "it just went down the wrong way is all."

Andi grabbed a napkin and wiped her face. "You're disgusting. I've lost my appetite."

Noah couldn't help but notice that his backup father was also just a little bit "off." His nose was a little crooked, as if he had a history of lost prizefights, and his ears were a bit too low on his head.

"Beautiful day!" he said as he glanced out of the kitchen window. "Say what you want about Himalayan weather, but a crystal-clear sky like this one makes it worth all the blizzards."

Noah cleared his throat to rid it of the last bit of yak milk, then turned to his sister. "Andi, could you come to my room for a second? There's something I need to show you."

Andi dubiously crossed her arms. "What?"

"I...uh...think I saw a yeti."

"In your room?"

"No, of course not. Why would there be a yeti in my room? It was outside my window."

Andi reluctantly got up. "Fine—but if it's just a mountain goat again, I'll be really annoyed."

"Don't take too long, you two," their backup-dad said. "The Sherpa should be here any minute to lead you down to school."

• ● •

"Explain," Noah demanded as soon as they were in his room.

"Isn't it obvious?" Andi said. "You were caught and turned back over to our side—and you should be grateful, because if you had been turned over to the other side, you'd be extremely dead right now."

"There is no 'our side,' " Noah insisted. "I'm on my own side. As far as I'm concerned, everyone else is the enemy."

"Not true," said Andi. "We have a vested interest in keeping you alive."

"Why? If you're from some other world, why do you even care?"

"That's not important."

"Of course it's important!"

"Well, it's not important that you know our reasons. In fact, it would be majorly counterproductive if you did. Big pictures are best left to bigger brains."

"Their brains can't be all that big if they forgot to erase my memory again."

"For your information, they *did* erase your memory. But I restored it. Don't make me regret my decision!"

"We need to find Mom and Dad!" Noah said. "Our REAL mom and dad. You said you'd help me."

"I will," Andi said. "We're going to need them, because these backups are less than competent. I don't trust them to keep you alive."

"Me neither. And what's with their faces anyway?"

"Their artificial skins aren't doing well in the Himalayan cold. But don't let on that you notice! We need them to believe they have everything under control until I can come up with a plan."

"And how long will that take?"

Andi took a moment to process, then said, "Well, it's Thursday now. My algorithms predict I'll have a viable plan of action by next week."

"No! I am not waiting that long," Noah said, stubborn as a mule, and not just because he happened to have mule DNA. "Your algorithms can take a flying leap."

"We can't just leave. After your last 'escape,' they'll be keeping a close eye on us. We'll have to wait for the right time. But in the meantime, just pretend like it's perfectly normal to be in a farmhouse on a Himalayan mountaintop."

Noah put his head into his hands. His stress level was rising, and that wasn't a good thing. He might just develop

249

horns and start headbutting everyone like the imaginary mountain goat Andi accused him of not seeing out of his window, when it was most certainly an imaginary yeti that he hadn't seen.

"The fact is, you are the last of four," Andi told him, "which means the situation is dire, and your safety is more critical than ever."

"The last of four what?" Noah asked, terrified that he might already know the answer.

"The last of four Noahs," she told him. "All the others were killed."

"So you're saying there are multiple versions of me?"

"*Were*," Andi reminded him.

Noah didn't know what to do with this information, other than file it away for a time when therapy would be more convenient.

Andi shook her head and sighed. "Mom and Dad should have taken you off-planet when they had the chance. True, you're still unstable, and we can't pull you off Earth until you stabilize—but judging by your side effects, you're almost there, so it might have been worth the risk."

Even though Andi was no longer a suitcase, there was an awful lot for Noah to unpack in that statement. He knew it was their goal to keep him alive, but no one ever said anything about removing him from Earth. And the reminder that his burgeoning powers were "side effects" pointed once more to that mysterious purpose Andi had refused to tell him about. And although he knew that, lately, he definitely had not been stable, he suspected that Andi meant a little more than his shell-shocked mental state. To them, he was like a cake in the oven, and he was not yet fully baked. He had no idea what would happen to him once he was.

Andi looked at him and pursed her lips, walking back all her off-planet crazy talk. "No, pulling you from Earth too soon could be catastrophic. You could end up like Noah Quattro."

"Uh . . . what happened to Noah Quattro?"

"You don't want to know," Andi told him.

"Maybe I do."

"Trust me, you don't."

And so, with no other choice, Noah took a few deep, cleansing breaths and went back to the kitchen, where the two parentish people were discussing plans for the weekend.

"Honey, we were thinking of taking a trip down to Kathmandu on Saturday—do you want to come?" the motherish one asked.

"Uh . . . not really," Noah told her.

To which his backup father responded, "I guess that's a Kathman-don't," proving that dad jokes were truly universal.

• ● •

The little red schoolhouse on the Himalayan mountainside was, like Arbuckle's Stonehenge, a creation of the

251

Department of Planetary Research. And although the ideas of homeschooling and distance learning were suggested, it was unpopular within the department. Once they decided there would be a little red schoolhouse, there simply would be a little red schoolhouse.

The problem wasn't its construction, but finding students to populate it. In the end, they decided that child-sized operatives in human suits pretending to be children would be much easier to manage than actual human children.

But the Sherpa, whose job it was to guide Noah and Andi to and from school in this odd little fiction, was not an alien. He was human—and an actual Sherpa—as it was decided that at least some authenticity was required.

He was in his mid-twenties and had spent much of his adult life guiding adventurous tourists up Mount Everest and, if they survived, back down again. However, added to those memories were false memories of the schoolhouse, and of escorting Andi and Noah along the treacherous ridge that led to it—a job for which the Sherpa was being paid more than enough so he wouldn't ask questions. (And to maintain the illusion, the aliens filled his bank account with enough money to prove he'd been doing the job for months.)

So, when the Sherpa arrived at Noah's house that morning, it seemed a perfectly natural thing to be escorting two American kids, who had no business being there, across a mountain ridge to a schoolhouse that had no business being there, either.

He did have a nagging feeling that something wasn't quite right, but he couldn't figure out what it might be. He had no idea that his employers were not human, and that the boy he shuttled back and forth to school was the last of four children who had been hidden around the world— and each of the others had died unpleasant deaths.

Two of those deaths were at the hands of Vecca and her team.

The other was Noah Qauttro.

His fate was a tragedy of epic proportions. Simply put, Noah Quattro, at the age of twelve, was taken from Earth long before he was "fully baked" and made to believe he was the victim of just some random alien abduction, rather than a highly specific and targeted alien abduction.

Noah Quattro was as excited as he was terrified when the mother ship's interstellar drive engaged, and he watched Earth disappear behind him. Unfortunately for him, his DNA had not matured sufficiently, and once free from Earth's gravity and the influence of his home planet's magnetic field, the many terrestrial species wound into his compressed genetic structure decompressed all at once.

Imagine an entire planetary zoo squeezed into the body of one hapless child, then suddenly released. It was, to say the least, not pretty.

His cells began to multiply at an alarming rate, and he

swelled bigger and bigger as all those creatures inside him began to express themselves. Then, once he reached a critical mass, poor Noah Quattro detonated in a massive explosion that destroyed the mother ship and killed everyone aboard.

When it was over, all that remained was an asteroid-sized glob of frozen flesh full of elephant trunks, cattails, and bird feet... but worst of all were the eyes. Thousands and thousands of eyes. It was so unpleasant to behold that it quickly made the list of the Top Ten Most Disturbing Interstellar Objects, right between the Great Quantum Blood Tentacle and the Cosmic String Spider Carcass.

And so Andi was right to tell Noah that he didn't need to know. However, there were quite a few things that he *did* need to know that Andi wasn't telling him.

23

A Crossroads of Dinosaur Death Marches

BACK IN ARBUCKLE, PREPARATIONS WERE WELL UNDERWAY FOR the upcoming Fossil Day Festival.

While National Fossil Day has existed for years, no one celebrated it like they did in Arbuckle, Oregon—because when it comes to the history of extinction, Arbuckle takes the gold. Nowhere else have so many species vanished from existence. Or, at least, according to local fossil records, which show that Arbuckle was once a veritable crossroads of dinosaur death marches.

All fascinating, except for the fact that Arbuckle's fossil record was entirely wrong.

The history of dinosaurs in Arbuckle began in 1872, after a wealthy settler became obsessed with early dinosaur discoveries. He had paid a king's ransom to purchase all the dinosaur bones that he could from around the world, and he opened the Arbuckle Museum of the Terrible Lizard, giving townsfolk their first glimpse of creatures that lived about 250 million years ago.

Unfortunately, these were the kind of townsfolk who did not like numbers like 250 million. They insisted that dinosaurs were nothing more than extremely large horses bred to pull extremely large carriages, and they did not take kindly to disagreement.

The controversy came to an end the night the museum burned down. Reportedly, it was struck by a meteorite that was a few hundred million years late to the dinosaur extinction party, although no meteorite was ever found. What was found, however, were a number of townsfolk with torches and pitchforks in the vicinity of the fire—but that was left out of the official report. And just in case it wasn't sufficiently left out, the official report mysteriously disappeared as well.

Over the years, the Museum of the Terrible Lizard vanished from memory and was lost to history. Then, nearly a hundred years later, a traveling paleontologist happened to find a *Megalosaurus* skull being used as a flower planter at the bed-and-breakfast where he was staying. The elderly couple who owned the place said they had dug it up a few years back but never thought much about it, assuming it was just the skull of an extremely large horse.

Within days, the property was seized by the National Park Service, the bed-and-breakfast was torn down, and the land became an official fossil excavation site, yielding hundreds of bones over the years and changing the face of paleontology as we know it.

And so, every year in mid-October, the town of Arbuckle celebrates its illustrious prehistory with Fossil-Fest, touting a parade of dinosaur floats, paleo-themed food trucks, and the appearance of a minor celebrity waving to the crowd from a carriage pulled by Clydesdales. Which are extremely large horses.

• ● •

For Sahara, the idea of returning to life as usual felt like an impossibility. How do you worry about grades, or focus on gymnastics, or even have normal conversations with friends when the world as you knew it has been pulled out from under you like a rug that was, admittedly, an ugly rug to begin with, but much less ugly than the blaster-scorched floor beneath it?

The answer is, you don't go back to business as usual. And yet Sahara's life moved on even though it had absolutely no right to do so. Sahara defined her current state as PASD: post-alien stress disorder. And her coping mechanism was to take even less crap from the world than she had taken before—because if her reality rug was that pullable, she didn't owe it anything.

Her new not-playing-the-game approach to life was now evident in all her conversations at school the next day, every one of which was now a mic drop.

"Hey, Sahara, did you see the latest post by [insert random vapid influencer here]?" asked her friend Celeste. To which Sahara responded:

"Sorry, I don't follow her anymore." Boom!

"Hey, Sahara, isn't [insert mildly attractive male classmate with fewer zits than most here] cute with his new haircut?" her friend Misty asked.

To which Sahara responded:

"Meh. Cuteness is for rabbits." Boom!

"Hey, Sahara, I saw you at the dance last week," said the mildly attractive male classmate with fewer zits than most. "You dance good! Wanna go to the movies or something?"

To which Sahara responded:

"No. But you should ask Misty." Boom!

And although honesty is supposedly the best policy, Sahara suspected that lies and fakeness were how the world really rolled. Her straight-line life had now taken some vicious and gnarly turns. She suspected her new approach to this uneasy road was paving the way to some lonely times ahead.

All that really mattered to her now was finding out what happened to Noah, and what the aliens were up to. But she suspected she never would find out.

"Hey, Sahara, could you be our main act on our Fossil-Fest parade float?" Her gymnastics coach asked.

Sahara's mic-drop reply might have been, "*You're*

confusing me with Sahara Solis from last week," but she took pity on her harried, stressed-out coach.

"Yeah, I'll do it," she told him. Because, in spite of everything, her team did need her, and just because she now had a take-no-prisoners approach to life, it didn't mean she got to shirk her legitimate responsibilities. Besides, what else was she going to with her time? Spend yet another day chatting with alien encounter groups online? She had tried that and quickly realized that the only thing she had in common with any of these people was the breathing of oxygen. And even then, some of them were clearly breathing other things as well.

In the end, Sahara had to admit that she was alone in this.

Except, of course, for Ogden.

But it wasn't reassuring to be in a club of two that neither member wanted to be in. Yet there they were, for better or worse, and all indications were leaning toward worse.

• ● •

Ogden was also suffering his own aftermath, but it was less PASD than it was FOMO. Wherever Noah was, he was now part of something larger than himself, and Ogden was missing out. He held Sahara responsible for his temporary FOGE (fear of getting eaten), which led to his escape from the most interesting situation of his life. Now Noah was experiencing mysteries of the universe that Ogden would never know.

And Ogden had lost his only real friend.

That hurt more than all the rest.

To make it worse, every time his mom saw him sitting alone in his room, she suggested he go over to Noah's.

"He's been abducted by aliens," Ogden finally told her when she pressed him one time too many. "I doubt if he's even on the planet anymore."

And since this was not an unusual thing for Ogden to say, she didn't bat an eye. "Well, I hope he's back in time for FossilFest. You always go together."

Well, not this year. Ogden would be going to his favorite annual event alone. But in spite of that, he resolved that he would enjoy it and find some consolation there. It was, after all, the only place he could release his inner dinosaur. And although Ogden was more of a stegosaurus than a velociraptor, on National Fossil Day no one judged.

And so, both Sahara and Ogden prepared to attend the festival, both hoping it would be the start of their new normal.

• ● •

Mountaintop life in Nepal was hard but rewarding. At least, according to Noah's backup father.

"Why do we live here again?" Noah asked him, just to see him literally squirm in his skin.

"Clean air and low taxes!" he told Noah, cheerfully.

Andi wasn't kidding when she said they were now under constant surveillance. She pointed out cameras that tracked them and the Sherpa all the way to school, and all the way back again.

The aliens did a fairly good job recreating a little red schoolhouse, and aside from some small glitches, such as the classroom having no pencil sharpener, and the teacher having no chin, one might think this was the way things were supposed to be. Noah suspected that all the kids were aliens in human skins, but the fake kids pulled off their act pretty well. In fact, they pretended to know him much better than he pretended to know them. Of course, there was that one girl who was having serious trouble tying her shoelaces, so Noah helped her.

"First day with the new hands?" he said, completely joking, but she did not see the humor in it.

"Absolutely not!" she told him. "I've had these hands for a good long time—and if anyone says otherwise, they are seriously misinformed!"

But aside from those few small things, it all seemed so oddly normal that, by the second day, Noah almost wished Andi hadn't un-replaced his memories, and he could live this rugged Himalayan frontier life in blissful ignorance.

On Friday afternoon, the Sherpa guided them back from school along the treacherous mountain ridge, getting them home just as a weather system moved in—and with a blizzard in the forecast, the Primes insisted he stay for the night. In return for their hospitality, the Sherpa commandeered the kitchen, to make a stew.

The wind roared outside, and soon everything beyond the window became a blizzard blur. "Will it be like this all weekend?" Noah asked his backup mom. "Because Bobby invited me over to his yurt tomorrow to watch cricket."

"Lemonade, Noah," she chided. "Lemonade." Although Noah suspected life wasn't giving them all that many lemons at this altitude. "Look at the positive," she said, straightening out her face. "Without the storm, our friend here wouldn't be cooking us a big pot of *Shakpa*—which I know is your favorite."

"Uh...right," said Noah. "I love me a nice bowl of Shakpa."

For the rest of the afternoon, Noah and Andi pretended to do homework at the kitchen table, which Noah found more mind-numbing than *actually* doing homework—but he knew he couldn't complain, because Andi had spent years pretending to do homework. Meanwhile, the Sherpa would occasionally say things in Nepali as he cooked, and Noah couldn't be sure if he was talking to them, or just doing that talk-to-yourself-while-you-cook thing that people do.

"Am I supposed to know the language?" Noah asked Andi, when their backup mom was out of range. Andi just shrugged.

"Not sure. Just do what human kids do whenever adults talk. Nod and pretend like you're listening." And then Andi leaned closer. "Stay alert, because I think this snowstorm will be our ticket out of here," she told Noah. "In a few minutes, you need to get Dad away from his workshop."

"Why don't you do it? It's freezing out there!"

"Because I need you to do it. And why are you worried about the cold? Before you get hypothermia, you'll develop blubber or something."

That made Noah laugh. She had no idea how right she was.

"Just get him to come back to the house, then keep him busy for half an hour or so."

She left Noah at the kitchen table to hit the books alone, and to nod occasionally when the Sherpa-turned-chef spoke in his general direction.

• ● •

Both the greenhouse and the workshop were precisely placed on the artificially flattened mountaintop to be in the same relative positions to the house as they had been before. Noah had to shake his head at these aliens' attention to detail for things that didn't really matter, while at the same time completely overlooking things that actually did.

Noah, clad in his heavy parka, braved the blizzard and

made it to the barn. Inside, his father's workshop was the same, except for the stall in the corner, home of the afore-mentioned yak—which mooed on his windswept entrance.

"Easy, Yolanda," his father said. "It's just the wind."

His backup dad was working on a new casket, but not doing a very good job. It wasn't surprising—it had taken his actual father years to master his craft.

Actual.

The word caught in his mind. Were his parents "actually" anything to him at all? He supposed he could think about it like being adopted. By aliens. Who lied to you about everything. From the day you were born. No, his "real" parents were never real . . . and yet they had treated him with loving care all his life, quite literally manipulating the world to keep him protected. Only now did it occur to Noah that the hockey rink and the motocross track closing had both been their doing. Any time Noah excelled in something that might draw attention to him—and therefore put him in danger—it was shut down. All to protect him, and to keep him hidden. Maybe he should have been grateful, but instead he felt bitter and betrayed.

When his backup father saw Noah looking at his unhandy-work, full of random gouges and splinters, he became sheepish. "I guess I'm having some trouble today," he said.

"You'll get it—you just need practice," Noah said—then caught himself. "I mean, with the new wood. That is a new kind of wood, isn't it?"

"Very observant of you," his backup father said. "It's local Himalayan deodar."

The wind blew, the barn shook, and Yolanda mooed again.

"Something I can help you with, son?"

Right—for a minute, he forgot he was on a mission. "Yeah, I know you're busy and all, but I was wondering if you could help me with my math homework."

His backup father put down his gouge—which wasn't doing anyone any good in his hands anyway—and gazed at Noah with a bleary expression.

"What's wrong?" Noah asked.

"Nothing at all," he said with an abashed little grin. "It just feels good that you . . . *need* me for something."

"It's just homework," Noah said.

"Well, it's still nice to be appreciated. As a father. As *your* father." Then he put his arms around Noah in a fatherly hug. It was goofy, yet Noah felt comforted in spite of himself. And so Noah hugged him back, allowing himself to be just a kid bonding with his backup father. Then, before the moment could get any stranger, Noah turned to go, and his backup father followed him to the house.

• ● •

It was just as the family was sitting down for dinner half an hour later that things got interesting.

"Where's your sister?" Fake Mom asked. "It's not like her to be unpunctual for the evening meal."

Noah shrugged. "Did you check her room?"

Then, from outside, above the wail of the wind, came the distinctive sound of breaking glass—and Andi burst in through the kitchen door, her parka covered in snow.

"Yolanda got into the greenhouse!"

• ● •

The proverbial "bull in a china shop" was nothing compared to a yak in a greenhouse. Yolanda was, to say the least, not happy at the moment. She was no stranger to blizzards, although she did love to vocalize back to the wind. This new circumstance, however, was alarming. She had been minding her own business in the corner of the barn when the little girl—who, by the way, did *not* smell like a little girl at all—had come in, taken her out into the storm, then pushed her into a place Yolanda had never been before. An amazing place full of flowers. No sooner had she begun to eat them than she began knocking things over around her, and no matter how she tried to maneuver in the tight space, every move made something else crash to the ground. Finally, her stress ballooned into a full-fledged panic attack, and she began kicking out windows to escape—but no matter how much glass she shattered, there seemed to be more. Honestly, what were these people thinking building such a structure here? Didn't they know that people who build glass houses shouldn't own yaks?

"Weren't you just out in your workshop?" Fake Mrs.

Prime said to her so-called husband as the entire family trudged out into the storm to see what was what. "Did you remember to close the barn door when you left?"

"I could have sworn I did!" he insisted, but a distressed yak call and the crash of more shattering glass said otherwise.

Fake Mr. and Mrs. Prime were doing their best to figure out how to help the poor animal. They weren't particularly worried about the greenhouse itself, for it had already served its purpose—but to play their roles correctly in front of Noah, they had to show an acceptable amount of concern.

"I'll go in and calm her down," Fake Mr. Prime said as another pane of glass was shattered by the thrust of Yolanda's heavy hooves.

"Be careful, dear," said his so-called wife. And when he was unsuccessful in calming the beast, she decided she'd better go in to help him.

Between the raging blizzard, and the raging yak, neither of them noticed that Noah and Andi were nowhere to be seen.

24

Welcome to the Rest of Your Life

FIFTY YARDS AWAY FROM THE YAK ATTACK, NOAH AND ANDI
stood at the edge of a sheer cliff, while Andi finalized calculations for a portal back to Arbuckle.

"I have enough battery power to create a portal now,"
she told Noah, shouting over the wind, "but this one is
special. I've never generated a *trans-core* portal before. It's
actually very exciting."

Noah was not all that excited, though, to be a guinea
pig in his android sister's learning curve.

"What if something goes wrong?" he asked.

"Death will be instantaneous," said Andi.

"Aaaaand this is a good idea why?"

"Because you are several thousand times more likely to
die slipping in the bathtub than crossing through a trans-
core portal. Just think of it as a doorway. Where the door-
frame is roughly seven thousand degrees Fahrenheit."

Andi reached up and began to trace a glowing circle with her fingertip.

"They're going to know we're gone," said Noah.

"Yes, but they'll think we got lost in the storm. They'll be searching for hours before they realize we've escaped."

More than once, the wind nearly blew them both off the edge of the cliff. Finally, Andi's circle was complete, and it was as if the skin of reality fell away like cellophane, revealing a blazing tunnel that seemed to have no end.

"It's going to be early morning in Arbuckle when we arrive," Andi told him. "You'll have portal lag. Deal with it."

She stood there for a moment more, hesitating. Behind them came the sound of more shattering glass, making it clear that their backup parents were still occupied.

"So . . . are we going?" Noah asked

"Yeah. You go first," Andi said, then pushed him in.

• ● •

The Sherpa, still in the kitchen, was understandably annoyed. He had slaved over a hot stove for hours, and now, thanks to that troublesome yak, dinner was getting colder by the minute.

He waited for the Primes to return, and when they didn't, he decided he might as well go out and get the animal back in the barn for them, as this family did not seem all that skilled in the care and maintenance of a barnyard animal.

When he went outside, the snow was so heavy, he could barely see a foot in front of him, so he followed a far-off light, which he assumed was coming from the greenhouse.

• ● •

Noah found that crossing through the trans-core portal wasn't like walking through a doorway at all. It was more like being punted through a swirling vortex of fire, then coming out the other side before the heat had a chance to realize what you were up to. Even so, Noah was glad that he was wearing his parka and gloves, because the microsecond he spent crossing through the portal left them melted and smoking, as well as singeing off most of his eyebrows.

"There, that wasn't so bad, was it?" said Andi when she emerged behind him.

"Compared to what?" Noah had to ask.

"Compared to bouncing off the moon," Andi said, as if it were obvious. "Lunar-transfer portals are the worst."

Noah looked around and found that they were in a construction site. A familiar one. And they were not alone.

• ● •

Mr. Ksh had seen many strange things happen at his construction sites over the years. He'd seen a dump truck disappear into a sinkhole without a trace. He'd witnessed a welder fall from the fifth floor, land in a pile of bricks, and walk away completely unharmed. But nothing compared to

270

a portal opening in a reinforced concrete wall. Amazing, yes, but in other ways, not entirely unexpected.

Being that it was early morning, no one but Mr. Ksh was present. While other people liked to commune with nature, Mr. Ksh had seen enough nature in his life, and he preferred to take morning walks through his construction sites, marveling that something could exist where nothing existed before—and that he could play a part in making that happen. What an extraordinary coincidence, then, that Mr. Ksh was standing directly in front of the portal when it opened, and the Prime children stepped out.

They stood staring at him, and Mr. Ksh stared back.

"Well, hello," Mr. Ksh said. "Would either of you care to tell me why there is a spinning nexus of death in my brand-new concrete wall?"

"Because it's better than bouncing off the moon?" Noah said, with a shrug and a smile that was really more of a grimace.

And then they ran off.

In ordinary circumstances, Mr. Ksh would have run after them, but the circumstances were far from ordinary. He would catch up with Noah Prime later. That he knew for a fact. Instead, he stood at the portal, peering into it. Waiting.

Then, just a few seconds after the kids had run from the construction site, someone else came through the portal. A man with a knitted Nepalese cap, which was now singed and smoking. Then the portal zipped itself closed behind him, as if it had never been there at all.

"Welcome to the rest of your life," Mr. Ksh said to the Sherpa, in perfect Nepali. "I've been waiting for you for a very long time."

• ● •

Friday was a school holiday in Arbuckle, as National Fossil Day was every year when it fell on a weekday.

Ogden did his best to build up his usual excitement for FossilFest, in spite of everything else that was on his mind. Nearly every science organization in Oregon would have a presence there. The Arbuckle Natural History Museum was planning an exhibit focused on carbon 14 as the most common method for dating fossils (WANT TO DATE A FOSSIL? a banner headline proclaimed). Another exhibit was going to be an authentic paleontology-like dig, set up in a giant sandbox by a local science club—with serious cash prizes for the best bones unearthed.

A giant paleontological sandbox with cash incentive? What wasn't there to love? Ogden wasn't about to let something as random as an alien encounter prevent him from attending. In fact, a secret alien presence could make it even more exciting.

When Ogden left for the festival that morning, he also hoped it would help distract him. But as he got closer, all he could think was *What if the bones they dig up in that sand-box are Noah's?*

He tried to shake off his growing concern. He'd already concluded that the aliens were friendly—at least to him. But to Noah and his family, not so much, as they did blow up his house. It seemed pretty clear that Noah's family were aliens as well. What Ogden didn't know was whether they were a rogue group of the same aliens, or a set of completely *different* aliens . . .

Was there some kind of intergalactic war going on, which Ogden had somehow stumbled into the middle of? The thought literally stopped him in his tracks, and he stood there at the side of the road, overwhelmed by the possible ramifications. Then he heard someone shouting.

"Excuse me! You, there!" He turned to see a big black Cadillac, which had slowed down in the street next to him, and he could see the driver through the open window, as well as a man in a slightly burned knit hat sitting in the passenger seat next to him.

The man driving the car shouted at Ogden, "Correct me if I'm wrong, but aren't you a friend of Noah Prime's?"

• ● •

Earlier that morning, Sahara found herself flying through a blue sky speckled with puffy, animal-shaped clouds. She knew she was dreaming, but at the moment she didn't mind. Then, all at once, the clouds changed from animals into various versions of Noah Prime—and then an alien spaceship descended toward her, playing "Baby Shark," which made it clear that this was a nightmare.

It took her a moment in her dream to remember that she'd set the supremely annoying song as her alarm, so she wouldn't be tempted to hit snooze, because then she'd have to hear it again.

As she swam back to consciousness, she remembered that today was FossilFest, and she was obliged to perform on the gymnastics float.

In the grand scheme of things, she now knew it didn't matter. She had inadvertently spied a larger universe, and now her participation in that larger universe was over. It no longer cared about her, and she had been puked back into the mundane. Her team was counting on her just as much now as they had before she knew aliens existed. So she killed "Baby Shark," shoved her dinosaur leotard in her gym bag, and got ready to leave.

She thought about how much her world had changed since she'd met Noah, and she wondered if she would ever find out what had happened to him. According to Ogden, he'd gotten away from the aliens. That was something to hang on to.

Okay, so there are larger forces out there, she thought as she rode off on her bike. *So what?* Perhaps it was wiser to just live quietly with the knowledge, and get on with her life.

These were the thoughts that troubled her as she pedaled her way toward the center of town. But as she came to a stop sign, a Cadillac pulled up next to her—the same one she had seen at Stonehenge. The one belonging to Mr. Ksh. A tinted back-seat window rolled down, revealing Ogden, of all people.

"Need a ride?" he asked.

"Thanks, but no thanks."

Sahara had no intention of joining them, until Mr. Ksh said the one thing that would get Sahara to drop her bike by the side of the road.

"I know where we can find your friend Noah."

"Is he okay? Where is he?"

"FossilFest, of course," Mr. Ksh said. "Please, we don't have much time—and your lives may depend on it."

Sahara took a deep breath. This was her second come-with-me-if-you-want-to-live moment this week. But at least this time it came from a human being. And there was something about Mr. Ksh that she trusted. It was as if he knew something the rest of them didn't.

"Fine," she said, "but if things get weird, I'm bailing."

"You mean things aren't weird already?" said Ogden.

She hid her bike in the brush by the side of the road, then hopped in next to Ogden.

There was someone else in the car with them, sitting shotgun next to Mr. Ksh. A man younger than Ksh but, like Ksh, of Asian descent. He was wearing an unseasonably heavy Sherpa jacket that looked a bit singed and a knit cap to match. His outfit was just out of place enough that Sahara wondered if he was another wardrobe-challenged alien. But those aliens all seemed far too sure of themselves. This man was not—in fact, he was nervous and wringing his hands. Then he said something to Mr. Ksh in a language Sahara couldn't name, much less understand, and Mr. Ksh responded in the same tongue.

"Who's your friend?" Sahara asked.

"Who, indeed!" was Mr. Ksh's reply, and he was more than happy to just leave it at that—which was beyond irritating. After everything she'd been through, Sahara did not have the patience for nonanswers. But perhaps she could goad him into saying something useful.

"You seem awfully calm for a man who saw his driver collapse into an anthill," she said to Mr. Ksh.

"What?" asked Ogden.

"Old news," said Sahara. "Try to keep up."

"No sense lamenting the past," Mr. Ksh said, in the same cheery tone. "The present is what matters. And, of course, the future."

Clearly, she was going to get nothing out of him, so she cut to the important question.

"So, where's Noah?"

"I don't have his precise location," Mr. Ksh said, "but I do know he's back, and he will make an appearance at FossilFest."

"Back from where?"

"Nepal—just south of the Tibetan border," Mr. Ksh said, as if it was a perfectly normal place to be back from. "The same area my *friend* here is from."

"And you know this how?"

To that, Mr. Ksh gave yet another nonanswer. "The same way I know that something is going to go terribly wrong at the festival today."

"If we don't stop it," added Ogden.

But Mr. Ksh shook his head. "No, we can't stop it. But maybe we can influence the outcome...."

• ● •

Mr. Ksh knew many things. Things he had no business knowing, but knowing them was good business for him. No one questioned his success, because it was most certainly earned with hard work and long hours.

He could have been even more successful than he was. A multibillionaire instead of just a multimillionaire. Greed, however, was not his driving force. There were two things driving him. First was a desire to leave something of value behind, and second was an abiding need to solve the greatest mystery of his life. Because although Mr. Ksh knew many things, what kept him awake at night were the things he didn't know. And at the center of those things was Noah Prime.

25

Official Victim and Designated Survivor

NOAH FOUND THAT SWINGING THROUGH THE TREES WITH ANDI clinging to his shoulders was much less stressful than performing miracle acrobatics in front of a mesmerized crowd. Now that he kinda sorta understood why he could do these things, he could manage it much better. It was kind of like riding a bull at the rodeo, when the entire rodeo's inside your own body. You just have to catch the rhythm, then hold on for dear life.

"You see how much easier it is for you to get started now?" Andi said.

It was true. He didn't need a crocodile chomping down on his arm, or some other massive shock to his system.

"Run as fast as you can and hurl yourself at a tree," Andi had said to him, after she had unexpectedly climbed on his back.

"Why would I do that?"

"Because you're in touch with your inner menagerie now, your subconscious won't let you hit the tree," she had told him. "Trust me."

And although his conscious mind told him this was a really bad idea, he trusted Andi far more than he used to. So he hurled himself at the tree, and suddenly he found himself climbing it and swinging through the canopy—he had a sense that he had done this before, but at the time he hadn't even been aware of it.

The forest was thick, and the trees were easy to travel. Noah found it . . . exhilarating. Like the way he used to feel riding motocross.

"By our trajectory, I can tell you're heading to Ogden's house," Andi said. "Bad idea. It might be staked out. Sahara's house, too."

"But you're sure they're okay?"

"Well, I've kept a running check on their parents' phone activity," she said, "and there are no calls to the police or mortuaries, so we can assume."

Noah came to rest on a sturdy bough near the intersection of two country roads. From this high in the trees, he could see the highway to his left and the center of town to his right.

Something clicked in Noah's brain. "He's not home anyway. Today is FossilFest!" Noah said. "That's where Ogden will be!"

"And I suspect there will be an alien presence there,

too, searching for clues to your whereabouts," Andi said. "So if we want to rescue Mom and Dad, that's a good place to start."

"But they'll recognize me the second I drop in," Noah pointed out.

"Not if we disguise you."

"Okay," Noah said. "What about that Halloween store next to the Walmart? We can find a disguise there."

"Oh, please! We're going to need something a little bit better than some Halloween costume. I'll have to make you a skin. We just need a subject to take it from."

Noah didn't like the sound of that. "You mean we have to peel someone's skin off?"

"Ew! No!" said Andi. "We just need to find a viable subject and do a biometric cellular intrusion scan."

"Does it hurt?" Noah asked.

"Like a root canal," Andi said, "if your whole body was covered with teeth, and they were all being drilled at once."

Now it was Noah's turn to say, "Ew!"

"The problem is," explained Andi, "I'm programmed to require informed consent. Whoever we scan needs to give us permission."

To that, Noah smiled. "I know just the subject."

• ● •

Kaleb Carpenter's parents always said their son was accident-prone, but it would be more accurate to say he was "accident-friendly." It began with his spatial awareness issues that left him bumping into objects and people, and misjudging things like, oh, say, the arc of a swinging hammer. But human beings are remarkably adaptable. At some point, Kaleb's body threw up its proverbial hands and said, "Fine, be that way," and, as Noah's mom might say, he learned how to make lemonade . . . out of some badly bruised lemons. As previously mentioned, Kaleb got into lots of fights that landed him in Saturday school. Many of those fights he lost, but he didn't mind, because he firmly believed life was a journey, not a destination. And if that journey was on a rocky path, barefoot, with occasional pieces of broken glass, well, he would make do.

Kaleb was just getting ready to head out to FossilFest, as he had been chosen to play the official victim in the jaws of the T. rex parade float. He had already dressed in his torn costume, splattered with mostly fake blood, when Noah Prime and his little sister showed up at his door for an unexpected visit.

"Kaleb, we need you to do a favor for us," Noah said. "My sister, Andi, will explain."

"I need a subject for . . . a science fair project," Andi said.

"Cool," said Kaleb. "What do you need me to do? But make it fast. I gotta get to FossilFest. I'm an official parade victim!"

"Which is why," Noah said, "we thought of you!"

Then his sister pulled out a strange-looking object. It looked somewhat like the business end of a vacuum cleaner, if the business end of a vacuum cleaner gave off high-voltage electricity.

"This is a Biometric Cellular Intrusion Scanner," Andi said.

"What's it do?"

"It creates a functional quantum copy of your dermal contours."

"It copies your skin," Noah explained.

"So, like, a skin for an avatar in a VR game?"

"Something like that," said Noah.

Kaleb reached up and brushed a hand through his slightly off-center Mohawk. "Where did you get it?"

"Um, eBay," Noah said.

"Kewl!"

"Yeah, but here's the thing," Noah said, a bit sheepishly. "The scan kind of . . . pinches a little."

Kaleb looked at the device a bit more closely. The sparks shooting across the wide nozzle did not look pleasant at all.

"How much?" Kaleb asked.

"Pain is subjective," Noah's sister said as she ushered them all into a bathroom and closed the door.

"Well, on a scale of one to ten," said Kaleb, "one being your nose getting caught in a mousetrap, and ten being caught in a bear trap and having to gnaw off your own foot . . ."

"How do you get your nose caught in a mousetrap?" asked Noah.

"It's possible," said Kaleb. "Trust me on that."

"Given that scale," said Andi, "it's a 7.3. I would say it's like being bitten by a shark, and surviving."

"Or a T. rex," suggested Kaleb. He crossed his arms and considered it. "So . . . 7.3, huh."

Andi nodded. "Give or take."

Kaleb took a deep breath, then shrugged. "Well, you gotta do what you gotta do."

• ● •

Noah had to look away—but not before seeing things he could not unsee. The scan seemed to rip Kaleb's flesh off his bones, then place it right back again, as Andi slowly ran the sparking wand over him. It took less than a minute, and when it was done, Kaleb looked as if he had been through the wringer—which was probably the right look for his part in the FossilFest parade.

"Wow," said Kaleb, still shaking. "That really hurt."

"Yeah, sorry," Noah said.

"No worries!" said Kaleb.

"Just one more thing," Andi said. Then she raised a finger, which began to glow ever so slightly, tapped it to his forehead—and Kaleb disappeared.

"What? Why did you do that?" demanded Noah. "Disintegrating Kaleb was definitely not part of the deal!"

283

"Calm down," Andi said. "I just oysterized him." Then she reached down, picked up something small from the floor, and held it out to Noah between her thumb and forefinger. A tiny sphere with an opalescent sheen. If Noah didn't know better, he'd say it was a pearl.

"He's fine," Andi told Noah. "He's asleep in his own private micro-dimension. We can bring him back whenever we want. Just add water."

"But . . . why?"

"Because we can't have two Kaleb Carpenters walking around FossilFest, can we?" Then she flipped a switch on the scanner, and its nozzle vomited forth something that looked like the shed skin of a snake, only human. "I'll wait in the hallway while you put on the skin. And don't tear it!"

• ● •

A quantum skin was not like a rubber mask. First, it covered one's entire body, and second, it didn't mask one's appearance—it actually bent space within it to match the subject it was copied from. It didn't matter how many toes or tentacles one might have; once you were sealed in a quantum skin, you were the exact shape, size, and appearance of the person whose skin you had copied. And while the scientists on Vecca's side of the battle hadn't mastered the concept of eyelids, the skin that Andi made was like the ones she and Noah's parents wore their entire lives on Earth:

284

indistinguishable from the real thing. Unless, of course, it got too hot, too cold, or was exposed to certain acids.

Once Noah pulled the skin over himself, he found the sensation unnerving. His own flesh began to crawl as if he was covered by a million tiny worms—the way you feel when your foot falls asleep, but over your whole body. It took a few moments for the sensation to fade, and when he looked at his hands, they looked like Kaleb Carpenter's hands—right down to the faded test answers written on his left palm. When he turned to the bathroom mirror, looking back at him was Kaleb Carpenter. It was even more unnerving than the squirming worm feeling.

"I'm not sure how I feel about this," Noah said as he stepped out of the bathroom.

"As if I care," Andi said, handing him the pearl. "Now, put Kaleb in your pocket, and let's go."

• ● •

"Tell me what you know," Mr. Ksh said as he drove Ogden and Sahara to the festival. "You must believe me when I tell you that I have a unique perspective on your situation."

"Why? Are you an alien, too?" Sahara asked, only half kidding.

"Certainly not!" Mr. Ksh said. "But I have had my own encounter with them in the past." He glanced over at his passenger. "So has my friend here—although his is much more recent than mine."

Even though they had no idea how Ksh had encountered the aliens before, Ogden and Sahara found having someone to talk to—someone who would believe them—was a relief. They told him everything, from the moment Noah dropped on Sahara from the trees, through the night Ogden locked them in the freezer, the destruction of the house, and their successful escape from the aliens—which Ogden was still a bit miffed at, since they had treated him with such hospitality. And when they were done, Ksh considered it and said:

"This is about real estate."

Which was something neither Ogden nor Sahara had reason to consider.

"How do you know?" Sahara asked.

"Because it's *always* about real estate," Mr. Ksh told them. "Here we have two forces competing for the same fertile planet. One force has created a human ark containing the genetic material of every living creature on Earth. And the other force wants to kill him."

"We kind of figured that much out," Ogden pointed out.

"Yes, but you must take it a step further," Mr. Ksh said. "An ark is not built without a dire need. Every culture and religion has such stories—and in all of them, it is because a flood is coming that will wipe out the world."

"Does it have to be the end of the world?" Ogden said. "Why can't it just be the end of Arbuckle? I could live with that."

"Flood myths usually encompass the entire known world," Mr. Ksh said. "And since the world is mostly known, I doubt anyone will escape it—except, of course, for your friend Noah, who I suspect is...how shall I put it...the designated survivor."

Sahara already felt as if she was drowning in this flood of new information. She had to remind herself that Ksh didn't know everything. It was just a theory, and an outlandish one at that. Even so, he seemed sure of himself, and it made sense—or as much sense as everything else in her life made in recent days, which was none at all. So at least it was consistent.

"So, your friend is the ark....The question is...why would someone want to destroy that ark?"

"Um...because they're the personification of absolute evil?" Ogden suggested.

But Mr. Ksh shook his head. "That kind of evil only exists in myths and politics. In this case, I don't think it's that simple. If we want to get to the bottom of this, we have to find out why they want to kill Noah." Then he sighed. "And my gut tells me we're not going to like the answer."

26

The Way of the Dinosaurs

Arbuckle used to have a dull and incredibly unimpressive Main Street full of struggling mom-and-pop shops peddling outdated products and performing functions that no one needed anymore, like film developing and typewriter repair. Places that had already gone the way of the dinosaurs, but whose owners refused to admit it.

Many businesses were killed in the crossfire of a vicious battle between Walmart and Target on either side of Arbuckle, leaving Main Street a virtual ghost town. Then, ten years ago, the town council was approached by a wealthy real estate developer with the idea of building an old-fashioned town square smack in the center of Arbuckle that would make it a hub of activity.

"My friends, it already exists," Mr. Ksh had told the council, with rare and compelling confidence. "All that remains is to build it."

And so, the corner of Main and Pine was demolished, along with all the buildings within a hundred yards of the corner, and a quaint town square was erected in its place, perpetually snarling traffic—which was actually a good thing, because everyone agreed that the annoyance of traffic was much better than the despair of a ghost town. So what if some of the buildings looked as if they would be more at home in, oh, say, Kathmandu. The Nepalese flavor added character to the square—which had become the pride and joy of Arbuckle—and it would remain so until the very moment of its utter destruction.

• ● •

"Fan out," Mr. Ksh told Ogden and Sahara once they arrived at the festival. "Your friend is here; it's just a matter of finding him."

"How can you be so sure?" Sahara asked.

"Because there's someone or something he needs to find, just as we need to find him. I can assure you his destination is here."

Sahara left in search of Noah, but Ogden lingered, because he had that strange sensation of intuition. The kind of feeling he had when he was about to solve a riddle, or come up with a new Theory of Everything.

Thinking outside the box was Ogden's specialty. Although when people suggested he was "thinking outside the box," it frustrated him, because he *existed* outside the box. It was the box itself that was a mystery to him; he had no idea what sort of thinking went on inside it, so it often felt as if he was excluded from a club. He had no illusion that the grass was greener inside the box—because without sunlight, any grass in there would be long dead or, at the very least, yellow rather than green.

"You think different," his mother always told him, which he knew was a good thing, but on gray days, he wished he could just think the same. It was, however, his outside-the-box thinking that led him to make an intuitive leap when he looked at Mr. Ksh and the befuddled dude in the Sherpa hat. The two men were not just similar but identical, right down to a mole on the left side of their noses. They were like twins born twenty years apart.

"He's you!" Ogden said, with a gasp.

And Mr. Ksh smiled. "How could that possibly be so?" he asked, but the man's smile betrayed that he was merely toying with Ogden.

Ogden began to piece it all together. "Before Stephen Hawking died—or was abducted by pan-dimensional beings, if you believe certain bloggers—he said that time travel was theoretically possible. And if it's possible, then someone somewhere knows how to do it." Then Ogden pointed at Mr. Ksh's companion. "The aliens are going to send him back in time somehow—and he will become you! *That's* how you know that Noah is here, and that's how you know something bad will happen—because for you it's already happened!" Then something else occurred to Ogden. "Knowing what's going to happen! I'll bet that's how you got rich!"

Ogden looked at the bewildered Sherpa—who was as far from a real estate tycoon as can be. But things change. People change. Especially when put in the pressure cooker of extraordinary circumstances. "He might not be big on stock futures, but that doesn't matter," Ogden observed. "You only need to know two words in the past to get filthy rich: Amazon and Apple."

"Well, it wasn't quite *that* easy," Mr. Ksh said, "but, yes, that's the long and short of it."

Confirmation! He knew it! This new information put things in much clearer focus. He looked at the younger Ksh and shook his head sadly. "Poor guy. Does he know what's going to happen to him?"

"Not a clue. Although I did tell him that I'm his long-lost cousin, and that I'm going to make him very rich."

Ogden crossed his arms. "So, what happens during the festival?"

"Nothing good, that's for sure. Just keep your eye out for an ambulance. Once it arrives in the square, all hell breaks loose."

"And then what?"

"That's the problem. I never really see what comes next. A few minutes later, I'm hurled twenty years into the past. For all I know, today could be the end of the world."

• ● •

The Sherpa, of course, had no idea what was in his future. He spoke no English, and so he only knew what his "cousin" told him in his native tongue of Nepali. He could not place exactly where on the family tree the man hung, and when the Sherpa asked, he was told not to trouble himself with it. It's not that he didn't believe the man—because he did bear a striking family resemblance—but the nature of their relationship was not the Sherpa's primary concern. He was more concerned with how he had gotten to the United States in the first place.

"Top secret government teleportation project," his cousin told him. "Best not to dwell on it."

Which was easy to say, but much harder to accomplish. How does one "not dwell" on such a thing?

Wisely, Mr. Ksh had not told him that his future was a one-way trip to the past. Ksh knew *when* it would happen. He knew *how* it would happen, but not why—or any of the circumstances around his leap through time. Only now, with the help of Ogden and Sahara, was he piecing together the bigger picture. He knew he couldn't stop his leap to the past—if there was anything Mr. Ksh had learned, it was that you can't change the past, no matter what you know about it. The universe simply doesn't allow it. All one can do is become part of what already happened. Or already will happen, as the case may be.

In spite of everything, there was a comforting balance to it. A wholeness. Mr. Ksh had learned to move in tune with the universe, and it had thus rewarded him with wealth and relative happiness. For instance, he knew, without a shadow of any doubt, that he would live to see this day. Knowing that you couldn't die no matter what you did was profoundly liberating. He had gone skydiving, and BASE jumping, and rock climbing with neither rope nor harness. He had lived an extraordinary life. If it ended today, he would say he was satisfied, although he certainly hoped that it didn't.

All he knew for sure about today was that the last thing his younger self would see, before getting hurled back in time, would be flames leaping from the earth, setting everything on fire.

• ● •

The festival was already in full swing when Noah arrived. The park was awash with tents and activities. Food trucks were selling dinosaur-themed eats, and musical acts performed on the steps of the museum.

"How will I know the aliens when I see them, if they're all wearing human skins?" Noah asked Andi.

"Their eyes—but even better, I've installed a diminished-reality app on Kaleb's phone for you," Andi told him.

"Uh . . . don't you mean *augmented* reality?"

"No, diminished—it's the opposite. It scrambles the

reality you see just enough to view what's actually inside of people. You're gonna see a lot of things you'll wish you hadn't—there are a lot of alien species here today—but what you're looking for are a whole bunch of tentacles squeezed into a human shape."

"You'll probably be better at spotting them than I am," Noah suggested.

"True, but you're the one in disguise. They'll recognize me if I don't make myself scarce."

So, without any further help from Andi, Noah moved through the festival with his phone raised, pretending to take selfies. He quickly came to realize the flaw to that plan—because there were a whole lot of tentacles crammed into human shapes. There was a veritable army of aliens here, and they were all here looking for him. Finding the one who had his parents—the one in charge—was not going to be easy with nothing more to go on.

The sound of a guy playing a dinosaur bone xylophone drew his attention. Next to the xylophone was a lemonade cart, which made him think of his mom.

"Lemonade, Noah. Lemonade."

But with the lemons currently in his possession, he suspected there was no lemonade to be had.

27

The Thing About Lemons

THERE ARE CERTAIN CONSTANTS THAT HOLD THE UNIVERSE together. The speed of light, for instance. No matter where you are, or what galactic mischief you're up to, the speed of light is always the same—and if you approach that speed, the universe is forced to slow time down, so that the speed of your ship's headlight beam doesn't surpass the speed of light. And, as a last-ditch effort to maintain its own sanity, the universe hurls you into hyperspace, so your faster-than-light antics can be somebody else's problem.

Another universal constant is the lemon.

No one knows where it came from, or why in creation there would be a fruit so acidic and sour—nevertheless, every planet where advanced life has arisen has lemons. And while Earth creatures somehow evolved to digest them—with humans going so far as to juice them for use in food and drink—to all non-Earth species, they are far too dangerous. In fact, their specific acidity is downright deadly to non-Earth life—and the lemons know it. In fact, it is generally accepted that citrus throughout the universe has a nasty collective consciousness that loves nothing more than making non-rooted beings miserable. If you doubt it, consider the grapefruit, and how precisely it spits into your eye.

On most other worlds, the toxin from the lemon has been distilled into a variety of poisons, and its zested rind is the key ingredient in numerous alien bioweapons. Thus, when an alien says, "If life gives you lemons, make lemonade," what they're really saying is, "If life gives you uranium, make nukes."

Which is one reason why most alien species are both awed and horrified by humanity: because eating lemon flesh and drinking lemon venom are proof to them that the human race is absolutely insane. All the more reason to be rid of it.

At this particular moment, however, Noah Prime found himself having a far more positive experience with the evil fruit—because he saw Ogden standing next to the lemonade stand.

• ● •

Noah was thrilled! Yes, Andi had told him that Ogden and Sahara were unharmed, but seeing Ogden flooded him with relief. He hurried over and grabbed Ogden by the shoulders, practically giving him a hug, but stopped himself before it got that far. "Ogden! You're okay!"

Ogden looked at him, blinking, and more than a little bit suspicious. "Yeah, why wouldn't I be? Hey, have you seen Noah? I'm looking for him."

It took Noah a moment to remember that he was in disguise. "Ogden, it's me! I'm Noah!"

"Umm, no you're not. You're Kaleb Carpenter," he said. "Are you pranking me, Kaleb—or are you actually having identity issues?"

"I'll prove it to you."

Ogden crossed his arms. "This ought to be interesting."

Noah sighed. Nothing was ever easy with Ogden. "Okay . . . In third grade, you accidentally set off a model rocket in Ms. Pollard's class. It ripped off her hair extension and pinned it to a *Clifford the Big Red Dog* poster, like pin the tail on the donkey, but with a dog—and since her hair was red, it was a pretty good match."

"This is true," Ogden said, weighing the evidence. "But you were in my third-grade class, too, Kaleb. So, as far as evidence goes, that's a fail."

Noah tried again. "Last week!" he said. "You locked Sahara and me in the freezer at the Fresh and Funky to see what would happen!"

But Ogden just shrugged. "Sahara could have told you that."

"Why would she?"

"How should I know? I don't have a window into her mind."

And so Noah tried one last time, pointing at Ogden. "Pull my finger."

Ogden shook his head "Nope. I know that trick."

"It's a different trick!"

"Kaleb would say that."

"Right—so if it's the same old fart trick, you'll know for sure that I'm Kaleb."

It was logic that Ogden approved of. "Fine." He reached out and reluctantly pulled Noah's extended finger.

And the finger came off in his hand.

Ogden yelped and dropped it to the ground, where it wiggled a bit, then died.

Noah couldn't deny that it hurt, but as he shook his hand, the pain quickly stopped, and when he looked, he was already growing a new finger in its place, poking through the hole in his Kaleb skin.

"The axolotl salamander!" Ogden said, a bit shell-shocked, "It sheds limbs when threatened, then grows them back. But that should take weeks!"

"What can I say, I'm an overachiever."

Ogden's entire demeanor suddenly changed, his face erupting in a very uncharacteristic smile. "Noah! It *is* you!" he said. "But why do you look like Kaleb Carpenter? And what's with the pink suitcase?"

Standing on the other side of the square, Sahara scanned the growing crowd for Noah. The Fossil Parade was soon to begin, which would make it even more difficult to spot him along the crowded route. Across the square, she saw Ogden talking to that creepy Kaleb kid. Then, from behind her—

"Sahara, there you are!"

Sahara flinched, as if caught, and turned toward the familiar voice. It was Misty, her teammate, who ran up to her with several other members of the gymnastics squad. "The coach was having a cow looking for you. The parade starts in a few minutes! Everyone's already on the float."

Sahara sighed. A gymnastics exhibition on a moving parade float was never a good idea, and Sahara was the only team member skilled enough to manage a moving version of the uneven parallel bars, which, in the test run around the school parking lot, had become increasingly less parallel and more uneven. That was, come to think of it, an accurate description of Sahara's entire life over the past few days.

"Katrina did a face-plant on the mat, so we're already down one," said Misty.

The coach decided the balance beam would make a much better centerpiece of the float, slightly less dangerous than the bars—so Sahara was slated to do her beam routine. Sahara realized that standing up there would offer her a better view of the crowd, making it that much easier to spot Noah along the route. She could be there for the team *and* look for Noah.

She nodded and said, "Lead the way."

• ● •

Quantavius T. Kratz had far better things to do than run the Guess That Dinosaur Smell booth at FossilFest. All he could think about was Noah and his camouflage skin—the military applications alone made him woozy. Imagine entire army uniforms made of Noahskin. No! KratzSkin—after all, he's the one who discovered the boy. He deserved the trademark.

Yet here he was, testing the sniffers of ridiculously unimaginative children.

"Ew! Smells like vinegar," the child facing him announced after sticking his nose in hole number eight.

"Wrong!" Kratz told him. "It's T. rex toe jam. You lose. Next!"

In reality, it was a pair of socks that Kratz had worn three days straight to get it just pungent enough for the day's event. Since T. rex toe jam was in short supply, one must improvise.

It was not a sense of duty that compelled him to run the booth—it was a sense of self-preservation. His principal was looking for reasons to fire him. In fact, the entire administration, and certain members of the school board, had been rallying against him ever since the cockroach incident. Not his fault! Who knew growth hormones and an electric current could cause an insect to grow to such gargantuan proportions?

"Let's see," said the little girl who chose hole number eleven. "Ugh! Smells like poo."

"From what dinosaur?" Kratz demanded.

"I dunno. Stegosaurus?"

"Wrong! Triceratops! You lose! Next!"

If Kratz had refused to take his turn at one of the school's FossilFest booths, he could be fired for dereliction of duty—and since his bright and glorious future was not yet in his grasp, he couldn't walk away from his teaching job just yet. Oh, but when he did, his departure would be stellar! But only if he delivered Noah Prime to the two shadow agents, as he promised.

"Oh, blechhhh! I'm gonna puke! It smells like dead body!" said the next kid.

"Yes—but which dinosaur's dead body?"

If there was one thing Kratz knew for sure, however, it was that Noah Prime's friend would be here. Odin, or Orin, or whatever his name was. The boy was an olfactory genius who could guess every smell, including which dinosaur Kratz randomly assigned to the odor. He had won the grand prize three years running. If anyone would know where Noah Prime was, it would be him—and now that Kratz had secret government objects of persuasion, the kid would sing like a canary!

"Brachiosaurus?"

"Wrong! That's the aroma of dead pterodactyl! Next!"

Finally, Kratz spotted Odin/Orin/Owen next to the lemonade stand, hanging out with that halfwit with the lopsided Mohawk, watching the parade, which had just begun.

"Guess that dinosaur smell!" shouted Kratz like a sideshow barker to get his attention. "Guess that smell, and win a prize!"

• ● •

Noah found that explaining everything to Ogden was like being trapped in quicksand. Even telling him why Andi was a suitcase led to more and increasingly specific questions from Ogden that threatened to swallow what was left of Noah's mind. In the end he told Ogden to get Sahara, and he would try to explain what he could to both of them. And so, while Ogden went to find Sahara, Noah waited by the lemonade stand, minding his business, and scanning the crowd for anyone who looked as if they might be the alien in charge.

The student volunteer working the lemonade stand was not an alien, although she could be mistaken for one. She had lopsided hair dyed a shade of black so dark it actually hurt your eyeballs to look at it, along with nails the color of dried blood. Noah recognized her from school: Stella Strife. She was serving other people lemonade but flatly refused to serve Noah.

"We reserve the right to refuse service to anyone," she told him, which was fine, because Noah wasn't in line.

"I didn't ask for a lemonade," he pointed out.

"Well, don't bother asking, Kaleb, because if you get any lemonade, it will be over my dead body, is that clear?"

"Oh. Oh, right." And Noah couldn't stop himself from asking, "Why?"

She looked at him, incredulous. "After what you said to me the other day, you're lucky I don't hurl lemonade in your face!"

"I'm . . . uh . . . sorry?" Noah offered.

She put her hands on her hips. "Prove it."

"Okay, sure . . ."

She eyed him suspiciously. "So, are you asking me out?"

"Wait, what?" Then it occurred to Noah that if he asked Stella out, it would ultimately be Kaleb Carpenter's problem, not his—and by the look of it, Kaleb deserved whatever sour lemons this girl had to give. Besides, these two were clearly meant for each other.

"Sure," Noah said with a big Kaleb Carpenter smile. "Let's talk about it in school on Monday."

What happened next was nobody's fault. Well, actually it was the fault of the clumsy festivalgoer who wasn't looking where he was going. He was too absorbed by some sort of mishap farther down the parade route. Something involving a gymnastics display gone horribly wrong.

The result of the man's inattention was an unfortunate foot stomp, which started a chain of events that no one could have predicted.

The moment Noah's foot was stepped on, he did not react the way most other humans would react: yelping in pain and spouting any number of colorful exclamations. Instead, he reacted as a stonefish does when stepped on. Huge, spear-like spikes erupted from his spine, shooting deadly venom. Had people been standing directly behind him, they would have been killed, but the only thing behind him was the glass tank of lemonade—which, when struck by Noah's sudden bony protrusions, shattered, drenching him in lemonade—

And although alien artificial skins were water-resistant, they had no power against the lemon. Noah's Kaleb Carpenter skin completely dissolved, leaving nothing but the remains of a Mohawk, lying in a lemonade puddle like a dead squirrel.

• ● •

Of the various people in the vicinity of the lemonade catastrophe, several were not people at all. They were aliens in disguise, although their disguises were easily spotted, as they were from other cultures and/or time periods. But since most people weren't looking for aliens, it was assumed that their clothing had something to do with FossilFest.

When the tank shattered, several of the disguised beings fled, screaming in terror—because the deadly lemon tincture was more lethal to them than stonefish venom—and so they didn't witness the unveiling of Noah Prime.

Except, that is, for the one who didn't run.

Or, more accurately, the fifteen masquerading as one.

They were members of a species of small hired assassins that existed entirely in committees, operating within a single human skin much the same way humans might operate in a submarine, if a submarine had absolutely no personal space. Which, perhaps, was why the human clothing they chose to wear was a toga, because, if nothing else, it provided much-needed ventilation.

Even though the fifteen shared a system of highly evolved neural connections, a decision to run in terror had to be discussed in open debate, then voted on, before action could be taken—and since the action was panic, they never even made it through the discussion phase. The result was that they were still close to the seething citrus calamity, and they were there to see the meltdown of Kaleb Carpenter into Noah Prime.

Once they realized that this was the target they had been looking for, it took mere seconds for them to discuss/debate/vote on a course of action. From a fold in their toga, they pulled out a disintegration gun that did not look at all like it came from ancient Greece, and they aimed it at Noah Prime, fully prepared to fire—

But before the trigger could be pulled, a heavy blunt object came down on the head of the committee chairman, knocking him out. And thanks to their highly evolved neural connections, the blow instantly rendered all fifteen unconscious.

How dare that drapery-clad cretin! No one was going to steal Quantavius T. Kratz's prize!

Just moments before, Kratz was shouting at the top of his lungs, trying to draw Noah's friend to the dinosaur-smelling booth—but to Kratz's disgust, the boy had gone off in the other direction. Then the lemonade tank shattered, and amid the mayhem—Was that . . . ? Had Kratz just seen . . . ? Yes! It was! It was Noah Prime standing up from the sticky mess, drenched and dazed.

Kratz had no idea where Noah had come from, or how he had just appeared there, but it didn't matter. Kratz couldn't believe his luck! He abandoned the booth and made a beeline toward Noah, pushing everyone out of his way. He raced into the path of the parade—and caused the "winged predator" float to stop short, launching a toothy papier-mâché pterodactyl out over the crowd, where it soared majestically before zeroing in on a small child, who screamed in abject terror at the attack, thus cementing for the child a future full of parade trust issues.

But Kratz did not care. Any misery he created was mere collateral damage in a greater battle. Then, as he neared Noah, he saw what must have been a government agent raising what looked like a classified weapon, preparing to fire on the boy.

Not going to happen! Noah was Kratz's discovery; if

the boy had to be killed in the name of science, that would be Kratz's prerogative—but only after Noah's harvested biological material ensured Kratz his fancy new job in his fancy glass office.

Thinking far more quickly than, oh, say, a fifteen-member alien committee might, Kratz ripped a femur from the dinosaur bone xylophone and smashed it over the usurping agent's head, thereby removing him from the equation.

Kratz stepped over the unconscious "agent" and finally reached Noah. The boy was bleeding. This was a good thing, because it provided Kratz with something he could use.

"Noah! You're injured," he said in a tone he used when forced to pretend that he cared. "Your wounds must be tended to immediately! Come with me—there's a first aid station in the museum."

Then he grabbed Noah and pulled him away.

"No, wait," Noah protested, appearing somewhat dazed. "My sis...suitcase! I need my suitcase!"

"Not to worry. I'm sure it will be here when you get back," Kratz told him...which wasn't at all true. Not because it wouldn't be there, but because Noah wouldn't be coming back.

28

Human Toothpaste

NOAH WAS STILL IN PAIN FROM THE SPIKES THAT HAD UNEXPECTEDLY erupted from his spine, and disoriented by the whole incident, when Kratz grabbed him; otherwise, he might have been able to resist. Although the spikes had withdrawn, they left holes in Noah's shirt, rimmed in just enough blood to make it look as if his back had been cut by the broken glass of the tank.

"Make way!" Kratz yelled, pulling Noah along. "This boy is injured!" Then he turned to Noah and gave him a smile that seemed almost-but-not-quite sincere. "Don't you worry, Noah. I'll make sure they take good care of you."

It was only then—when Kratz called him by name—that Noah realized his disguise had melted off. That meant that any and all aliens searching for him could spot him easily. So he let Kratz spirit him into the museum, keeping his head down all the way. Kratz didn't know it, but he was doing Noah a favor by dragging him out of view. Or so Noah thought.

With most everyone watching the parade, the museum was nearly deserted. Once they were inside, Noah tried to pull away from Kratz—but Kratz's grip was too strong.

"Are you dizzy? Nauseated? Are you going into shock?" Kratz asked.

"I'm okay, really."

"Nonsense!" said Kratz. "Just look at all that blood. You're going to need stitches."

"No," insisted Noah, "it'll heal by itself." In fact, it already had, but Kratz was a man with a mission.

They turned a corner to a deserted part of the museum: a domed rotunda between the north and south wings, presided over by a statue of famed physicist Luis Alvarez, who, with his son, was the first to theorize that the dinosaurs were killed off by an asteroid. The physicist's stern bronze gaze made it clear he was not pleased to be stuck in a rotunda in a museum in a small town he had never visited, nor ever wanted to.

In the wall beside the statue, there was a door. That's where Kratz stopped.

"Ah, here we are. The first aid station."

Which didn't make any sense, because the sign on the door read JANITORIAL SUPPLIES. But before Noah could object, he was hurled inside, and Kratz slammed the door behind him.

• • •

What Kratz needed was a place to store Noah until he could track down the two government agents who had contacted him. The closet seemed as good a place as any.

Noah tried to turn the knob on the other side—but Kratz gripped it and kept it from turning. Noah pounded on the door. "Hey! Mr. Kratz! Let me out!"

Clearly, the boy didn't comprehend the severity of his current situation. Noah turned the knob again, and Kratz, realizing the door wasn't designed to lock someone in, resorted to an old trick he had occasionally been the victim of in his prep school years. He kicked the doorknob over and over until it broke off—causing the knob on the other side to come off in Noah's hand. Without a mechanism to turn the latch, the door was as good as locked.

"I'm sorry, Noah, truly I am," he shouted through the door. "It's nothing personal. I will do my best to make the various experiments you'll be put through less painful than I suspect they will be. But I can't promise anything." Then he raced off in search of the two agents who could return him to scientific glory.

• ● •

Noah pounded on the door, but it wouldn't give. He had access now to more and more biological responses, but he was still just learning. Trial and error had nearly gotten him eaten by a crocodile. The result was that he could now turn his ribs into weapons against an attacker, but the pain of that response wasn't something he wanted to experience again, any more than he wanted spikes to shoot out of his spine again.

There were definitely traits of other animals he had yet to tap into, however. *What I need is a battering ram*, he thought. *Aha! A ram!* He was already nearing an adrenaline frenzy, so he should be able to activate. The only way to find out was to try. And didn't Andi say his subconscious wouldn't let him hurt himself? So, with all his force, he hurled himself against the door headfirst—

And he learned that bad ideas never seem bad until after they're attempted. It's a lesson that one can only learn the hard way. If Andi were present now, she might have pointed out that his subconscious certainly wouldn't stop him if it was his clear *intention* to smash his head against the wall.

What Noah didn't take into account was that headbutting for rams is a mating ritual—much like the emperor penguin dance he had found himself involuntarily doing for Sahara. Perhaps if he'd been in the middle of another awkward situation with Sahara—and there was another male of the species around—his headbutt might have worked. But it was, instead, just an extremely painful bad idea.

Noah fell to the ground cradling his head in his hands,

wondering if he had given himself a concussion, and cursing his latest set of poor choices, including how he had wound up stuck in a janitor's closet.

Kratz! Was he one of *them*? Was he an alien sleeper agent in deep cover? Noah considered the idea for a whole five seconds, then dismissed it. No—Kratz couldn't be one of them. It was clear he wasn't just pretending to be a miserable human being; he actually *was* a miserable human being. Whatever Kratz's deal, he wasn't dealing it from an extraterrestrial deck. Or even a full deck, for that matter.

But what if the aliens who had taken his parents were now employing locals like Kratz to do their dirty work? All the more reason to escape. And so, rather than hurling himself at the door again, Noah slowed down to consider his options logically.

The iron spindle was still attached to the doorknob in his hand, but when he jammed it into the hole, it just spun freely, not engaging at all. What he needed was a tool to trip the latch.

He looked around the little storeroom and found a dusty toolbox. Inside, among the feathery remains of last year's spiders, was a screwdriver. He grabbed it and peered into the hole in the door, hoping to get a glimpse of how the latching mechanism worked—

And he found, a moment later, that his right eye was on the other side of the door. Not just that, but his nose was beginning to make the journey, too.

This was an interesting, if unsettling, development.

Noah recalled that an octopus, if given enough time and motivation, can squeeze its entire body through a space no larger than a dime. Is that what was happening here? For a moment, he couldn't breathe, but then his right nostril emerged from the hole, and he sucked a deep breath through it. All right, then, octopus it is.

Forcing himself through the hole didn't hurt, exactly, but it certainly felt strange to go entirely boneless inch by inch, only to have his bones reform on the other side. *This must be what it feels like to be born*, thought Noah. Then it occurred to him that he might not actually *have* been born. Maybe he was hatched, or grown in a tank. Then it occurred to him that perhaps being stuck halfway through a hole was not the best time to think about this.

Five minutes later, Noah was beginning to feel this was falling into that huge category of really bad ideas. It was taking way too long, and Kratz could come along at any moment, catching him. Perhaps an octopus might have the Zen sort of patience required for this maneuver, but Noah didn't. When he was finally able to wriggle his arms through, he used his hands to push against the door, giving him leverage—but he couldn't push too hard, or he'd rip himself in half. Yes, he had the amphibious ability to grow back fingers, and maybe entire limbs, but he doubted he'd survive his entire bottom half being torn off.

It was right about then, in the midst of the struggle,

that he realized there was another issue he had that an octopus wouldn't. It was something he hadn't considered, and it was too late to consider it now. Because although his body had the ability to squeeze its way through the hole, sadly, his clothes did not, and they were slowly peeling off of him like he was human toothpaste squeezing out of the tube.

• ● •

As soon as Kratz left Noah, he went back outside and sought out the toga-clad man he had bonked with a dinosaur bone. The oddly dressed festivalgoer had regained consciousness and was standing in a daze, as if having a debate with himself over what to do now. Kratz grabbed him and got in his befuddled face.

"I need to talk to your superiors, and I need to talk to them now!" Kratz demanded. But the man did not respond right away—so, to increase his motivation, Kratz pulled out the stolen "laser pointer" and aimed it at him. "If you don't tell me, I will use this!"

The man registered at least fifteen different expressions of panic. "Are you crazy?" he said. "Waving around a thing like that in a place like this?"

"You have five seconds," Kratz informed him.

So the man reached into a fold of his toga, produced a very high-tech-looking phone, and gave it to Kratz. "Call them yourself," he said.

"Fine—tell me the number."

"Pi."

"To what decimal?"

"All of them."

"But pi is infinite."

"Then use speed dial."

But before he could do so, he saw the two agents in charge pushing toward them through the crowd.

"Where's the boy?" Vecca asked. "The museum, you say?"

"I . . . I didn't say anything."

"You will," Rom said. "Go on, make the call."

"But . . . I don't have to—you're already here."

Rom rolled his eyes. "Yes, but we won't have already been here if you don't make the call."

"That's a temporal-loop phone, set seven minutes in retrograde," Vecca explained. "And since it took us almost seven minutes to get here, you should be making that call right about now. So do it!"

And so he did.

• ● •

"He was in there, I swear to you!"

Kratz stood with Vecca and Rom beneath the disapproving bronze gazes of the celebrated physicist Luis Alvarez and his son Walter who famously followed in his footsteps. Kratz's own voice echoed back to him in the lofty space of the rotunda like an accusation.

"You have to believe me! He was here!"

How could Noah have gotten out? The agents had to disintegrate the door to gain access, for goodness' sake! Yet once they had gotten into the janitor's closet, they found Noah had done a disappearing act. All that remained were his clothes, as if he had melted like the Wicked Witch of the West.

"He couldn't have gotten far," Vecca said. "Rom, you take the north wing of the museum; I'll take the south."

And since the museum only had two wings, Kratz had to ask, "What shall I do?"

They both regarded him with a cool gaze he had seen many times before: that "why are you still here?" look.

"Rom, make him go away," said Vecca.

"But . . . we had a deal," insisted Kratz.

"Yes—provided you gave us Noah Prime, which you have not."

"Shall I oysterize him, Vecca?" asked Rom.

Whatever that was, it did not sound even remotely pleasant to Kratz, so he pulled out the "laser pointer," because it seemed to instill fear in the alien outside, and he took aim.

"Hey, that's mine!" said Rom.

"Are you out of your mind, Kratz?" yelled Vecca. "Waving around a thing like that in a place like this? Put it down so we can talk."

"No!" said Kratz. He was not the kind of fool who

would fall for a trick like that. He was a different kind entirely. "If I put this down, he'll caramelize me!"

"*Oysterize*," corrected Rom.

The laser pointer thing Kratz now held seemed to have multiple settings to go with its various buttons. He had no idea what it did besides producing a chess piece, but a weapon was a weapon, and whatever it did would be sufficient. So, before Rom could aim his own weapon and ostracize him, Kratz raised the laser pointer and fired a wide, bright beam of distorted light.

Rom, with lightning-fast reflexes, dove out of the way, and the beam hit the wall behind him, dissolving a hole to a forest beyond. Except there *was* no forest beyond. The museum gift shop should have been on the other side of that wall. Of course, there *had* been a forest there twenty years ago.

But before Kratz could even begin to comprehend the ramifications of creating a portal through time, Rom lunged at him. "Put that thing down before you hurt somebody!" he yelled. Which was a senseless thing to say, because hurting somebody was precisely what Kratz wanted to do.

They struggled over the weapon, and Kratz pressed a different button this time—but Rom pushed his arm down at the last instant. The blast was directed downward, creating a hole in the floor. But it was more than a hole: It was a pit that seemed bottomless.

This time, thanks to Kratz's trial-and-error button pushing, he didn't create a portal in time. Instead, he created a portal through space—and a short portal at that, only about thirty miles to the other end. The problem was, those thirty miles were straight down.

Vecca ripped the weapon away from Kratz. "We should throw you in and be done with you!" she snarled.

Then a bright orange light began to bloom in the depths of the pit, growing brighter.

"Vecca," said Rom, backing away. "I think we have a problem."

Vecca dared to glance into the pit, which was emitting growing waves of heat. Then she turned to Kratz with a terrified glare of accusation. "What have you done?"

It was in that moment that Kratz finally managed to do the math. He had a weapon that could create a hole in the wall that opened on a forest that wasn't there. And a pit that was growing hotter and brighter by the second. That was when it occurred to Kratz that maybe these two weren't government agents after all.

29

In Plain Sight

PEOPLE WEARING CAMOUFLAGE OUTFITS DON'T GET RUN OVER any more than people in ordinary clothes. That's because unless you're a soldier in the desert, or a hunter in the woods, camouflage is utterly and completely useless in hiding your presence.

On the other hand, Noah Prime's unwanted, and entirely unexpected, birthday suit was the absolute best outfit for his survival in the museum. Because, as Kratz had noted with incredible tunnel vision, Noah's skin could change color and texture, truly camouflaging him when he was under severe stress, and could be the basis of actual camouflaged fabric prints if Kratz had his way.

But he wasn't going to get his way—because although the bronze statue of famed physicist Luis Alvarez paid absolutely no attention to the confrontation between Vecca, Rom, and Quantavius Kratz, the bronze statue of his son

Walter did. That was because there *was* no statue of Walter Alvarez in the Arbuckle Museum of Natural History. It was, in fact, Noah Prime, hiding in plain sight, having taken on the exact visual appearance of a bronze statue.

Noah saw the argument play out between Kratz and the aliens in a state of heightened reality. Every sight and sound, every smell, every movement of the air focused his awareness. He could feel the defenses of multiple creatures ready to activate within him, giving him a broader picture of everything happening. He could read that Kratz fully intended to kill the two aliens even before he pulled out the weapon. But oddly, he could also sense that the aliens had no intention to kill Kratz. Which confused him, since they seemed to have such disregard for human life. Or at least Noah's human life. But then Noah wasn't entirely human, was he? It was Noah's first real indication that the carefully curated greenhouse of his life had even more glass to crash against.

The moment Kratz began blasting, Noah saw his moment to escape. He couldn't get back to the closet for his clothes without crossing their line of vision—and if he did that, no amount of camouflage would hide him—so, using the shadow of the real statue as cover, he slipped into the north wing, where he quickly found the display on early humans. And although musty furs and animal skins weren't exactly his style, this was definitely a case of "any port in a storm." He did draw a line at the bear-tooth

320

necklace, though, leaving it on the mannequin. But seeing it made him think about the ridiculous string of pearls the alien woman wore, looped around her neck at least three or four times. Definitely a fashion statement from another era. It made him think of Kaleb Carpenter, who was still in the pocket of his jeans, in the broom closet, and would have to be rescued later—

But wait a moment.

A pearl necklace...that looked like a hundred Kaleb Carpenters...around the neck of the alien in charge. For all of Noah's increased perception, he hadn't had the vision to even consider it. Could it be that the woman actually *wore* her captives? Could Noah's parents be right there in a literal chain gang around her neck?

Noah, now dressed as a caveman in winter, raced back to the rotunda, but when he arrived, all three were gone. And the room had grown far too hot for the heavy furs he wore.

• ● •

Meanwhile, Mr. Ksh and his younger self meandered through the greenery and displays of the town square, enjoying the sights and sounds of FossilFest as if they had all the time in the world. They didn't, of course—they had precisely the amount of time Mr. Ksh already knew they had: not a second less, not a second more.

The Sherpa was at that place in his confusion where he realized his only option was to go with the flow.

"Look at this architecture," Mr. Ksh said in their native Nepali, pointing out the buildings around the perimeter of the park. "It's beautiful, is it not? Remember it. Remember all of this. Every single building around the square."

"Yes, but I thought we were looking for Noah Prime," the Sherpa said.

"We are," admitted Mr. Ksh. "But we won't find him yet, so why waste time looking? Enjoy the moment while we have it."

To the Sherpa, FossilFest reminded him of the Buddha Jayanti Festival in Kathmandu. The flowers and bright colors. The painting of faces and the worship of devout pilgrims from near and far. The Sherpa was no stranger to the idea of ancestor worship—just not the worship of ancestors as ancient as dinosaurs. Leave it to Americans to take things a bit too far.

"When we find Noah, am I to bring him home?" the Sherpa asked.

"No," said Mr. Ksh. "Noah is never going back to Nepal." Then he sighed and put a gentle hand on the Sherpa's shoulder. "And, sorry to say, my friend, neither are you."

• ● •

It took Ogden some time to find Sahara among the debris field of the gymnastics float disaster. Apparently, the truck pulling the gymnastics platform had jackknifed

322

while negotiating a corner, turning the entire float on its side. The half dozen kids doing synchronized floor exercises had found themselves knocked off their feet or their heads, whichever they happened to be standing on at that moment, and Sahara, on the balance beam, scanning the parade route for Noah, was launched skyward. She managed to do a perfect flip, but since she came down through the open sunroof of a parked car, she did not stick the landing.

The parade, though now challenged, rerouted itself around the disaster, treating it like an accident on the side of a freeway—complete with traffic cones, lookie-loos, and that one mysterious shoe that always seems to be there in the aftermath of any accident.

Sahara, who had climbed out of the car, was trying to assist a fellow gymnast, who had somehow gotten stuck in a tree, when Ogden found her.

"Noah's by the lemonade stand!" he told her. "Let's go!"

• ● •

Sahara followed Ogden to the lemonade stand—which appeared to have had its own disaster.

"I don't see him," said Sahara.

"You wouldn't," Ogden told her. "He was in disguise. But something must have happened to him, or he wouldn't have left Andi!"

"Andi? She's here? Where?" When Sahara last saw

Andi, her decapitated body was holding her head in her arms and leading them to safety. Sahara didn't know whether she was looking for a disembodied head or a headless body. Turns out it was neither.

"Right there," Ogden said, pointing at a small pink suitcase.

"She's in the suitcase?"

"No, she *is* the suitcase," Ogden said, kneeling down to it. "Noah told me she's an android who can disguise herself in this form."

"So . . . she's a Transformer . . . who turns into . . . a *suitcase*?"

Ogden sighed. "Well, Optimus Prime she's not."

Ogden tried to figure out how to transform a suitcase back into an annoying little sister, but travel accessories were not his expertise. Then a digital readout appeared on the handle, and it read:

PUSH THE PINK BUTTON, BOZO!

"Yeah, that's her," said Sahara.

Once Ogden pushed the pink button on the handle, the suitcase turned inside out like a puzzle box vomiting, transforming into Andi before their very eyes. Sahara supposed this ought to have shocked or even panicked her. Instead, she took comfort in knowing that she wasn't crazy; the world was.

"That took long enough," said Andi, looking around to make sure her transformation had gone unnoticed. "Where did Noah go?"

"We were hoping you'd know," said Sahara.

Andi glared at them. "In case you hadn't noticed, suitcases don't have eyes."

"They don't have ears, either," Ogden pointed out, "and yet you heard us."

Their conversation was interrupted by the loud wailing of an arriving ambulance, dispatched to triage the sprained ankles and bruised egos of the gymnastics team, as well as tend to the child who had been attacked by the papier-mâché pterodactyl and had still not stopped screaming.

That's when Mr. Ksh arrived at the scene with the bemused Sherpa in tow.

"The ambulance!" said Ksh. "It's time!"

"What?" said Sahara. "Noah's in the ambulance?"

"No! He's in the museum!"

Then Ogden remembered that Ksh had told him everything goes wrong shortly after the ambulance arrives.

"Now we will find Noah in the museum," Ksh said.

"How do you know that?" demanded Andi.

"Because, as I've told Ogden, I've been here before," explained Ksh, pointing to the Sherpa, who was clueless, but only because he was currently experiencing the clues his future self would need. "Let's go," said Ksh, leading the way to the museum. "He'll be dressed like a caveman."

• ● •

True to Ksh's word, they found Noah dressed like a caveman, in a rotunda that was ridiculously hot.

"Noah!" shouted Sahara the moment she saw him. She wanted to throw her arms around him, thrilled that he was actually here and alive—but she resisted the urge. Partially because it would have been a really awkward moment, and partially because she was morally opposed to fur. "Why are you dressed like that?"

"I'll explain later," said Noah, meaning never, "but right now we have to find two aliens and Mr. Kratz!"

"Mr. Kratz?" said Ogden, incredulous.

"Yes! Mr. Kratz!"

But before they could make any sort of plan, the room erupted. Literally. The hole that, for some reason, was in the middle of the stone floor began to spew red-hot magma.

"Watch out!" yelled Sahara. "The floor is lava!" And she pulled Ogden and Noah away from the lava surge. They could all feel the small hairs on their arms begin to singe.

Meanwhile, Ksh and the Sherpa had backed away from the lava into a corner. It was the corner that held the second portal, to what appeared to be a forest far, far away, but wasn't far away at all. It was, in fact, this exact spot, but twenty some years earlier, before the museum was built.

Ksh turned to his frightened and confused younger self and said, *"Hatāra garnuhōs! Tyahām̐ bāṭa jānuhōs!"* Which roughly translates to "Hurry! Go through there!"

To which the Sherpa responded, *"Ma jānē chaina! Malā'ī tyō jaṅgala manapardaina!"* Which roughly translates to "No way! I don't like the looks of that forest!"

But with the approaching lava, Ksh had no time for idle conversation. So he grabbed his younger self and threw him through the portal—but first, Ksh whispered six words into his ear:

"War Emblem. Proud Citizen. Perfect Drift."

And while those might sound like passwords that came with your internet router, they were, in fact, the names of the first-, second-, and third-place horses in the Kentucky Derby nearly twenty years earlier—names he never forgot. It was a trifecta that paid $18,373.20 on the dollar, providing a young Mr. Ksh with all the money he needed to begin his real estate empire.

Once the young Ksh was through, the portal destabilized and collapsed, stranding him in the past to begin his new life. The elder Ksh sighed with intense satisfaction— but also some fear. Because lava had already covered half the floor of the rotunda, the space was getting increasingly oven-like. And the statue, which was right at the leading edge of the lava, was not looking at all well.

"Now what?" asked Ogden.

"I don't know," said Ksh. "From this moment on, I have no idea what happens next."

"I do," said Sahara. "Unless we want to be roasted alive, we get out of here!"

"Not yet!" said Noah. "We can't leave Kaleb Carpenter!"

"Kaleb Carpenter?" said Sahara. "He's here?"

"In my pocket," said Noah. "I'll explain later," meaning never. Then, with a single kangaroo hop, he leaped over the rising lava, retrieved the pearl from his pocket in the broom closet, and leaped back just as the statue of Luis Alvarez keeled like the *Titanic*, then melted into the flaming, bubbling ooze.

30

Mount Arbuckle and the Duck Pond Apocalypse

THERE WAS NO QUESTION THAT THIS YEAR'S FOSSILFEST WOULD be one to remember, provided there was anyone left to remember it.

First came the flying papier-mâché reptile of death.

Then the gymnastics float disaster.

And then the museum spontaneously combusted. Every window burst into flames simultaneously—it seemed as if the bricks themselves were burning. Because they were.

The burning museum quickly became the featured attraction of the festival. It had gone up in flames so quickly, it was hard to believe it was just an ordinary fire. Then the central dome collapsed, and a geyser of lava shot up that set everything around it ablaze. Neighboring buildings, the stalled parade floats—everything was catching fire. Lava burst through the museum doors and flowed down the granite steps, consuming the steps themselves and everything else in its path.

People ran, aliens teleported right out of their skins—it was mayhem the likes of which Arbuckle hadn't seen since the Great Fireworks Mishap of '93—but even that paled when compared to a random volcanic eruption.

The Clydesdales pulling the float with the minor celebrity had never seen lava before, but they instinctively knew it wouldn't be good for their health. They reared, and kicked, and finally tore free from the float and escaped— while the minor celebrity took out her phone, called her agent, and fired him on the spot.

• ● •

Vecca stood with Rom at the far edge of the park, watching the eruption, frustrated beyond belief.

"Well," said Rom, "there's something you don't see every day. Unless you're from Rigel 3."

"We can't let this distract us," Vecca said. "Noah Prime is here somewhere. Let's just find him, terminate him, and be done with this place once and for all."

• ● •

Noah's caveman garb did not have the modern con_venience of pockets, so as he and his friends fled the burning museum, he gave the oysterized Kaleb Carpenter to Ogden, whose pockets were famous for being bottomless.

"Don't lose that," Noah told him.

"I never lose anything," Ogden assured him. "I only misplace things indefinitely."

Noah's senses were still hypercharged. All of his animalistic responses were resting on a hair trigger. He finally felt as if he could access any of them. So many times in the past, they presented themselves without warning or control. That happened when he panicked—but now he knew that if he kept himself focused, he could ride the response instead of letting it ride him.

What he needed now was a way to single out the head alien in the crowd of festivalgoers and fire gawkers. There had to be responses that would do that for him!

"Noah, slow down!" shouted Sahara—but Noah was focused on one thing and one thing only.

"We have to find her! The alien with the pearls. She has my parents!"

He didn't *think* about leaping into the trees like a spider monkey—he just knew he needed a better view of the crowd.

From up in the trees, he could see the entire square: the park, as well as the buildings around it. But clearly, the sense of sight wasn't enough. He needed to employ all of his senses. He didn't *think* about sniffing the air like a bloodhound—nevertheless, his sense of smell kicked into overdrive. Immediately, he was overwhelmed by the aromas of spilled lemonade, failing underarm deodorant, and sulfur from the eruption. All twelve stenches from the Guess That Dinosaur Smell booth assaulted his nostrils—he could tell exactly what each of them was, and that none of them were what they claimed to be. But then, sliding sneakily beneath those odors, was one he had sensed before. In the museum. It was undeniably her scent!

Then, like the golden-cheeked warbler, he sensed the exact direction of the wind, and with the acute vision of a Harris's hawk, he spotted her near the duck pond at the edge of the park. So he leaped down from the trees, hit the ground, and raced with the speed of a cheetah toward the pond.

• ● •

Vecca was not expecting Noah to be searching for her. Her strategy was all about rousting him out of hiding—so when he showed up right beside her, instead of pulling out her disintegration gun, her demolecularizing ray, or her one-touch death spritz, she just stared at him, stunned.

"Hi there," said Noah. Then he reached out and ripped the pearls from her neck.

The chain that held them was a cosmic string fragment. Unbreakable—except, of course, at the one spot where it was fused into a loop. Thus, even cosmic string necklaces could suffer a broken clasp.

The pearls spilled off the string, rolling on the ground at the edge of the pond.

There were too many to count. Dozens bounced away,

spreading out from where they fell. What Noah needed was some way to quickly gather them. And before he even knew what he was doing, out shot his tongue, which was now, like a pangolin's, even longer than his body. It lapped out, and as it sucked in pearl after pearl, Noah's cheeks expanded like a squirrel's.

"Look what you've done!" yelled Vecca. "Give those back to me immediately!"

But Noah had other plans. He had no idea which of the pearls were his parents, but he knew how to find out.

Just add water, Andi had said.

Pushing past Vecca, he squeezed his cheeks together and shot all the pearls out into the duck pond like a shotgun. In seconds, the water began to churn.

• ● •

Kratz, who had managed to lose Rom and Vecca before they could oysterize him, watched the museum eruption from a distance, hiding behind a hedge. He had hatched a brand-new theory, and it wasn't a happy one. He was now convinced that the two so-called government agents were, in fact, demons, and they had lured Kratz into opening the doorway to hell. The fire-breathing fledgling volcano that had once been the Arbuckle Museum of Natural History was proof enough for him. Kratz had triggered the apocalypse, and he fully expected to see the devil himself, with sharp teeth and twisty black horns, rising from the flames, and perhaps thanking Kratz for being released—which, come to think of it, might put Kratz in an advantageous position, so maybe he should stick around, not run. But when a refrigerator-sized chunk of flaming rock landed on the hedge concealing him, he decided that running for his life was still the best course of action.

• ● •

Sahara saw Noah swing through the trees with every bit of grace he had shown when performing on the rings at his unexpected gymnastics exhibition. She was the only one of them on the ground who was able to keep up with him, and she arrived at the duck pond just in time to see Noah get down on all fours, unfurl an impossibly long, prehensile tongue, and lick up pearls from the ground until his cheeks bulged beyond human proportions, then spit the pearls out into the duck pond.

She took it on faith that Noah had an excellent reason for this odd behavior, but when creatures began to bubble out of the pond, she began to wonder if Noah had any idea what he was doing at all.

• ● •

Noah watched the de-oysterized mob of aliens closely, searching for his parents among the beings escaping from the duck pond.

He saw a green lobsterish thing that looked like it

was covered with radioactive jam. A buzzing swarm that seemed to be made entirely of levitating eyeballs. A being that collapsed space around itself, and breathed out little puffs of alternate dimensions. And a cat. Just an ordinary cat—but with an expression of such long-suffering despair, you could swear it was about to start spouting bad poetry.

But within the mob of odd critters, Noah didn't see his parents. Or at least the human skins in which his parents were cloaked.

If Noah had been watching the other creatures a little more closely, he might have noticed a certain urgency propelling them. The kind of urgency that doesn't bode well for a festival full of plump, meaty humans.

• ● •

According to the instruction manual for the Model 35B Polydimensional Oysterizing Ray, the device mimics a natural process. Oysterizing—in an actual oyster—concentrates the oyster's own minerals into a pearl, thereby protecting it from the irritating grain of sand at the center of the pearl.

Under normal circumstances (that is, normal for aliens), an oysterizing ray convinces the universe that the individual it is aimed at is, in fact, a major irritant, and thus the universe responds exactly the way an oyster does, turning the individual into a pearl. To reverse the process, the same oysterizing ray should be used to rehydrate, allowing the natural reabsorption of minerals.

But when an oysterized individual is reverted by other means, such as dunking them in water, that washes away a huge amount of minerals. Leaving the individual suddenly conscious and very hungry.

Ravenously hungry.

Eat-your-own-foot kind of hungry.

So, when the various alien prisoners that Vecca kept wrapped around her neck were freed, they were extremely ready for their next meal.

• ● •

When Kratz, who was now on the other side of the duck pond, saw the creatures, it only reinforced what he already believed. Demons! He had brought forth demons! And one of them had spotted him. A fire-breathing thing with teeth the size of picket fences.

As it came toward him, he pulled out the levitation pen, and the moment it saw the weapon, it stopped.

"*Klaatu barada nikto*," it growled. Which roughly translates to, "Are you out of your mind, waving around a thing like that in a place like this?"

Kratz hit a button, and the creature was sent shooting skyward like a rocket.

• ● •

Mr. Ksh, Ogden, and Andi didn't know the particulars of the alien onslaught. Only that dozens of monsters of multiple horrific varieties were climbing out of the duck pond like clowns out of a car, and they knew they'd better find some cover from the onslaught.

While Andi and Ogden hid nearby, Ksh ran back to his car, planning to drive away and leave the mayhem behind. He had done his part, after all, and assured his own long, healthy life. Or at least until this moment. No telling now when his health or longevity would end. Hence the reason he had ordered a coffin from Mr. Prime, just in case something terrible happened. Such as having his entire car picked up by an angry, muscular creature that, unable to get to the tasty treat inside, hurled it in frustration toward the town's old water tower.

• ● •

Sahara was the only one close to Noah—but he had not seen her before she was set upon by a creature from the pond that seemed to be made entirely of feathers. It didn't do much damage, but it tickled something terrible. It kept her from getting to Noah, and the feathers dancing and flicking around her blocked her view. But she heard every bit of what happened next between Noah and Vecca. And she didn't like the things she heard.

• ● •

Vecca backed away from the flood of alien beings jumping out of the pond. All of her old enemies, now free. Drakl from Cygnus 4, H#Ø§@! from Terminus 6, and Mittens the cat, who had the death sentence in twelve systems. Vecca and her team had only been one step away from completing their kill-all-N.O.A.H.s mission, however this final N.O.A.H. was proving much more difficult than the others. But now, here he was, his back to her, within killing distance! And she would have killed him right then and there, had Mittens not run off with her weapons belt.

Killing Noah Prime with her bare hands—or bare tentacles—was out of the question, because unlike the previous N.O.A.H.s, this one had full access to, and perhaps even some control over, his multispecies traits. If she tried to grab him, he might very well inject her with poison quills, or spit venom in her eye, or something else equally deadly. No—this was best delegated to one of her underlings. Sadly, however, most of her team had abandoned the mission. Well, she still had Rom—but when she looked for him, he was nowhere to be seen. Then she spotted him a moment later, being dragged away by none other than Praxxis the Planet-Mauler—one of her most prized pearls. Praxxis had taken Rom hostage and was using him as a (non)human shield.

She had hoped that one of the escaping prisoners might spot Noah and eat him, but no such luck. They were bounding away from the duck pond, setting their sights on other potential lunches.

Vecca spared a moment for the deepest of sighs. There

was no question this was not one of her better days. She began to wonder whether saving this planet was really worth all this trouble...

• ● •

It was right about then that a team of actual government agents showed up, led by Agent Rigby—the head of the Federal Office of Biological Experimentation (FOBE). It was the same office that Kratz used to run, before he accidentally gave an unwanted appendage to half the personnel. So, when she spotted Kratz in the crowd fleeing from the epicenter of the disaster, she wasn't entirely surprised.

"Kratz!" she yelled when she saw him. "What's going on here?"

Kratz stopped short, seeing his former assistant— toward whom he still held a grudge, since she had been the one who ratted him out.

"Why, hello, Eleanor," he said, as a fireball zoomed overhead. "What brings you to Arbuckle?"

But she was in no mood for small talk. "Is this one of *your* disasters?"

"Of course not!" Kratz said with supreme indignation. "It was like that when I got here."

"We were dispatched to investigate reports of radiation anomalies consistent with either solar flares or a gravitational wormhole—but now it appears to be nothing more than volcanic activity."

"Ha!" said Kratz with a rueful chuckle. "That's what *you* think!"

Rigby instructed her team to take readings and record the geological event. "I want every detail!" Rigby ordered.

Then Kratz leaned in close. "The devil is in the details, Eleanor," he whispered. "And I do mean that literally." Then he turned and took off into the woods.

• ● •

Noah leaned over the pond, looking at the settling water, hoping beyond hope that his parents were still in there, trying to climb out.

But the last of the aliens had left.

"Are you really that selfish?"

Noah turned to see the head alien—the one called Vecca—watching him with weary contempt. "So selfish that you'd sacrifice everyone you love, everything you know—your entire world—just so you can continue to live?"

"I don't know what you're talking about!" Noah said. "Now give me back my parents, or I'll go Wolverine on you. Or worse than Wolverine—and believe me, there's plenty worse in me!"

But Vecca's expression changed: from contempt to surprise. "Do you really not know what I'm talking about? They never told you?"

"Told me what?"

340

Then her expression changed again: from surprise to pity.

"You poor, poor lesser being," she said. "Don't you understand that you hold within your DNA the entire biodiversity of animal life on this planet?"

"I already know that—I'm not an idiot!"

"Well, has it ever occurred to you why someone would create a thing such as you?"

Noah resented being called a "thing." So he dug down and answered with pride at the being he was. "To advance human evolution!" he declared. "And you want to stop it!"

To that, Vecca laughed. "Is that what they told you? Or did you come up with that yourself?"

He couldn't stand how smug this alien was. "I know what I know."

Then she looked at him with such pity that it made him even angrier. "What you know is a drop in the bucket compared to what you don't know," Vecca said. "The truth is, my little test tube, that you were created to preserve a sample of every animal on Earth...after life on Earth is destroyed."

"You mean...you're going to destroy the world?"

Vecca sighed. "No, your *parents* want to do that. I'm here to *save* the world. By destroying *you*."

Noah found his head swimming and bubbling like the duck pond, with alien thoughts too horrible to consider. So he shut them down. He refused to even think about it. She was lying. Trying to trick him. It had to be! There was no room for any other truth.

"I'll make a deal with you, Noah," Vecca said. Her voice regained its silky smoothness. "If your parents mean that much to you, you can have them."

Then she pushed back her hair, reached for her pearl earrings, and took them off.

"I'll free them right now," Vecca said, holding the two pearls out to him. "In exchange for you."

Noah couldn't take his eyes off the two pearls glistening in her palm.

"Your life for theirs."

31

Prepare to Die

THE UNIVERSE IS FULL OF TERRIFYING THINGS. ROGUE BLACK holes hurtling through space at five million miles per hour. Cannibalistic galaxies slowly devouring one another. The Screaming Skull Nebula, furious at the fact that in space, no one can hear it scream.

Fortunately for Earth, most of the truly terrible things are terribly far away. Too far away for them to even notice that Earth exists. But every once in a while, something truly awful does notice. Such as a species of terraformers, looking for a nice planet to completely erase, then remodel to its own liking.

Of course, a species that advanced would also have a very high code of moral conduct and follow some very strict and unbreakable rules. Rules like:

Never kill a planet without first preserving a sample of all forms of life there.

That way, the planet's biodiversity would not be lost—it would be stored in living samples that could then be used to create a zoo. A zoo that would contain a bit of everything from the murdered planet. It was a hard-and-fast rule of planetary terraforming. Without getting that sample, life on the planet could not legally be erased. And even a murderous civilization would only murder legally.

With that in mind, anyone who wanted to save Earth—or at least delay its destruction—could do so by killing those precious samples. Which is precisely what Vecca and Rom had been trying to do: Kill Noah, to save Earth.

• ● •

"Your life for theirs," Vecca said, holding out Noah's oysterized parents to him.

Noah might have made the deal. He was tired of fighting, tired of running—and the seed of uncertainty Vecca had planted in him about his reason for existing . . . well, it was just enough to tip the scale toward sacrificing himself.

But before he could make the deal, a blast came out of nowhere and ripped Vecca right out of her human skin, revealing her true form: a mass of tangled tentacles, and on each tentacle, a terrible, sharp-toothed mouth.

Noah turned in the direction of the blast, to see that it was none other than his backup father who had fired the shot, arriving not a second too soon.

"No deals!" his backup father said, firing again, but

the creature that was Vecca grabbed a lamppost with one of her tentacles and pulled herself out of the way, dodging the second blast.

"I take it you have your memories back," he said to Noah.

"And I know you're not my father, so you don't have to pretend."

"It's no pretense, Noah. Being your backup parents is our sole purpose in life." He shot again, but the Vecca-thing was quick, and she dodged again.

"Come with me, Noah!" his backup father said. "I'll get you off-planet to safety!"

Off-planet, thought Noah. *But what happens to the planet once I'm gone?*

Noah never got to ask that all-important question, because a blast out of nowhere hit his backup father square in the chest, ripping him out of his human skin as well.

It was Rom—who had managed to escape from Praxxis's grasp—and unlike the blast that had grazed Vecca, this one left a wound the size of a baseball, out of which bloomed a warm blue light. Without his skin, his backup father wasn't a glob of tentacles like Vecca's species. He was *all* blue light. Beautiful . . . calming . . . and dying.

Noah knelt on the ground next him, but he didn't know what he could possibly do.

"Hurry," his backup father said weakly. "The ship is waiting for you, just one klick north. You can make it, I know you can."

345

Noah had so many questions, but the only one he could think to ask was, "How far is a klick?"

His backup father chuckled in his pain. "I wish...I wish I could have gotten to know you better, Noah. And that maybe you might have come to see us as more than just a replacement for your real fake parents. But know that we loved you as much as anyone could..."

And with that, he closed his eyes, then dissolved into a pool of light that made the grass grow three inches in a matter of seconds.

Noah felt his grief and anger—along with the strength of all the predator DNA in his blood—well up inside him. His nails sharpened to points, his teeth became fangs, his hair became quills. He rose to his feet and glared at Rom.

"My name is Noah Prime. You killed my backup father. Prepare to die!"

He ran toward Rom, ready to tear whatever was inside that skin into tiny pieces of shark bait.

Rom raised his weapon and fired, but Noah was too fast, evading each blast as he got closer—and when Rom realized that no amount of weapon technology was going to save him, he turned and ran, screaming like a small human child. (Later, he would claim it was the war cry of his species, but no one would believe him.)

Then Noah turned toward Vecca, who had recovered the two pearls.

"Give them to me!" Noah demanded. But although he had scared Rom, Vecca was not so easily intimidated.

"This isn't over, Noah." Which is what villains usually say when it is. Then she scuttled backward on all twelves until she was out of sight.

• ● •

The hungry creatures were not having much luck catching humans, which were unusually stubborn when it came to self-preservation. Then one of them noticed the festival's abandoned food trucks and began to rip one open like a tin of canned ham. Before long, the others caught on and did the same.

Meanwhile, Ogden and Andi fought bravely against the swarming eyeball creature—Andi blasting the ocular menaces with laser precision, and Ogden smacking them away in a display of his advanced whack-a-mole skills. They made it back to the duck pond just in time to see lava spill into it, causing it to boil.

A strange, feathery creature that seemed somewhat humanoid was struggling toward Noah, who sat despondent in a patch of overgrown grass. Andi powered up her lasers...but something about that creature gave Ogden pause.

"Wait," he told Andi. She hesitated just long enough for Sahara to emerge from the flock of feathers, which then flitted off toward the food trucks. Sahara ran to Noah and pulled him away from the edge of the pond before the lava could reach him.

Noah felt beaten. Vecca still had his parents, his backup father had given his life to save him, and things were no better off than when this whole thing started.

He could have just sat there and let the lava consume him—but Sahara wouldn't have it. She pulled him to his feet.

"After everything we've been through, I'm not letting you give up now, so don't even think about it!"

Ogden and Andi joined them, and they escaped the burning, boiling park. They didn't stop running until they were in the safety of the nearby woods, where they took a moment to catch their breaths. Andi did a scan of the immediate area to confirm that they were alone.

"We have to get Noah to safety," Andi said. "You might have scared Vecca off for the moment, but it's her mission to kill you, and she'll be back with reinforcements."

Then Sahara approached Noah. She wasn't even sure how to ask, but she knew she had to. "Noah, I heard what that alien said to you. Do you think it's true?"

Noah backed away, as if the suggestion itself was a betrayal. "You saw what she was! Underneath that human skin, she was a disgusting monster! You saw!"

But Sahara kept her cool. "Just because something's ugly . . . that doesn't mean it's evil. . . ."

"Are you kidding me? She wants to kill me!"

Ogden raised a hand, as if in class. "I've sometimes wanted to kill you."

"But she actually tried. She killed off a whole bunch of other versions of me! Andi—tell them! Tell them what that monster said is a lie!"

Andi shrugged. "I didn't hear what she said."

And so Sahara explained Mr. Ksh's ark theory—and how it was right on target. You don't create an ark . . . unless something is about to be destroyed.

"Ha!" shouted Ogden, as if he had just solved a particularly difficult equation. "Your parents are the enemies of humanity! It makes perfect sense!"

"No!" insisted Noah, still in denial. He could feel tears beginning to come to his eyes, but he fought them back. "It makes no sense! How could you . . . how could you even suggest it? You know my parents, Ogden! They're good people."

And no one dared to suggest that, technically, they weren't "people" at all.

"If it's true," said Ogden, pacing as he worked it out, "then there would need to be samples of all kinds of life. Not just animals, but plants, and insects."

Sahara gasped. "Like your mom's greenhouse! I've never seen so many beautiful flowers! And didn't you say she had a prize orchid?"

As much as Noah tried to block it out, a memory came

to him. His mom so tenderly, lovingly cultivating those plants. How carefully she collected the seeds from her special one. *"It's all about the seeds,"* she had once told him. Could the seeds from that orchid have contained DNA from every plant on Earth?

"And the manslaughter hornets!" blurted Ogden. "They looked like a little bit of a whole lot of bugs. And remember how your dad never wanted to get rid of the hive."

"Because he respected nature...," Noah said, but he was losing his conviction. The more light his friends shed on his life, the harder it was to deny. The more he wanted to run from it, the larger the truth loomed before him.

Could what Vecca said be true?

He thought of his father's workshop. The care his dad took working the wood of his designer caskets. His dad would always speak to Noah about his work: warm philosophical musings about the cycle of life. The way things must die to make room for other things. What was it he said? *"This world is an impermanent place. Nothing lasts forever, and nothing should."* Noah assumed it was his father's way of making peace with his purpose. Well, maybe it was. Because maybe he wasn't just building wooden coffins—maybe he was preparing a virtual coffin for the entire planet.

Noah wanted so badly to talk to his parents—to have them tell him that it just wasn't true. That they were the good guys, and that monstrous, hideous Vecca was the enemy.

Through all of this, Andi was silent. It was that silence

more than anything that pushed Noah toward seeing the facts for what they were. His tears began to flow now, and he didn't even try to stop them.

"Tell me the truth, Andi," he said "I deserve to know! Was it our parents' mission not just to protect me . . . but to also destroy the world?"

Andi hesitated far too long before answering.

"Define 'destroy,'" she said.

Noah turned away. He had denied the truth—convincing himself that Vecca was lying. But here was proof that she wasn't. He couldn't look at Andi anymore—couldn't look at any of them. His world had already been turned upside down. He thought nothing could be worse. But now it was being turned inside out as well.

Andi approached him and tried to put a hand on his shoulder, but he pulled away. She began to speak gently.

"We got the seeds and the hive off-planet before our house was destroyed and Mom and Dad were captured," Andi said, "but we couldn't remove you from your environment until you matured. You weren't ready—but given the events of the past couple of weeks, your genetic matrix has been fully activated."

Noah squeezed his eyes tight, trying to stem the flood of tears, but he couldn't. He wished he could become something else, anything else. But no animal trait took hold—because it was his humanity that was the best defense against this dark, terrible moment.

"There's a ship waiting for us, Noah," Andi told him. "Just over the next hill. We need to go." Then she glanced at Noah's friends. "I'm sure there's room for Ogden and Sahara on the ship, too."

Noah finally looked at her. "But what about their families? And all our friends? And our town? And our world? What about everyone else, Andi?"

Andi sighed. "Like I said, I'm sure there's room for Ogden and Sahara."

And so that was it. The whole horrible truth of his existence. Noah lived so that everyone else—every*thing* else—could die.

There was only one thing left he could ask.

"Why?"

Andi took her time in answering. "When you build a house, do you ever stop to think about the ant colonies you destroy?" she said. "The millions of things that die just so that you can have a sparkling new place to live?"

"This is nothing like that!"

"It's exactly like that!" Andi insisted. "Your species has always been about devastating indigenous life, large and small. Even your own kind. Well, the ones who made me are the same. They want to build something new on this planet. To them, you're all like the ants and the worms churned up by bulldozers."

"And our parents believe that? YOU believe that?"

"What I believe doesn't matter," Andi said. "And if it

352

were up to me, you would never have known. We would have taken you away from here to live an amazing life. A single vial of your blood would create a beautiful earth habitat that you could visit whenever you wanted. You would be like royalty out among the stars."

"And I would never know what happened to Earth . . ."

"You would never know," admitted Andi. "To protect you from the pain of it."

Noah tried to let it all sink in, but it was more like a flow of lava: It didn't sink in; instead, it scorched everything in its path.

"If it means anything, Mom and Dad do love you, Noah," Andi told him. "They honestly and truly love you."

Finally, a new determination began to fill him. "Love me, love my world," Noah said. "They can't have it any other way. I won't let them."

Then he stepped away from Andi and his friends, and began shouting to the forest at the top of his lungs.

"*Vecca!*" he yelled. "*Vecca! I'm here! Hurry! Hurry up and kill me before it's too late!*"

Ogden and Sahara had stood back, watching the heartbreaking conversation between Andi and Noah—but when Noah started calling out for Vecca, they knew they had to do something. It took both of them to bring Noah down, but because he had so little fight left in him, they were able to pin him to the ground. Sahara clamped her hand firmly over Noah's mouth so he couldn't scream.

"Quiet!" she told him. "I have an idea."

Noah finally stopped struggling, and she took her hand from his mouth.

"What?" he asked bitterly. "What could possibly fix this?"

"Simple," said Sahara. "You, Noah Prime, have to die."

32

Idiot's Guide to the End of the World

THE DEEP-EARTH PORTAL FINALLY COLLAPSED, CUTTING OFF THE source of the lava, and the fiery flow stopped as suddenly as it had begun—but not before leaving a volcano that stood twice as high as the trees, now the tallest point in Arbuckle.

Mr. Ksh—who had survived his Cadillac-hurling ordeal, thanks to a combination of luck and second-generation airbags—managed to climb out of his car through the sunroof. The vehicle was now firmly wedged in the water tower, looking somewhat like a sinking ship, if ships sank in a sea of rusted metal. Bruised and bleary, he sat perched on the trunk, taking in the view and pondering what was to come next for him.

For more than twenty years, he had always known what would happen next. Few specifics, but certainly all the major disasters and triumphs that befell the world—and the knowledge that he would build the very town center that he just saw utterly destroyed. What a strange feeling to suddenly be subject to the unknowable flow of time once more. But he had to admit there was magic to the mystery of the coming moment.

From his perch, he could see the volcano that now dominated the landscape. Beyond the ruins of the square, more trees and several homes were burning. But now that the lava flow had stopped, firefighters were quickly bringing it all down to a steaming sizzle.

He couldn't see any of the creatures that had emerged from the duck pond. They had all gone their merry ways, stepping out into the world to do whatever it is such unearthly creatures did.

He had no idea what had become of Noah Prime and his friends. After Ksh figured a way down from the water tower, he would have to find out, because if they had survived, he expected they might still need his help. And what kind of Sherpa would he be if he couldn't lead them off this particular mountain?

• ● •

While Rom tried to explain away his untimely surge of cowardice, Vecca was attended to by several underlings who sewed her back into her human skin.

"We could just make you a new skin," one of them suggested.

"Out of the question," Vecca said. "A new one will be far too stiff until it's broken in. Besides, this skin and I have been through a lot together." Vecca was proud to wear its battle scars—which, in this case, was a thick line of stitches that ran down one side of her face and all the way to her toes.

While she would much rather not have to wear a skin at all, it was necessary here on Earth, because this world was not kind to her kind. The harshness of hard surfaces bruised her—and those hideous things called trees! The way they dropped daggers on her! Those pine needles were like broken glass on the ground, shredding her tender tentacles. Escaping from a fully activated Noah Prime without the protection of a human skin had been an agonizing ordeal. *Ugh! This place!* No wonder her terraforming enemies wanted to erase it all.

But just because something was ugly, that did not make it bad. Repugnant or not, life on Earth deserved to exist. Her whole species believed that. Thus, they waged an endless war against terraformers. She had to remind herself that there was a noble reason she was putting herself at risk to preserve life on this planet. If she succeeded in killing the last N.O.A.H., no one on it would know what she and her team had done for them . . . but that was all right. That was as it should be. She hardly needed human praise; if she succeeded in her mission, she would be acknowledged and respected by those in the universe who truly mattered.

Meanwhile, Rom had given up making excuses for his behavior, and he attempted to redeem himself by doubling his efforts in getting the mission back on track.

"I've located a faint spatial distortion in the woods just over that hill," he informed Vecca.

Vecca perked up "The terraformers' ship?"

"It would seem so, yes."

Vecca jumped into action, ordering her team to fan out and take strategic positions in the woods around the enemy ship. "We can't let them find the boy before we do," she told them. "If they get him aboard that ship, it's over."

The mission was hard enough before—but now that Noah Prime's genetic matrix was activated, he could be removed from the planet. And a Nascent Organic Aggregate Hybrid—a N.O.A.H.—that was "fully cooked" was the last step before planet-wide destruction.

"We have to kill him before he gets to that ship!" Vecca declared. "I will not lose this world like we lost the last ones!"

• ● •

Vecca and Rom's previous mission was the very definition of a galactic fail. It involved five lush and verdant moons orbiting a giant gas planet. Each moon teamed with life, some of which was highly evolved—but not evolved enough to conceive what was about to happen to them.

Each of the five worlds had multiple N.O.A.H.s to

track down and destroy. Vecca never even came close to finding them all before they matured and were spirited off each world. Then, in one blazing moment, the terraformers ignited the gas giant into a star, which instantly killed off all life on its moons. Vecca lost half her team in the firestorm. Those five moons had now become five dead planets orbiting the new sun. Planets that were slowly cooling into a habitable range.

Vecca and her team had been able to uncover the plan for Earth, which was no less catastrophic. Instead of fire, however, Earth's doom would be water—in the form of a redirected comet. The terraformers weren't planning anything so inelegant as a comet strike. Instead, the comet—which was mostly ice and frozen water vapor—would be guided into a low Earth orbit and irradiated. As it melted, it would flood the entire planet with radioactive rain, which would submerge the continents and poison the sea. The deluge would leave the planet ready for whatever the terraformers wanted to do with it.

Which, in this case, was to turn it into a water park.

• ● •

The woods around Arbuckle were awash in the bitter stench of sulfur—a product of the eruption. Somewhere in those woods were escaped beings that had no business being here on Earth but were determined to make better life choices than the ones that had left them incarcerated around Vecca's neck. They made plans for an earthly future, figuring out how to adapt and peacefully blend in.

Kratz was still in the woods, too, racing to distance himself from the creatures he still believed to be demons. To Kratz, that smell of sulfur—also called brimstone—proved his theory, because it was well-known that brimstone was the stench of hell, and he wondered what was in store for him now. There were how-to books for nearly everything, but there was no *Idiot's Guide to the End of the World.*

Elsewhere in the forest, the refreshing sulfuric breeze blew past Vecca and her team as they desperately tried to reach Noah before he could be spirited off-world in a ship that bent light around it, rendering it invisible to eyes that only saw in three dimensions.

Long tongues of lava that had spilled out into the woods had begun to crust over and harden. Now they looked like steaming black rivers of volcanic rock. They no longer flowed, but they still radiated waves of heat.

It was near the hot edge of one of those black-rock rivers where Vecca caught up with Noah Prime. He and his friends were making their way to the hidden ship, but they couldn't cross the hot stone, which would broil them the second they tried. In other words, they were trapped!

Vecca's team emerged from the woods, attracting their attention, while Rom snuck in from the side, catching Andi by surprise. He tapped a button at the nape of her neck, promptly collapsing her into a suitcase before she could activate any of her defensive weapons. Then he ripped out the beryllium sphere and hurled it into the woods.

Noah and his young accomplices were now weaponless and outnumbered—and although the boy's animal defenses might have been enough to fend off Vecca before, she knew he didn't stand a chance against her entire team.

She was about to order her team to fire at will, but before she could utter a syllable, a distorted version of a familiar face arrived to save the day. Or, more accurately, to save Noah and destroy the day. Noah's backup mom and a squad of terraformers swooped down from their hidden ship above, to wage a major assault against Vecca's team.

Vecca had feared it would come to this: a face-to-face gunfight with the enemy. Her team turned their weapons on the enemy squad, while Noah and his friends dropped to the ground to keep from being caught in the crossfire.

"No!" Vecca yelled to her team. "Don't let them draw your fire! We have one target and one target only!"

But her team was already too caught up in the battle. Only Vecca kept her eyes on the prize. Ignoring the flashing melee, and her rapidly disintegrating comrades, she made eye contact with the troublesome N.O.A.H., raised her weapon, and fired.

Vecca was an excellent shot—but Noah, tapping into the phenomenal reflexes of the star-nosed mole, bounded away just in time.

"Run, Noah!" shouted Sahara. But he had nowhere to run—he was backed against the river of crusted lava, too hot for an ordinary human to cross. However, as everyone already knew, Noah was no ordinary human.

He leaped like an impala, cutting an arc over the crusted lava. For a moment, it looked as if he might escape—but this time, luck was on Vecca's side, because halfway into the leap, Noah smashed his head against a low-hanging branch. He fell, coming down right on top of the superheated lava rock. His caveman furs began to catch fire.

Vecca dodged a blast from one of the terraformers, then turned back toward Noah, who rolled off of the blazing-hot rock, crying out in pain.

His backup mother changed her weapon setting and fired an ice ray that froze the air around Noah to cool him down. Then Noah, both singed from the heat and shivering from the sudden cold, lifted his head weakly.

"I . . . don't feel so good . . ."

What happened next was awful to watch, even for Vecca.

Noah's flesh began to bubble and churn as if there were giant beetles beneath his skin. Then he started to swell and stretch, his body filling with blubber in response to the freezing ray. His eyes practically disappeared into his swelling face.

"His genetic matrix is failing!" shouted his backup mom. "We have to stabilize him before it's too late!" She moved toward him, but Noah sprouted spiny spikes like a sea urchin's, making him impossible to even approach.

Vecca saw him open his mouth to scream, but instead he expelled a projectile puke of squid ink as thick as motor oil all over Vecca, while at the same time spraying his backup mother from his other end with rancid skunk funk. He seemed to turn inside out right before their eyes, over and over again, his wailing voice changing pitch and octave, sounding like a one-man stampede of a thousand animals.

Then, just at the moment it seemed as if he might explode, he began to deflate like a balloon... until all that remained was the lifeless body of a boy, bloated and blue, seeming to decompose like a dead whale on a hot beach.

Noah Prime was... dead?

All was now silence. No one dared speak. The only sound was the buzzing of flies that were beginning to swarm. The putrid stench of decay was so overpowering, the others had to back off. Only Sahara was willing to endure it. She knelt in tears beside Noah, mourning her friend.

"Goodbye, Noah...," she whispered.

Vecca could not help but gloat in her victory, grinning even as she wiped squid ink from her face. "Mission accomplished."

"So what?" Noah's backup mom snapped. "This is nothing. A setback, that's all." She pulled on her left ear to straighten out her face, but it only succeeded in making her nose point north.

"Oh, really?" taunted Vecca. "How long will it take you to prepare a new set of N.O.A.H.s? Thirteen earth years? Fourteen?"

"Earth years are short," Noah's backup mom said, trying to hide the sting of defeat, but not doing a very good job of it. "You haven't saved this world; you've just delayed the inevitable."

"Well then," said Vecca, "I'll be back in fourteen years to delay it again. And again, and again." Then Vecca signaled to Rom. "Rom, please erase the humans' memories."

"Well, I would," said Rom, "but my cerebral hypercube appears to be missing."

Vecca sighed. "Of course it is." Then she turned to Ogden and Sahara. "Fine, keep your memories. At this point, it doesn't matter, and I don't want to spend another second on this awful little rock you call home. I saved it, and now I'm happy to leave it."

Then she and her team withdrew, as did all the terraformers, except for Noah's backup mom, who, like Ogden and Sahara, mourned Noah's death. When the wind changed enough for her to approach Noah's body without gagging, she knelt beside Sahara. "I wish...I wish I could have known him more than I did," she told Sahara. "He was an exceptional human being. Special in so many ways."

Then Ogden stepped forward. "Well . . . can you at least take me?" he asked. "So it's not a total loss?

She tugged her drooping chin to a more pleasant angle, in an attempt to smile. "Not today," she said. "But you were both true friends to Noah. I understand that Andi promised you passage to safety. When the time comes, there will be room for you and Sahara on our ship, just as Andi promised."

Ogden and Sahara turned to glance at Andi. She lay there in the dirt, like a forlorn carry-on that never got carried on.

"Poor thing," said Noah's backup mom. "You'll recycle her, won't you?"

Sahara stared at her, not sure she heard correctly. "Wait—you're just leaving her?"

The motherish alien shrugged. "There are newer models. You know how it is with old technology."

Sahara scowled. "The *real* Mrs. Prime wouldn't just abandon her."

"Well, 'the real Mrs. Prime' isn't here, is she? She and her partner were foolish enough to allow themselves to be captured. Perhaps they failed because they got too sentimental." Then she adjusted a setting on her blaster and aimed it at Noah.

"What are you doing?" demanded Sahara.

"Disintegrating his remains, of course. It's the least I can do."

But Sahara stood between Noah and the blaster. "Don't you dare!" she growled. "At least allow him the dignity of a human burial."

The mother-ish alien considered it for a moment, then put her weapon away. "You may engage in whatever death ritual you see fit. As I recall, there's a casket just his size at our backup house in the Himalayas, should you wish to retrieve it."

Then, without as much as a goodbye, she climbed up a set of stairs that couldn't be seen and vanished into a ship that wasn't observably there.

The roar of an engine, a whoosh of wind, and the ship was on its way back to a star that human astronomers had yet to discover.

Sahara and Ogden knelt reverentially by Noah, as if paying final respects to their fallen friend. Then Sahara said, "They're gone."

And the rotting corpse of Noah Prime sat up like the walking dead.

"Ugh," he said. "I have such a headache."

33

FOBE

THERE ARE ALWAYS TWO SIDES IN ANY BATTLE.

Both are adamant in their beliefs, and both are willing to do anything—not just to win, but to make sure that the other side loses. Whatever the situation, wherever in the universe the battle unfolds, it's the same. And even worse, both sides are eternally convinced that the end justifies the means, no matter how terrible the means might be. Sadly, it is always those who find themselves caught between the two warring sides who suffer the most.

With that in mind, there was only one way to save both Noah and the earth—and that was to make *both* sides believe Noah was dead.

Sahara was the mastermind who planned it—but it took all four of them to make it work. It required Ogden's knowledge of weird earth critters: knowledge that neither the Noah killers nor the terraformers bothered to learn.

Such as the fact that the Pompeii worm could withstand temperatures that would boil any other living thing. Or the way the hognose snake can fool predators by not just playing dead—but also *smelling* dead. It took Andi's tactical triangulation of both enemy forces to move the four of them through the woods in such a way that both sides would converge on them at the same time. And it took Noah's skill at calling up dozens upon dozens of animalistic reactions to simulate a total meltdown, while surviving an actual meltdown when he dropped on the crusted lava.

Noah particularly enjoyed squirting Vecca with squid ink. Yes, she was here to save the world, but that didn't mean Noah had to like her.

Then, when he had finished his grand performance, Noah stopped his heart like a wood frog and held his breath like a sea turtle, as he played the hognose snake stinking of rot.

When his backup mom knelt beside Sahara, he was tempted to jump up and go "Boo!" But luckily, he restrained himself.

"I knew you could do it!" said Sahara.

"Not me," admitted Ogden. "I was about ninety-nine percent certain of failure. I hate being wrong, but this time I'll live with it."

Noah took a few deep breaths, pushing away the last of the animal responses, becoming fully himself once more—although he could never again be sure what his true self was. He was a little bit of so many things.

"Ogden, why don't you go get Andi's beryllium sphere," Noah said. "Rom threw it that way."

"Is that a good idea?" Sahara said. "I mean, yes, she helped us, but now we know she's not exactly on Earth's side."

"She's my sister," Noah said. "And she's on *my* side. Besides, once she finds out they were ready to toss her away like an old iPhone, there's no way she'll help them."

Ogden retrieved the sphere—but even before they could reactivate Andi, their situation took a final unexpected turn. Out of the trees came yet another armed, battle-clad team, weapons trained on them.

"Oh no," said Ogden. "What now?"

It took a moment for them to realize that this squad didn't just appear human, they *were* human. Kevlar armor and rifles—they were some sort of SWAT team, or black-ops regiment. Then, once the kids were surrounded, a woman with a severe expression, a severe haircut, and an even more severe suit came striding out of the woods.

"Noah Prime, you are being taken in for questioning," she said. "And we certainly have a lot to discuss."

"Who are you?" Noah demanded.

She flashed her badge. "Agent Rigby. Federal Office of Biological Experimentation."

"Government agents? Are you serious?" Noah looked around at the absurdly human black-ops team, with their absurdly human weapons, and he began to snicker. Which made Sahara and Ogden begin to giggle, and before long it blew up into a full-fledged laugh attack.

Agent Rigby was not amused.

"I assure you, Mr. Prime, this is no joke. This is very serious business."

But that just made them laugh even harder. This was like the mall cop showing up after Godzilla had left.

"Sure, why not?" said Noah, holding his hands out to her. "Cuff me or whatever. I'll play along!"

Which just made Ogden and Sahara roll on the ground in a side-aching guffaw fest that showed no signs of ending anytime soon.

• ● •

"Well, at least nobody died," Noah Prime said. *Or at least no one human*, he thought—although he couldn't really be sure of that. He offered Agent Rigby a half-hearted grin and tried to shrug, but the various cuffs and chains that held him firmly to the chair made shrugging difficult.

"Believe me, Mr. Prime, in this world, there are worse things than death."

Noah was already getting tired of this. After all he'd been through, he did not want to put on a show for however many government agents were watching him from the other side of the huge one-way mirror. He had to be careful of what he said. If he gave too little information, they'd just hold him longer, and if he gave too much information, they'd never let him go.

"I suppose you want to know about the volcano," he said. "And the monsters that crawled out of the duck pond."

From her expression, it was clear she didn't even know about the monsters yet. Darn.

"You could also tell me how that Cadillac ended up stuck in a water tower a hundred feet from the ground," added Agent Rigby. "But let's start with why you're dressed as a caveman."

"Uh . . . it's the newest look," he said. "You should give it a try."

• ● •

Agent Rigby had run many interrogations in her day. The fact that this boy was not unglued by the things he had experienced was beginning to unnerve *her*, but she couldn't let that show. He asked for a bathroom break, but she would not oblige. Not until he gave her at least some information.

"When you were six years old, you drowned."

"*Almost* drowned."

"*Should* have drowned."

Noah had been on her agency's radar since he was inexplicably found beside a salmon conveyor upriver that day. He was by no means a center of attention, just a file that

371

slowly grew with each odd incident they logged. Clearly, he was not clueless about all these incidents, but the more she pushed for answers, the fewer he gave. She couldn't help but feel that Noah Prime was treating this whole thing as a charade. He dodged and parried, bantered and evaded. At one point, he asked about his friends, who were being held in a different wing of the facility. Agent Rigby hoped she might be able to use them as a bargaining chip to get some information from Noah, but still he didn't bite.

"Noah, whoever interrogates you next won't be nearly as pleasant as I am," she told him. "For all of our sakes, please tell me what you know."

Noah looked her in the eye—a troubling gaze that made her shiver. "What I know is a drop in the bucket compared to what I don't know."

Just then, one of her colleagues burst into the room.

"Agent Rigby, excuse the intrusion," he said, "but we have a code crimson, followed immediately by a code turquoise."

"Crimson and turquoise? Are you serious?"

"I'm afraid so."

"Do those things have anything to do with my friends?" Noah asked.

The intruding agent gave no answer.

"I'm not done with you," Agent Rigby said—which is what government agents always say when they are.

"Can't I at least go to the bathroom while you're gone?"

She considered it for a moment, then called in one of the guards who was just outside the room. "Take him to the bathroom, but keep him cuffed," she ordered. "And with an escort of five armed guards."

"Five?"

"You heard me! Five!"

Then Agent Rigby stormed out, her heels clicking a rapid, steady beat on the linoleum floor.

Her agency had a convoluted and complex color-coding system for unexpected events. A code crimson was an incident involving artificial intelligence. A code turquoise was a prisoner escape by use of advanced weaponry—and although at one point in her life Agent Rigby was a rocket scientist, it didn't take one to figure out what had happened.

"Tell me," she said to the other agent as they made their way toward the sound of blaring alarms. And he informed her that Noah Prime's suitcase—which they had been trying to open—was, in fact, not a suitcase at all but an intelligent weapon system.

"When they installed the power source, it activated!" explained the agent. "From what I understand, it was some sort of terrifying doomsday machine!"

Apparently, this diabolical device burned holes in steel walls like a chunk of Swiss cheese. Only after it had escaped did they realize that it didn't escape alone. It had managed to take Noah's friends with it.

When Agent Rigby arrived at the scene, she quickly surveyed the damage. By the precision of the laser blasts, she could tell this was incredibly advanced technology. Perhaps Russian or Chinese.

"We've scrambled all resources searching for them," the head of security told her.

"The only thing that will be scrambled will be the brains of whoever let this happen!" Agent Rigby told him—although she knew that this happened entirely on her watch, which meant it was all on her.

Well, at least they still had the focus of their investigation.

But when she got back to Noah Prime's cell, he wasn't there. He was still in the bathroom, with the five-guard escort waiting outside the door.

"You mean you didn't go in with him?" she asked, incredulous.

"Uh . . . it's the bathroom, ma'am."

Exasperated, she ordered them to unlock the door— and when she pushed it open, her worst fears were realized. Noah was gone.

"No, that can't be!" said the lead guard. "There are no windows, and we've been out there the entire time!"

A quick inspection revealed that the toilet was clogged. More than clogged, it was stuffed with those strange, singed caveman furs Noah had been wearing. And at the bottom, Agent Rigby fished out a pair of handcuffs, still clamped shut.

"Impossible!" said the lead guard. "No one can fit down a hole that small!"

Agent Rigby had to admit she was as impressed as she was furious. "I want every single agent down in that sewer now!"

And as if all this wasn't bad enough, yet another agent entered with yet another bit of bad news.

"Agent Rigby, we have a crisis that requires your immediate attention."

"Seriously?" She pointed to the clogged commode. "Can't you see that I'm dealing with a code brown?"

"We have a developing crisis back in Arbuckle."

"Yes, the volcano. And the reports of monsters. And something about a child attacked by a pterodactyl."

"Not that. Something else."

"What code?" demanded Agent Rigby.

"We . . . don't have a color for this . . ."

That stopped Agent Rigby cold. In her experience, everything fit into one category or another. This did not bode well. Not well at all.

"Tell me," she said.

"Okay," said the other agent. "But you may want to sit down . . ."

34

I Am He,
As You Are He

QUANTAVIUS KRATZ HAD NO IDEA HOW HE CAME TO BE IN THE place he was. One moment, he was in his apartment, lying low, hiding from the apocalypse, and fiddling with the cubic device he had taken from Rom...and the next moment, he was in someone else's living room, watching cartoons.

He rose to look around. Had the device teleported him here? Is that what had happened when he twisted the cube?

Just then, a woman who appeared to be extremely tall emerged from a kitchen doorway that appeared to be extremely high and glared at him in what appeared to be extreme disgust.

"Who are you?" Kratz demanded. "And why am I here?"

"I would ask you the same thing," the woman said, "but I doubt I'd get a reasonable answer."

The woman was rude. Kratz could not abide rudeness, and so he left without as much as goodbye.

There were several things troubling him at this point, although he was a bit too befuddled to address his concerns in any meaningful way. First was the fact that, when he spoke to the woman, his voice sounded the way it might if he had drawn breath from a helium balloon. Second was the fact that everything around him seemed so large. And third was the fact that he was wearing SpongeBob pajamas.

As he made his way down the street, people were storming out of their homes, as if offended. They all glared at one another, and they argued as people do. Kratz didn't pay it any attention. If he had, he might have wondered why the arguments all sounded so similar.

The street signs at the corner helped orient him. He wasn't far from his apartment, so he took to running, and he found that he had a bit more energy than usual.

The air still smelled of brimstone, but the odor was fading. Through the trees, he could catch glimpses of the newborn volcano—enough to see that it was no longer erupting. Could it have been a false alarm? Could the demonic doorway have been closed in time to save the world? If so, could he take credit for it?

As he made his way home, he found that there were many other people heading in the same direction. It troubled him, but as with the other troubling things, he found he didn't have enough mental bandwidth to process it.

It wasn't until he turned the last corner that he began to sense the depth of his predicament. There was a crowd around his apartment building—a crowd that was growing larger by the second, as if half the town had suddenly decided to form a flash mob on his street. The National Guard, which had been dispatched to deal with the unexpected volcano, was now trying to maintain order in this new chaos.

"Calm down!" one of the military types yelled. "We'll get to the bottom of this. Just calm down!" But no one in the crowd was having it.

"I demand you allow me to pass!" a woman insisted.

"Let me in, or I will report you to the authorities!" an older man threatened.

"*Arf! Arf!*" yapped a miffed Pomeranian.

Kratz pushed to the front, fighting his way through the crowd that towered around him like a forest.

"Excuse me," he said to the National Guard leader, in that same odd, high voice. "I live here, so kindly step aside and let me through."

The soldier in charge laughed. "Right. Do yourself a favor, and find your mother, kid."

Kratz was beyond indignant. "Who are you calling 'kid'? I'll have you know that I am Dr. Quantavius Kratz!"

"No, he's not!" said a man with a long beard. "*I'm* Dr. Quantavius!"

"They're both lying! It's me," said a woman in fuzzy slippers. "*I'm* Quantavius!"

"*Arf! Arf!*" yapped the Pomeranian.

The soldier ordered them all to step away, which just made the crowd angrier—and finally, Kratz began to piece things together. He looked at his hands and noticed how small they were. He reached to his face—none of his features felt right. It was all so shocking, he could barely resist the urge to stomp and cry and throw a full-fledged tantrum.

Just then, someone came to the window of his apartment. Someone who looked exactly like him! The entire crowd went wild.

"There's the culprit!"

"He stole my body!"

"No, it's *my* body he stole."

"*Grrrrr, bark, grrrrrr!*"

Meanwhile, inside that apartment, the man who actually *was* Q. T. Kratz was starting to sweat. The small Rubik's Cube–like device he had taken from Rom seemed so innocent. Perhaps he shouldn't have twisted it when he had no idea what it was. He had no way of knowing that it was a memory-stealer—or that a counterclockwise twist would turn it into a memory *projector*, imposing Kratz's memories on everyone within range. All he knew was that half the town now firmly believed themselves to be Quantavius

379

Theodore Kratz. And since every single one of them was now as stubborn as Kratz himself, nothing would convince them otherwise.

"Arrest the impostor!" they yelled. "Pull him out of there!" "Tear him apart."

While out in the street, little-boy Kratz put his thumb firmly in his mouth, realizing that there were worse things than the end of the world.

35

A Perfectly Normal Thing to Do

A MONTH LATER, IN A ROOM THAT DIDN'T EXIST, NOAH, ANDI, Sahara, and Ogden got together to play a board game that Ogden had designed—which, to no one's surprise, involved rounding up various extraterrestrial creatures that had escaped from a cursed pond.

It was a challenge to do in Ogden's game, but nowhere near as challenging as it had been in real life—and to the best of anyone's knowledge, none of the de-oysterized beings had been captured. Sightings were popping up everywhere on social media, but then such sightings always were, even before any of those sightings were real.

"You get to roll as many dice as your character has hands, or tentacles, or whatever," Ogden explained.

"How is that fair?" Sahara complained. "Noah's character has twelve!"

"Yes," said Ogden, "but dodecapeds lose their turn if they roll above thirty-six, so it balances out."

While the others rolled and made their moves, Noah took a moment to appreciate the view. It was spectacular: a sun setting over a rain forest canopy, frozen in that perfect moment that turned everything golden. It made him think about all the creatures beneath such a canopy. Noah was very much like a rain forest himself. Too many species to number—predator and prey—coexisting in a deceptively tranquil ecosystem.

Andi poked him. "Pay attention! It's your turn."

Noah rolled a 49 and thus, by Ogden's rules, lost his turn, but he didn't mind. It was all about being with his friends.

"So how have things been in Arbuckle?" Noah asked Sahara.

"Even weirder than Ogden's laundry," she told him.

"Ogden's laundry?"

"Well, I kinda forgot that Kaleb Carpenter was in my pocket," Ogden explained, "and when my jeans got washed, he came climbing out of the washing machine, ate everything in my dad's fridge, and ran off."

Noah grimaced. "And you're saying there are even weirder things that that?"

Ogden and Sahara shared a "should we tell him" kind of glance. Then Sahara said, "They're not letting anyone in or out of Arbuckle—military blockades everywhere—and yet we're supposed to go about our business as if nothing was wrong."

"So . . . Agent Rigby never went after you?"

"She's too busy dealing with everything else that happened," Sahara explained. "But just in case, Andi gave us skins for when the Feds are around—and they're perfect disguises."

"Yeah, I keep mine in a jar by the door," Ogden said. "Just in case."

"And your parents don't freak out when you put them on?"

Ogden laughed at the suggestion. "Are you kidding me? They don't even notice!"

Sahara sighed. "Our homes are in the Quantavius Zone. All our parents think they're Mr. Kratz, so they don't pay much attention to anything we do."

"The 'Quantavius Zone,' huh?" said Noah. "So Kratz finally got something named after him."

From what Noah was able to piece together, about half the town had been Kratz-ified, and the actual Kratz had been taken away "for his own safety," but really to be studied and experimented on.

"It's soooo annoying," Sahara said. "Now all my parents do is argue and blame each other."

"Yeah," agreed Ogden. "I haven't noticed much of a difference."

"Don't worry, memory projections fade," Andi informed them. "At least for people who weren't close to the epicenter. But anyone who was within a hundred yards of him when he flicked that switch? They're screwed. Those people are Kratz for good."

The thought of it made Noah grimace. "I wouldn't wish that on my worst enemy."

"To be honest, I'm surprised they didn't evacuate the whole town after the eruption," Sahara said.

"Sounds like they're more interested in keeping what's in Arbuckle in, rather than getting the people out," Noah observed.

"Besides," said Andi, "geologists will have already determined that there is no lava pocket beneath Arbuckle. Once the portal collapsed, the instant volcano became an instantly dead volcano. They'll be trying to figure that one out for years."

"Mr. Ksh told Andi and me that he's already planning to build a new town square," Noah said. "With the volcano as the centerpiece."

"Yeah," said Andi, "he thinks Arbuckle is going to become a big tourist destination. Stonehenge West. Monster sightings. It's a no-brainer."

As they played, they spoke of things larger than life and small things as well. The nature of reality, and what school's been like with Arbuckle cut off from the outside world, and with several teachers thinking they're Kratz. They discussed everything from cosmic string theory to Sahara's new gymnastics routine to the memorial that sprang up around Noah's locker, since everyone thought he was dead.

"Oh, and Ogden's adopted a cat!" Sahara said.

"She's incredibly smart!" Ogden told them. "She's got an attitude, but what cat doesn't?"

Ogden won the game—which was no surprise, since he was the only one who knew all the rules. And although the sun hadn't gotten any lower in the sky, the hour was getting late.

"Same time next month?" Noah asked, and everyone agreed. But before they went their separate ways, Sahara came over to Noah, speaking quietly.

"Are you sure you're okay?" she asked.

Noah gave her his best "better-than-ever" smile.

"I'm fine," he told her, even though they both knew he would never be entirely fine. But that was okay. That was life.

"And your parents?"

"I'll find them," Noah said. "And when I do, they'll have a lot of explaining to do."

Then they stood there, not sure what to say, the moment getting awkward.

"We saved the world," said Noah. "So, what now?"

Sahara smiled, then leaned closer and gave Noah the slightest of kisses. "Because that night in the greenhouse, we never got the chance," she said.

"Wow," said Noah. "I could almost actually feel that."

Then Sahara—and Ogden and the room and the sunset— winked out, leaving Noah and Andi alone in the dark. Andi flipped on a light.

"Sorry," she said. "Spotty internet."

"Even so," said Noah, "VR without VR goggles is a pretty good trick."

"Not really," said Andi. "Your people will figure that one out in a couple of years."

The balmy night air and sound of surf reminded him of where they actually were: one of Mr. Ksh's many homes—this one in the Florida Keys.

"Don't get too comfortable," Andi said. "Next week we're in Iceland."

It had been Mr. Ksh's idea to keep them mobile. Never in any one place long enough to draw attention to themselves—which could attract the Feds, but even worse, alert the aliens on either side to the fact that Noah was still alive. So, before people could get curious, Andi would pop a portal and take them to some other place that Ksh owned. But for now, they were here, and Noah was determined to take advantage of it.

"It's a nice night," he said. "Let's take a walk on the beach."

"Do I have to?" moaned Andi.

"*You* don't have to do anything, but I'm going."

But of course Andi would join him, because she rarely let him do anything alone. It was both annoying and endearing.

"I'm beginning to think staying with you is worse than the recycle bin," Andi said.

"Ah, come on, admit it. You love me!"

If disgust was radiation, Andi's expression would be a core meltdown and a nuclear winter rolled into one. "Don't say that! Machines don't love, so shut up about it!"

It was just the two of them on the beach, no sounds

but the surf and the caws of seagulls that Noah felt a vague urge to call back to, but he didn't.

"So, do you think they're already making new N.O.A.H.s?" he asked.

"I'm sure," Andi answered.

"Will they all look like me?"

Andi gave him her most judgmental gaze. "I swear, you are SO self-centered! N.O.A.H.s never look alike. And they're not all boys, either."

Noah shrugged. "Makes sense," he said. "At some point, we should try to find them. Rescue them."

"Really?" said Andi. "So, kidnap them from their homes, traumatize them with the truth of what they are, and raise them in secret somewhere. Yeah, that won't draw any attention."

Noah sighed. Nothing ahead of them was going to be easy, was it?

The surf drew back, revealing tiny silver fish flipping against the undertow, and then a wave crashed, sending foam and fish washing past their feet. Noah felt an impulse to join the tiny creatures in the water, and this time, he didn't fight it. He took off his shirt and kicked off his sandals.

"What are you doing?" Andi asked.

"Going for a swim." Then, before she could object, Noah ran into the surf and dove into a wave.

When he surfaced, he heard Andi calling to him from the shore. "Salt water and I are not friends!" she shouted.

"If something happens to you, and I have to come out there, I'll be really irritated!"

Noah dove under again, and he found that the sea floor dropped off quickly. He was in over his head, but he was becoming used to that feeling in so many ways. Deeper and deeper he swam, until his lungs began to ache. Then he forced out all his air and breathed in water. For a moment, his monkey brain panicked, but he pushed past it—feeling the sudden surge of adrenaline that had become so familiar. He raised his arms, and gills opened up in his armpits, forcing the water out. He breathed in through his nose, out through his armpits, until he found a comfortable rhythm. Until it felt like a perfectly normal thing to do.

He opened his eyes to stinging, murky darkness. Humans were, by nature, afraid of the dark—but the dark was where other things thrived. He made a clicking noise—and found, to his delight, that he could echolocate. It was a sense so much clearer than sight! He pinged on a fish. A rock. Swaying fronds of seaweed . . .

But there was more here. Echolocation was only the beginning. Adding a new, remarkable sense opened yet another pathway within him. One might call it a sixth sense, but for Noah it was a seventh.

Intuition.

Knowledge beyond perception. Not so much telling the future but knowing, with absolute certainty, its direction. Not the destination, but the things he would encounter on the way.

He and his friends would not be parted for long.

Their journey together was just the tip of something much larger.

And without any question, he *would* find his parents again.

Noah instinctively knew that this precognition wasn't from any one creature woven into his DNA. It was the culmination of all of them—and it told him that there was more to this than any of them, even Vecca, knew!

Noah couldn't linger long with Andi waiting impatiently on the shore for him, but he allowed himself a few more moments. In spite of all the threats, all the things he and his friends had faced, and would still have to face—in spite of all that, he felt an oddly charged contentment. In this perfect moment, he felt all his parts finally come together. If Ogden were here, he'd say the whole was greater than the sum of the parts. And Sahara would point out that it was the same for the four of them. Noah, Ogden, Sahara, and Andi were each part of a greater whole. A team to be reckoned with.

Noah smiled, grinning wide like a dolphin, laughing like a chimpanzee. Whatever happened next, they were ready to take it on.

So go ahead, Vecca, and Rom, and anyone else out there hiding in the darkness of space, Noah thought, in a bold, brazen dare to the universe.

Go ahead. Shock this monkey!

I dare you!

ACKNOWLEDGMENTS

We are thrilled to be writing together again and want to thank and acknowledge everyone who helped us bring our little walrus to market. First and foremost, we'd like to thank our editor, Liz Kossnar, who worked tirelessly with us to whip the book into shape, editor-in-chief Alvina Ling, publisher Megan Tingley, deputy publisher Jackie Engel, and editorial assistant Lauren Kisare.

But there are so many people at Little, Brown who go above and beyond! In production, Marisa Finkelstein and Kimberly Stella. In marketing & publicity, Stefanie Hoffman, Alice Gelber, Savannah Kennelly, Cheryl Lew, and, of course, the incomparable Victoria Stapleton!

A shout-out as well to Little, Brown's remarkable sales team, including Shawn Foster, Danielle Cantarella, Karen Torres, and Claire Gamble.

Thanks to artist Jim Madsen and designer Karina Granda for that iconic cover! And speaking of the cover, we'd like to thank Neal's daughter, Erin Shusterman, who came up with the initial concept art for the cover and has created bespoke *I Am the Walrus* swag for us!

We also want to thank editorial superstar Stephanie Lurie, who worked with us early on when the book was with Disney • Hyperion.

Thanks to our literary agent, Andrea Brown, for everything she does, as well as our entertainment agents, Steve Fisher and Debbie Deuble-Hill, at APA; our contract attorneys, Shep Rosenman and Jennifer Justman; and our managers, Trevor Engelson and Josh McGuire.

A special thanks to attorney Barbara Zimmerman for navigating the legal waters of the title. Thanks, Barbara— you are the eggman!

Neal would like to thank Barb Sobel and Kim Thomason for all the various lifesaving assistant work that keeps critical things from falling between the cracks, and for fending off evil plumbers. Thanks to research assistant Symone Powell, social media managers Mara De Guzman and Bianca Peries, and Jarrod Shusterman and Sofía Lapuente for helping Neal's TikTok go viral.

And we'd both like to thank our new tour coordinator, Claire Salmon, for organizing us on the road, and all the fans whose names we used!

Thank you all for serving up our book animal-style!

GABY GERSTER

NEAL SHUSTERMAN is the *New York Times* bestselling and award-winning author of more than forty books, including *Challenger Deep*, which won the National Book Award; *Scythe*, a Michael L. Printz Honor Book; *Dry* and *Roxy*, both of which he cowrote with his son Jarrod Shusterman; *Unwind*, which won more than thirty domestic and international awards; and *The Schwa Was Here*, winner of the Boston Globe–Horn Book Award. His latest book is *Courage to Dream*, a Holocaust-themed graphic novel, illustrated by artist Andrés Vera Martínez. Neal invites you to visit him online at storyman.com, Facebook.com/NealShusterman, and @nealshusterman on both Instagram and Twitter.

LOU MELUSO

ERIC ELFMAN is a screenwriter, a private writing coach, and the author of several books for children and young adults, including the Accelerati Trilogy, cowritten with Neal Shusterman (*Tesla's Attic*, *Edison's Alley*, and *Hawking's Hallway*); *Almanac of the Gross, Disgusting & Totally Repulsive* (an ALA Recommended book); and three *X-Files* novels. He has sold screenplays to Interscope, Walden Media, Revolution, and Universal Studios. Eric currently lives in the San Francisco Bay Area. Visit Eric online at ElfmanWorld.com, or on Twitter @Eric_Elfman.